FALL FROM GRACE

MORECAMBE BAY TRILOGY 2

PAUL J. TEAGUE

ALSO BY PAUL J. TEAGUE

Morecambe Bay Trilogy 1

Book 1 - Left For Dead

Book 2 - Circle of Lies

Book 3 - Truth Be Told

Morecambe Bay Trilogy 2

Book 4 - Trust Me Once

Book 5 - Fall From Grace

Book 6 - Bound By Blood

Morecambe Bay Trilogy 3

Book 7 - First To Die

Book 8 - Nothing To Lose

Book 9 - Last To Tell

Note: The Morecambe Bay trilogies are best read in the order shown above.

Don't Tell Meg Trilogy

Features DCI Kate Summers and Steven Terry.

Book 1 - Don't Tell Meg

Book 2 - The Murder Place

Book 3 - The Forgotten Children

Standalone Thrillers

Dead of Night

One Last Chance

No More Secrets

So Many Lies

Two Years After

Friends Who Lie

Now You See Her

PROLOGUE

11:32 pm December 31st, 1999

Kate wiped her hands on the handkerchief. Even in the darkness of the arcade, she could see that it was drenched in blood. For a moment she considered pushing it to the bottom of one of the nearby industrial waste bins, but if she did that, her police colleagues would find it soon enough and follow the trail back to her and her brother. No, she'd burn it later. She couldn't risk them finding it, with blood from both of them seeping through the fibres.

She was trembling with the shock of what had just happened. Could she still go through with the plan? Fireworks sounded in the distance; if it wasn't midnight already, it must be getting close. She was probably too late.

Kate pushed the handkerchief deep into her pocket. She could never conceal what she'd been doing that night if it fell into the wrong hands.

She had to rush to the promenade. Tiffany had been

there for at least twenty minutes. Why had everything got screwed up at the last moment?

She checked around the arcade. One silly slip and it would all be over. Had she dropped anything? No, it was clear as far as she could see, given the darkness. She moved along the shadowy side, alert for any voices and movement from the pavement beyond.

More fireworks flashed in the sky; midnight was fast approaching. She checked both ways before darting out. Anybody intent on seeing in the new millennium would either be at a party or heading for the pub right now. The road along the sea front was deserted, save for the silhouette of a dog walker far off in the distance. Kate kept her head down as she rushed towards the Midland Hotel, willing the car to be there.

The distinctive curvature of the now derelict hotel rose up ahead, its dilapidated form a ghostly presence. There was a sense of anticipation out here, as if the world was wound like a tight spring and would explode at midnight in a cacophony of merrymaking. She felt none of that excitement. Kate crossed the road without paying much attention, since nobody was out driving. The sea was wild that night. When she was in her sea view flat just along from The Battery pub, she would often open her window to enjoy the crashing of the waves and the sound of the wind rushing inland. Now the sea was her foe, an enemy for whom she had the utmost respect.

The car was parked at the top of the slipway, just like Brett had said it would be. But was she too late? She prayed Tiffany would still be alive. The dark grey waves were lapping at the concrete slipway in front of her car, an invading force gradually encroaching on the promenade. But something wasn't right; even at a distance, she could tell the car was running. She raced towards the vehicle in a state of panic, sensing they'd done something terrible. And Brett? What of her brother? Would he even survive the night, now they knew what he'd been planning?

The sky erupted with the crackling of fireworks and a burst of cheering from the hotels along the promenade and right across the town. The entire resort must be celebrating the new millennium.

As Kate reached the car, she could see the windows were steamed up and somebody was inside. There was only one person it could be. She checked all the windows as fast as she could. A body was slumped in the passenger seat, completely still. Kate opened the doors to allow the sea air to rush in and banish the spectre of death. Tiffany was still alive, but who knew how long she'd been there since she'd spoken to Brett?

Every drop of frustration, rage and anxiety came flooding out through her tears as she looked at Tiffany, willing her to be alive. There was an overwhelming smell of car fumes. This man was the devil; he'd stop at nothing. He'd left Tiffany to die here.

Kate leaned in, switched off the engine, wiped the end of the key with her sleeve and unclipped Tiffany's seat belt. Something died in her soul that night as she saw the empty child seats in the back. Were the children safe? Had Brett made it in time? Or did *he* have them?

She put her arms around Tiffany, groaning at the dead weight as she pulled at her and apologising repeatedly in case she was hurting her. It was a struggle, but gradually she manoeuvred the woman until she was free of the car. Tiffany vomited. That was good, wasn't it? It would help to get the toxins out. Kate gently laid Tiffany on the ground and left her in the recovery position.

This was more than she could cope with on her own. Her head was swirling with doubt, self-recrimination, anxiety and fear. She was close to collapsing beside Tiffany, overwhelmed by it all.

'Oh God, I was too late. I'm so sorry, Tiffany. I'm so sorry I didn't get here in time.'

Tiffany's phone was in the footwell. Kate grabbed it, walked to the back of the vehicle and dialled 999 to give an anonymous tip-off. Then she wiped the phone for prints and returned it.

'I've called an ambulance, Tiffany. You'll be okay. I've got to go now, or they'll realise it was me. I'm so sorry I was too late.'

The children had vanished. Where were they? As she turned to make sure Tiffany was safe on the slipway, she caught sight of some bright objects bobbing about in the waves. Something made her stop and look closer; they were children's soft toys. She recognised one: a teddy bear, the one that Rowan was never without.

As the millennium fireworks lit up the sky over the sea in a joyful splash of colour, all she could think of was that she'd never felt more wretched. She'd failed everybody and probably ruined her own life in the process.

It was time to go. The ambulance would be here soon, and she was meant to be on shift. Kate began to run along the promenade at the rear of the derelict Midland Hotel, towards The Battery end. Her flat on the sea front had provided the perfect cover, allowing her to disappear for an hour or so during the mayhem of the night. Soon she was due back on shift. She had her police radio on, set to a low volume, and she'd checked in. Nobody had missed her. But it was time to get back in uniform and be seen by her colleagues, as a way of providing cover.

As she passed the far end of the Midland Hotel, a man was sitting on the wall, his head hanging down as if he'd drunk too much. Kate turned away to obscure her face, running faster to get back to her flat. She washed herself, taking care to rinse around the sink, then bundled her clothes and the handkerchief into a supermarket bag and pushed it under her mattress. Her first job of the New Year would be to burn the lot without anybody knowing.

Kate put on her uniform, which she'd left on the bed earlier, ready to resume her shift after her break. She'd been so proud to wear that uniform, the culmination of years of hard work and more than a few tears. Now she felt like a fraud in it, a pauper wearing a king's gown. She checked herself in the mirror, but there were no visible signs of what had happened earlier.

By the time she got back to the Midland Hotel, the ambulance had arrived and the first police car was on the scene. She was one of the first officers there. That was good; she could check that she hadn't made any mistakes and be sure that Tiffany was going to survive. She needed to find out what had happened to the children. And Brett... please let Brett be safe.

She was allocated the menial tasks: cordoning off the area with police tape, encouraging the growing crowd to step back and allow the ambulance crew to get on with their work, and fielding queries from bystanders, many of whom were inebriated and exposed to the cold wind in party gowns and tuxedos.

'What's going on?'

'Who is she? Is she okay?'

'Looks like she tried to top herself, judging by that length of hose sticking through the side window. Poor thing probably couldn't face another year.'

Kate watched as the emergency response team checked Tiffany over and placed her in the ambulance. The celebratory fireworks were replaced by the flashing lights of police vehicles. In the bay, the lifeboat crew members were already searching for bodies. They didn't know what they were looking for, but her colleagues said they'd been warned to prepare for three children and Tiffany's husband, David.

She could never tell them what they'd planned that night, or her part in it. If they found out how she'd helped, she'd be suspended from her job before the night was over. Still, she assisted her fellow officers as they worked the scene, following instructions as the most junior person present. It was only when she was asked to pluck Rowan's teddy bear out of the water that she broke down. An officer who'd been among the first on the scene shouted over to her, seeing how distressed she was.

'Try not to let it bother you, love; there'll be worse to come if they end up fishing three tiny bodies out of the water tonight. You'll be seeing a lot worse than this in your policing career, believe me.'

She should have tried harder to maintain her composure. Maybe she just didn't have it in her; perhaps she'd never make a decent cop.

She handed over the bagged toy to one of the senior officers and returned to deal with the gathered crowd, taking up a position in front of the tape with her back facing them so she could pull herself together.

If they could do this to Tiffany, what would they do to her brother if they caught him? She prayed that he had found a safe place to hide; if they found him, he was dead.

CHAPTER ONE

Charlotte stared at the incoming caller ID on Hollie's phone, unable to fathom it out. 'Callie Irwin? How the hell does she know Hollie Wickes?'

Jed looked confused. Of course he did; there was no reason for him to have heard of either of the women. How could the girl who was supposed to be stalking her husband have anything to do with what happened to the Irwin family? It didn't make sense. The call ended before she had time to answer.

The battery on Hollie's phone was hanging on for dear life. There was no chance Jed would have anything in the house that was compatible with that model. The property was so trapped in a time warp, it was a wonder he had electricity, or even glass in the windows. She reckoned the mobile had one, maybe two calls' worth of power left. So, who should she contact, after almost drowning on the causeway and staying away from home overnight?

She should let her family know she was safe. But somebody had tried to take her life, and as soon as they found out they'd failed, they were bound to try again. The only people with the ability to do that were Vinnie Mace and Fabian Armstrong. Could they be tapping her phones? She hadn't a clue how it was done, or if it was even possible in the UK unless you were involved in law enforcement.

Charlotte made a decision which she hoped she wouldn't regret. She called Nigel. It was far too early in the morning, and a gamble, but if the phone died, he could tell Will what had happened. His was the one mobile number she could remember off the top of her head. Nigel answered straight away, as if he was waiting for her call.

'It's Charlotte. I'm calling from a different phone.'

'What the hell happened to you last night?' he asked, not bothering with the pleasantries.

'Somebody tried to drown me. I'm at Sunderland Point with Jed—'

'Jesus, Charlotte, I thought you were going to back off.'

'I haven't done anything... nothing that might hurt Fabian Armstrong. I don't know why—'

'Are you okay? What the hell did they do? No, forget that. I need to tell you something.'

'Like why you're up so early in the morning?'

'Yes, basically,' Nigel replied. 'By the way, Will called me last night, worried sick about you.'

'Did he call the police?'

'No, not yet. Well, he did, but they told him to wait overnight to see if you turned up this morning.'

'Nice of the police to care so much.'

'There's been an incident out by the stone graves. The police aren't saying anything yet, but I'm heading over there now.'

Charlotte glanced at the phone screen to check the battery. It was just about to run out.

'Look Nigel, this phone is about to die. I'll meet you

over at the tombs and you can give me a ride back home. Please call the guest house and tell my family I'm okay. Tell them I'm safe and just got caught up in something last night. Please don't tell them what happened—'

The phone clicked off.

'Damn it! I'm going to need a lift,' Charlotte said, glancing at Jed.

'I thought you might. It's okay; I've towed your car back to the car park at the end of the causeway. You'll need to get somebody to retrieve it.'

Her problems were mounting up again. The window needed sorting at the guest house. Now the car would be a write-off, after being flooded with sea water. And she still needed to give her statement at the police station. Charlotte's legs weakened at the thought of it all and for a moment she thought she was going to fall.

'Are you okay?' Jed asked. 'You had quite a shock last night. Shouldn't you think about getting checked out at the hospital?'

Charlotte was almost embarrassed to go back to the infirmary with more injuries. She ran a quick inventory on the damage she'd sustained. Her head was sore, but there didn't appear to be any serious damage. She walked over to an old-fashioned mirror hanging on a chain across the room. There was some bruising and a few scratches, but nothing that needed stitches. Her body was stiff and sore, and her skin was cracked from being submerged in the icy sea water. She wouldn't be winning any modelling contracts, but she'd live.

'Have you got something I can eat on the go, like some bread rolls? I'll make it up to you.'

'Yes, there's bread, butter and jam on the worktop

downstairs. Help yourself. You don't need to make anything up to me. Where do you want me to drive you?'

'St Patrick's Chapel at Heysham. It's not too far; is that okay? I'm sorry for all this trouble, Jed, but it's a good job you were around. It sounds like you and Kate saved my life.'

Jed seemed embarrassed by the compliment. His life must be much quieter than this normally.

She cut off a thick wedge of bread from the loaf on the wooden bread board, smothered it in butter and jam and picked up her mobile phone, which she'd spotted drying by Jed's Aga. She checked it for life. Dead, of course. It was the same make as Hollie's; a battery switch might work, creating a Frankenstein's monster of a phone. Perhaps she could even swap the SIM cards.

Jed led her to his battered 4x4 outside the house. It was parked alongside his tractor, which also looked like it had seen better days. She wondered why Jed struggled on with a job like that, risking his life out at sea in his small boat, scratching out what must be a difficult living in the bay. Still, she was thankful; she couldn't imagine anyone better suited to come along and rescue her from the causeway. She had only known this man for half an hour and she already owed her life to him.

'Thanks for what you did last night, Jed,' she said as he started the car and they made their way along the narrow road in front of the houses.

'You have Kate Allan to thank,' he said, glancing ahead at two young men in wet suits walking in front of them. They looked cocky, as if they'd be more at home on Bondi Beach than on the shingle at Sunderland Point. Charlotte clocked the expression on Jed's face.

'Who are they?' she asked.

'A couple of nephews of some guy who lives up this

end. They're a darned nuisance; they come here for two weeks at a time. It's their jet-skis I object to, buzzing away all day up and down the peninsula. We don't need that sort of thing here. I dread them coming.'

Charlotte clocked their muscular bodies and kept her thoughts to herself about how they helped to improve the landscape just a little. She suspected she might soon make an enemy of Jed if she dared to share that fantasy.

The visual distraction was welcome as they entered the causeway. The events of the night before were still on her mind. She still hadn't oriented herself; it seemed unbelievable that so much could have happened in less than twelve hours. They passed her car, parked on the slope in front of the car park noticeboard. There was no evidence of the events other than some seaweed which had become entangled around one of the rear wheels. How would she explain all this to Will?

All she remembered was the movement behind her when she was in the car, then waking up and being surrounded by water. She had a vague recollection of voices and lights, but she couldn't be sure if she was just imagining it from what Jed had told her about the rescue. Then something clicked about what Jed had just said.

'Jed, you referred to DCI Summers as Kate Allan back there; why do you call her that? She's been Kate Summers for years now.'

Jed was silent as he manoeuvred the car to avoid thick patches of mud which had collected on the road. At either side of them were the soggy channels of the salt marsh, still puddled with water, the only remaining sign of the danger she'd been in. It looked so beautiful when the tide was out, yet she was all too aware how perilous it could be.

'Do you know Kate?'

'Me and Kate go back a long way,' Jed said, keeping his eyes on the road. 'I still call her Kate Allan, even though she's married now. All those years ago, she was the only one who listened to me.'

'But you said the police checked the pillbox and dismissed it from their investigation. I thought they listened to you?'

'There was something I didn't mention the other day. I've been ignored so often, I sometimes think I imagined it myself. When I went back to the pillbox after we first discovered it, I saw something else inside. It was gone by the time the police arrived. But I swear to you, there was a packet of disposable nappies in the pillbox. Whoever was hiding in there had a baby with them.'

CHAPTER TWO

Charlotte stared at Jed in amazement.

'You mean nobody followed up on it?' she asked.

'Remember, I was just a kid then. One of the cops suggested to my dad that I had an overactive imagination. I even doubted myself. It wasn't there by the time the police checked out the pillbox, and I've often thought about it since. I reckon whoever was hiding out there saw me and made a run for it. They took all the evidence with them; they wouldn't be stupid enough to leave it. You've seen the state of my mobile phone now, but we didn't even have them back then. These days you'd take photographs and the police would have to believe you.'

'Even though you were a kid, they should have followed up the lead.'

Jed picked up his mobile phone, glancing at it occasionally while keeping his eye on the causeway.

'This is where we found you last night, on the bridge.'

Charlotte glanced from side to side, taking it all in as Jed slowed for her. The small bridge crossed a wide, muddy channel. She knew nothing about peninsulas and marshes, but this looked like a place where the tide would come in first. She shuddered at the thought of it. It was probably a good thing she'd been out cold and had missed the drama of her rescue.

'Thanks again, Jed. I can't tell you how grateful I am.'

'Do you want to call anybody on my phone? The signal has just kicked in; it's yours if you want it.'

Charlotte held out her hand and took the phone.

'I think I'd better make a call home. I know I asked Nigel to do it, but I should call Will myself.'

She checked the time. It was still early. She couldn't remember Will's mobile number, so she called the guest house phone instead. Isla answered.

'Hi Isla, it's Charlotte—'

'Oh Charlotte, thank God, we've been going crazy here—'

'Did Nigel call?'

'Yes, but Will's going out of his mind. We all are. What happened to the window in the lounge?'

'It's a long story, Isla. Can you get Will for me? I'll bring him up to date and he can pass on the news. I'm safe though, as you can hear.'

'Take care, please, Charlotte. You're precious to everybody around here. Please keep yourself out of trouble.'

'I will, Isla. Thank you.'

There was some shuffling and calling in the background and two clicks, a sign that Will had picked up the phone extension in the family accommodation and Isla had replaced her handset so they could speak privately.

'What the hell happened?' Will asked, his voice frantic and annoyed at the same time.

'I honestly didn't bring this on myself,' Charlotte

replied. This was going to be tricky; by the sound of it, Will was already on a short fuse.

'But the window, Charlotte... and now Nigel tells me you got caught up in something last night. You were away all night, Charlotte, and I was going crazy back here. You just can't do this to us, it's unfair on the kids.'

'I know.'

She was silent for a moment. He was right. But she'd gone to help a friend. She had backed off from Fabian Armstrong, intent on doing nothing to exacerbate the situation. Then a thought occurred to her. What if it wasn't even Vinnie Mace who'd organised the smashed window? What if it wasn't Vinnie who'd tried to drown her at Sunderland Point? It could be somebody else, perhaps the person who'd set off the fire alarms in the hospital.

'Will, I promise you, whoever is responsible for the window and for what happened last night, I did nothing to provoke anyone after we spoke at the weekend. I thought I was going to meet DCI Summers, but it turned out to be a hoax. Somebody tried to lure me there—'

'You have to speak to the police.'

'But Kate Summers warned me off. She said there's a bad apple in the force and she can't work out who it is. That's why I was going to see her; at least she's someone we can trust.'

Will gave a long sigh, heavy with doubt. She hated herself for putting him through this again. But she hadn't caused it, and there was no single event which would have put a stop to it. As George had told her some time ago, evil people did bad things and they would continue, regardless of what she did or didn't do.

'What happened last night? Where were you? Nigel said you'd explain.'

So, Nigel hadn't given Will all the details. She and Will had promised they wouldn't keep secrets from each other again. But this seemed like the right time to spare everybody the full truth. Only three people were aware of the events out on the causeway. She wasn't involving the police, not until Kate told her who she could speak to. So she opted for a sanitised version of the story.

'I got caught in the tides at Sunderland Point last night. The car got saturated, and I was cut off. A man rescued me, someone we met out there while reporting for the newspaper the other day. He's driving me over to Heysham now—'

'Is the car a write-off?'

'Will, I'm sorry, yes. Jed towed it back to safety for me with his tractor and gave me a place to sleep for the night. I should have phoned, but I was exhausted.'

'Okay, okay,' Will answered. She could almost picture him raising his hands in despair. He was surrendering, and she was free to go.

'I'll contact the garage as soon as I can to get the car checked out. We'll need a crime number from the police station to get the insurance sorted on the window. I'll take care of everything, Will. Leave it to me.'

'So long as you're safe, Charlotte. We can sort the window and the car. I can't bear the thought of losing you.'

They remained on the line in silence. She got the message. Hopefully he understood she felt the same. She said it, just to be certain.

'I love you, Will. I wouldn't do anything to put you or the kids in danger. You must know that.'

He sighed again.

'I do. Only I thought we'd lost you once. I can't face that again.'

It would have been the perfect point at which to end the call. But there was Hollie Wickes and the missed call from Callie Irwin.

'Will, I need to tell you something. You won't want to hear this, but it might place you in danger—'

'For God's sake, Charlotte, please don't say there's more.'

'I'm sorry, Will. That woman, Holly Wickes, who you warned me about. She knows Callie Irwin, the girl who was found on the slipway on the promenade.'

'Is this the one who they're saying disappeared from the infirmary on the news this morning?'

'Yes. I don't know how they're connected, but this means you're involved too, Will. Just be careful, that's all—'

The call waiting sound beeped three times before Will spoke again.

'I'd better just check this; it might be a booking or cancellation. Stay on the line, I'll see what they want.'

Charlotte moved Jed's phone away from her ear while she waited for him to check the call.

'Everything all right back home?' Jed asked.

Charlotte nodded, but Will was back on the line already.

'It was Nigel again,' Will told her. 'He was asking if you're on your way to the chapel ruins at Heysham. Some chap's body has been found out there. His name was Evan something... Evan Parish or Farrish.'

CHAPTER THREE

December 1999

Kate sipped her Rum and Coke and scanned the pub. It was a curse of the job, spotting ne'er-do-wells and other members of Morecambe's lowlife community out for a night on the town. Most of them seemed to take it in good spirits; it wasn't as if she was dealing with Jack the Ripper types. As a beat bobby in Morecambe, she had to accept that it went with the territory. Occasionally they'd tease her about never being off duty or else they claimed their innocence, but it had always been something that she could brush aside. Besides, most of them were three sheets to the wind, so if she didn't run into any belligerent drunks, she was fine.

'So, are you going to try and pull a fella tonight or what?' Shannon asked. 'You've been in a drought for weeks now. It's nearly Christmas and it's easy to get hold of a bloke at this time of year. Are you in or out?'

Kate laughed at Shannon, who was already worse for wear. She'd been acutely aware of the differences between them ever since returning to the resort to take up her first post. It was a proud moment for her and an immense achievement, becoming a police constable with the Lancashire Constabulary. In her home county, no less. She'd got herself fit, passed every test and challenge they'd placed before her and now she got to walk the streets of her hometown in the uniform she'd dreamed of wearing. When her friends at primary school had dressed in princess costumes, she had made for the plastic police hats and truncheons in the dressing-up box from an early age. It all came from having a father who'd served so long in the force. If only he could see her now. Some part of her believed he was still watching over her, even though she wasn't religious anymore.

Shannon was wearing too much make-up and the right-hand strap on her vest top kept slipping down, advertising the fact she was bra-less. Hitting the town like this had seemed like great fun when they were younger and working together in the shop in Lancaster. When her father was shot and killed, she wised up and got her act together. That life seemed so far away now. Although it was painful, she could see she'd soon be observing Shannon and Dawn in her rear-view mirror. As Kate watched Dawn walking back from the rest rooms, her leggings so tight and revealing they might just as well have been another layer of skin, she realised this was probably the last time they'd be out on the town like this.

The truth was, she was a professional now. She kept asking herself if she was being snobby, looking down her nose at her old friends. She didn't want to be, but she'd come to realise Shannon and Dawn were a liability in her line of work. The final straw had been Shannon sleeping with a young guy she'd arrested at the Woolworths store on the sea front. She had been so embarrassed, standing in front of her police colleagues while they gave him a police caution, only to have him smirking at her throughout, as if goading her with his intimate knowledge of her friend. That was the point at which she realised she needed to cut the ties.

She could have a laugh with the other coppers, including several new constables based at Morecambe from Kate's intake. It was rapidly becoming her social life now. Besides, she'd got her eyes on a young guy in the civilian employee ranks, so the local lads in the resort had long since ceased to be an appealing option.

'So, what do you say?' Dawn continued, having caught the tail end of the conversation. 'How about we chat up those three lads over there, for old time's sake? Last one to get a snog is an old witch.'

Kate looked at the chosen targets for the night. The Battery was not exactly the best place to go scouting for Morecambe's finest male specimens. The three lads in question were identikit models, with their gelled hair, loose-hanging shirts and pints of lager. She was certain they'd be surrounded by a thick cloud of Lynx Africa deodorant.

This had never been her scene. On nights out with Shannon, Dawn and their entourage, she'd always ended up as the old witch. Her curse was the admiration she had for her dad. He'd always been a great role model, bringing up her and Brett on his own, in spite of the antisocial shifts and punishing case load. He would take some matching; the guys and their prevailing aroma of Lynx deodorant were unlikely to measure up.

'I'm sorry ladies, I'll have to forgo the knee trembler tonight,' she said, fixing a smile on her face so she didn't come across as disapproving of her friends. It had never bothered her what they got up to; that was none of her business. It just wasn't the path she'd chosen.

'I'm meeting up with Brett tonight. Much as I'd like to join you... you know, family—'

Shannon helped her out, even though she could see the disappointment on her face. They'd probably worked out that this would be the last hurrah, too.

'Great, I can take the spotty one and the one who's spilled lager down the front of his trousers. At least I hope he has. Maybe he's just pleased to see me.'

Shannon and Kate shrieked at the joke, a carefully timed ploy to catch the group's attention. Like highly trained sniffer dogs, the men could catch even the mildest scent of available females, and they had gathered like a group of starving vultures within the minute, sensing they might be in for a feast.

'Hello girls, what's so funny then?' one of them asked, unaware of the damp patch of lager around his groin. The waft of over-sprayed deodorant had arrived before they did.

Shannon and Dawn moved into predator mode and Kate decided it was time to make her exit, especially as the guy with bad acne had obviously selected her as his target for the night.

'Nice to meet you chaps. I'll have to leave you in the company of these lovely ladies; I need to be somewhere else, I'm afraid.'

Dawn put her arms around her and gave her a big hug. If the atmosphere hadn't been so smoky, Kate would have sworn she had tears in her eyes.

'I love you, Kate,' she whispered. 'Take care.'

Kate felt the tears welling up. This was the end for them. They'd still be friends, but nothing would be the same again. Their lives were on separate paths.

'Hey, I didn't realise that was on offer too!' the third guy said. 'Mind if I join in, girls?'

One of the advantages of being a police constable was that it had expanded Kate's ability to deal with all types of people and different situations. She was far from perfect, but she was improving.

'Me and Dawn are an exclusive couple,' she said, 'except when it comes to Shannon, of course.'

Kate put her arms around Shannon, noticing how tense she was. It didn't matter, she was getting a hug. It made Shannon thaw a little.

'Are you going on anywhere?' Shannon asked.

'I'm meeting Brett in Crystal T's,' Kate answered. 'I'll maybe catch you there?'

'Yes, have a great night.'

They both knew they wouldn't be meeting in Crystal T's.

Kate watched as Shannon moved the spotty guy's hand onto her behind. She wanted to tell them they could do better, but it was wiser to keep her mouth shut. Shannon and Dawn were sacrificial lambs, willingly hurling themselves at a destiny as old as time: unwanted pregnancy, unwanted marriage, unwanted life. They were both capable of so much more, but they couldn't see it.

'Bye then,' she said. They didn't even notice. The men had dismissed her as a non-prospect, and the girls were brazening out their choices, as if they were passengers laughing while the Titanic sank.

Kate pulled on her jacket. Her flat was not far up the road from The Battery pub, and she'd rather have gone back home for a hot chocolate and a decent book. But it was a while since she'd seen Brett and he seemed keen to talk.

She decided to walk along the promenade, even though

the weather was wild; the biting wind would revive her. The cables from Adventure Kingdom's cable car ride still stretched across the road, as a final protest against the closure of the amusement park the year before. It reminded Kate of summer evenings spent with Brett and their dad, candy floss in hand, howling with laughter as they splashed to the bottom of the log flume. Life was so simple back then; her father had always made it seem so easy.

The walk was quite long, but life pounding the streets on the beat had built up her resilience. It was nice to be off shift, having a night out. Brett was always good company; she'd have liked to see more of him if she could.

She crossed the road opposite the Winter Gardens and took the side street leading to Crystal T's. The moment she stepped into the nightclub's radius, it was like entering a brand-new level on a computer game. The pounding of the music from within the club reverberated out on the street and around the entrance were kissing couples and groups of friends, seeking sanctuary from the wall of sound inside. They were playing Prince's 1999. Even though the song had first been released in the '80s, the pop star was no doubt raking in the royalties from the forthcoming arrival of a new millennium.

Kate made her way in and scanned the dance floor and bar for Brett. She spotted him immediately, but he hadn't seen her, giving her a chance to stand back and watch him. He was talking to a woman, and they seemed relaxed and comfortable together.

Brett caught her watching him. He whispered into the woman's ear; she glanced around, then disappeared into the crowd of drinkers standing around the bar.

Kate gave her brother a wave and walked towards him. He looked sheepish.

'Hi Brett,' she shouted over the music, 'Sorry I'm early. I made a fast exit from The Battery; it was getting too frisky in there for me.'

'Hi Kate, it's great to see you. Your hair's a bit wild; I gather the wind's whipping up?'

He smiled; Brett always smiled. He'd lifted her through some dark times.

'So, who was the lady I saw you chatting to? She looks like more than a friend. Do tell.'

The smile went from Brett's face the moment she said the words. It was like the DJ had just faded out 1999 and started playing the Funeral March instead.

'You won't know—' he began.

'No, but I might be meeting her soon, judging from that body language.'

'I don't want to talk about it, Kate, so please drop the subject. She's just someone I met, okay?'

CHAPTER FOUR

Charlotte reached out for the car dashboard to steady herself, feeling a need to hold on to something to combat the panic. Jed saw the expression on her face and slowed the vehicle.

'Are you all right? Do I need to stop the car? Your face has just turned white.'

'I'm fine. Keep driving, please,' Charlotte answered.

Will was still on the phone.

'Who's that you're with now?'

'It's Jed. He's driving me to Heysham. I stayed at his place overnight.'

There was silence at the end of the phone. She could tell what Will was thinking, but she didn't care. Sure, she'd sheltered at some strange man's house the night before without calling home to let anybody know where she was. But Evan Farrish was dead. She couldn't grasp the information; it was like trying to hold water in her hands.

'Will, I've got to go. I'm okay, I'm safe. Can you call the garage before you go to work? I've parked the car outside the public conveniences at the end of the Sunderland Point causeway. I'll deal with the car, the window and the insurance when I get back. But I'm due at Heysham right now—'

'Damn, I just realised I was going to take the car tonight. I have to be on campus for the presentation event. Never mind, I'll figure it out. I might catch a taxi or see if I can get a late bus. Don't worry about it; I'll tell you my plans later.'

Charlotte couldn't miss the dig at her. She couldn't face telling him the full truth yet; it would have to wait. It was bad enough dealing with all the problems on her plate without having to treat Will with kid gloves.

She ended the call and passed the phone back to Jed. It may have been old-fashioned, but it worked well enough and it had a battery life to die for.

She checked the battery on Hollie's phone, which was perched on the parcel shelf. It was on life support; she wouldn't be able to squeeze out another call. Silently, she leaned over to retrieve her own phone and began to remove the plastic backs, take out the batteries and the SIM cards and attempt to create some hybrid model, using the best pieces from each. Her own battery was still dry; she hadn't expected that.

Charlotte spent the whole time thinking of Evan Farrish. The man had survived a career in policing and now, retired and enjoying life, he'd been murdered by some psychopath whilst out walking his dog. They'd all taken it for granted that they could walk along the cliffs, not even considering the remote location might make them vulnerable.

Jed was switching between watching the road and checking on Charlotte. For a man who spent so much time on a boat at sea, he was showing a remarkable ability to know when to keep quiet. His silence gave her a moment to think, to figure things out.

She'd put her battery into Hollie's phone, switched over the SIM card and pressed the power button. To her surprise, the screen lit up.

'I've managed to raise the dead,' she said.

Jed looked confused.

'The phone, I've got my phone going again.'

'Great, well done,' he replied. 'You still look like someone just drained all the blood out of you. Are you sure you're okay?'

'Yes, thanks. My husband's just given me some shocking news, but I'll explain everything after I've made a call.'

She dialled Nigel, not bothering to announce herself when he picked up.

'Evan is dead?'

'Yes, his body was discovered this morning by some dog owner who walks the cliffs at an ungodly hour every morning. He was drowned in one of the stone graves at the church ruins and his body was left in one of the hollows. I'm almost there now.'

Charlotte could scarcely find her voice. She'd been clinging to a tiny hope that Will might have got his wires crossed, but he obviously hadn't.

'Are you still there, Charlotte?'

It was as if somebody had placed her on standby and she couldn't reactivate. At last she unfroze.

'I just can't believe it. They must have killed him after they came for me last night. It must be linked to our conversation at Half Moon Bay. You realise you might be in danger too, don't you, Nigel?'

'That penny was just beginning to drop, Charlotte. I think we may have brought this upon ourselves. Evan Farrish must have had some information that somebody would rather we didn't know. I hope Rory Higson is okay.

He covered the case as a reporter at the same time as Evan. Let's hope he doesn't have information that puts him in danger.'

'Oh God, please tell me they won't go for Rory. I must try to raise Kate Summers. She told me not to speak to the police, because she reckons there's a rogue among them. But what can we do? We can't allow whoever it is to go around killing people. It's got to be Vinnie Mace.'

Even as she said it, Charlotte thought about the mystery person who'd paid a visit to the ICU in Lancaster. Was there somebody else in circulation who was doing this?

'If it's too much for you, don't come to the stone graves. Go straight home and catch your breath.'

Charlotte was tempted, but she needed to be at the place where Evan had lost his life. Had she and Nigel brought this upon him?

'No, I'm coming. We owe Evan that much—'

'You realise his body is still on site, don't you? They'll have called the forensics team, so it'll all be cordoned off, but they won't move him until they're certain they have what they need from the crime scene.'

'Nigel, it's fine. We're just passing through Middleton now; we'll be with you soon.'

She ended the call.

'Do you mind if I take this leaflet?' Charlotte asked.

Jed glanced at what she'd just taken out of the car door storage compartment. It was a curled-up pizza brochure.

'Help yourself. I found it stuck in the wipers last week.'

Charlotte used the paper to make a storage packet for Hollie's SIM card. She had Callie's number on the call log and the device would no doubt hold other useful information. The moment she could catch a break and get the phone battery re-charged, she'd go through it. She abandoned any lame attempt at preserving Hollie's privacy; the student was fair game.

Jed had shown remarkable patience for a man who'd only recently stopped to answer a few harmless questions from two local newspaper journalists. Now he was in the eye of a storm likely to be more threatening than anything he'd ever encountered at sea. Charlotte talked him through it, leaving out certain choice elements of information. It turned out Jed shared her opinion of DCI Kate Summers. The thought of her doing anything wrong was unconscionable.

'Tell me about these nappies. I hate to sound like the police, but you are sure you saw them? You were very young at the time; you might have been mistaken.'

For the first time since she'd met him, she sensed Jed prickling. She decided to change tack.

'Okay, I'm sorry. I'm just trying to get everything straight. There are so many fragments of information here, I can't fit it all into my head. What with Callie Irwin showing up and your memory of the pillbox, this all adds up. Do you think it might have been Callie in the pillbox? And if so, who had taken her? I can't believe the police didn't pick this up at the time.'

'They were convinced the children and the husband were washed away to sea. But about a year ago, the paper covered a big news story about the local MP being caught up in all sorts of horrible things. I don't get the paper, sorry, but I read it on the shelves of the supermarket in town.'

'What does this have to do with Edward Callow?' Charlotte asked. 'Did you realise I was caught up with all that?'

'No,' Jed replied. Judging by his expression, he didn't seem too surprised. 'I didn't take much notice, but there was a photo in the report which made me look more closely.

When I was a kid, one of the coppers slipped me a five-pound note to stop bothering them. I can still remember his words; *Here's a fiver, now bugger off and leave us to get on with our investigation.* I'd been trying to get them to listen about the pillbox. They checked it out then seemed to forget all about it, like it wasn't important. But I remember the guy who gave me the money; I didn't like him. He was in that article about Edward Callow. I recognised him in the photo. It was a man called Harvey something. Harvey Turnbull, that was his name. I'd remember that nasty piece of work anywhere.'

The mention of Harvey Turnbull made Charlotte angry. What was it about these men? They poisoned so many lives, yet people seemed powerless to stop them. She thought it through, desperately seeking a rational explanation. Harvey had been a policeman in the resort at that time. They'd since found out he was a crooked cop, but it was possible he'd been working the case at the time, when nobody knew he was on the take. It still left a foul taste in her mouth; here was a young lad with crucial information who'd been told to get lost. She wondered if Turnbull had known Fabian Armstrong then. The possibility of a connection was too strong to ignore.

'We're here now,' Jed said as they saw a police cordon up ahead, blocking the older part of the village. 'If I drop you off here, will you be okay to find your way home?'

He stopped the car ahead of the police vehicles which were crowding the route, their blue lights flashing an alert. The residents in this part of the village were going to have a disrupted day. Charlotte turned to Jed as she unclipped her seat belt.

'The past twelve hours have been crazy, Jed, but I can't thank you enough for what you did to help me. I want you to know how much I appreciate it. When things calm down a little, I'll thank you properly.'

Jed's face turned red and he looked down at the steering wheel. Charlotte didn't push it any further; she opened her car door and stepped out into the road.

'Just throw my clothes away,' she said before heading off. 'They're all soaked, so don't bother trying to save them. I'll get these clothes laundered and bring them over as soon as we get mobile again.'

He nodded.

'Oh, check the pockets first, please. Did you retrieve all my personal bits and pieces from the car?'

'They're still drying on the Aga; I'll get them back to you. What shall I do about the car?'

'If all my personal stuff is out, just leave the doors open so the pick-up truck can get to it. Leave the keys on the driver's seat. Nobody is going anywhere with it, are they?'

'Not a chance of that,' he replied. 'The engine was completely submerged last night.'

She thanked Jed once again and walked up the road towards a young officer who had been stationed in front of the cordon to prevent people like her from getting anywhere near the crime scene. If they asked for her ID she'd be stuck; she'd forgotten to bring it with her.

'Good morning, Miss. Are you a resident?' the officer asked.

'No, I'm local press, I work on The Bay View Weekly.'

'Do you have your press card please?'

Charlotte fumbled for her phone, thinking she'd have to get Nigel to come over and vouch for her.

'It's okay, Officer, you can let her through,' came a voice

from beyond the cordon. It was Toni Lawson. What an opportune moment for the police press officer to be around. Once she was waved through, she made her way over to Toni, who seemed pleased to see her.

'I always remember a friend who passes me toilet tissue underneath a cubicle,' she said with a smile. 'What happened to you, Charlotte? Did you choose your outfit from your husband's wardrobe this morning?'

Charlotte hadn't even thought about her clothing, Jed's loose-fitting jeans and a heavy, chequered shirt. He'd found her a pair of trainers, but they were too big, and she was walking awkwardly in them. She burst out laughing as she imagined what she must look like.

'It's a long story,' she said, smiling at Toni and feeling the tension melt away. 'Let's put it this way, they'll be wearing this on the Paris catwalks next year. You got to see it here in Heysham before anyone else.'

It was Toni's turn to laugh now.

'I take it you're not here for a delightful cliff top walk?' Toni asked.

'No, I'm not. And I take it you're here to brief people like me?'

'I am,' Toni replied, giving the prompt to walk with her. They came to the edge of the narrow lane which led up to St Peter's Church, as the spectacular bay view opened out over the tops of the graves. There were worse places to be at that time of day. If only Evan Farrish hadn't lost his life.

'What do you know so far?' Charlotte asked. She figured she might as well get an informal briefing while she had the press officer's full attention.

'A 69-year-old former police officer was discovered in one of the stone graves at the end of this lane. Cause of death still has to be confirmed, but it's most likely drowning and possibly strangulation. No witnesses have come forward; his dog was found wandering the village. He's well known around here, so one of the villagers alerted the police immediately. We're unsure of the time of death. It could be last night or this morning. Nobody reported him missing. You can spare yourself a briefing now; go home and put your feet up.'

'What do you think it's connected to?' Charlotte asked. 'Do you have any ideas yet?'

'We're not sure. It could be something random, but that's unlikely. You don't get a lot of major crimes around here. We'll be sifting through his old cases to see if any bad 'uns have been released from prison who might bear a grudge. It's too early to say.'

'I might be able to help,' Charlotte said, stopping.

Toni followed her lead. The voices of the assembled press pack could now be heard.

'We were speaking to Evan Farrish only yesterday morning. He was telling us about his involvement in the Irwin case. Were you aware he was the case lead?'

'No, I wasn't,' Toni replied, the scent of curiosity hanging in the air. 'I'll make sure I report that to DI Comfort. I'm pretty certain he'll want to talk to you about it. Okay, I've got to love you and leave you now; it's time for the main show.'

Toni walked off to speak to the uniformed officers who were gathered in front of the assembled members of the press.

Charlotte scanned the scene for Nigel, but he'd seen her already and was approaching.

'Did you dress in the dark this morning?' he asked.

'Oh, very funny. Toni Lawson got in first with the wisecracks.'

'Well, apart from your sartorial choices, you don't seem any the worse for wear from your escapades overnight. I'm pleased you're okay, especially after what happened to poor old Evan. We've got a lot to catch up on. Everything has gone crazy since we last spoke—'

Charlotte wasn't listening. She'd just had a terrible thought. Her brain hadn't kicked in after the shock of the morning's events. Lucia couldn't be left alone in the guest house, not after what happened to Evan Farrish and the threat to her own life. She had to get her daughter out of there. If they'd come for Charlotte, it wouldn't take them long to come for her children.

CHAPTER SIX

December 1999

Kate walked through the arcade, watching an elderly woman on the slot machines. She must have been in her late eighties, with a tightly permed blue rinse, wearing pink circular glasses and looking every bit the identikit granny. Yet every other time she placed a 10p piece into the slot, the machine seemed to pay out. She'd gathered a small crowd of people around her, most of whom had no doubt lost their own money and were now resigned to watching this lady win it all back. Kate walked past and smiled, putting on the friendly face of the beat constable. It was all about connection and relationships, that's what her Sergeant had reminded her about, and most of the time it was easy in Morecambe.

The resort had begun to struggle since Kate had grown up, what with the recent closure of the theme park on the sea front, the relocation of the railway station, the demise of many of the pubs and the Midland Hotel falling into disrepair. The town needed to find a new trick, or it would struggle to survive. Still, she loved the place, and she was happy walking the streets dealing with the largely petty crime issues that came up day-to-day.

Harvey's was one of the casualties she missed most; it was the place where she'd spent many of her teenage nights, not all of them at the legal age. Crystal T's was not her favourite location to meet, but for some reason Brett preferred the noisiness and anonymity of the place.

She was pleased to have a moment alone to work out what she thought about the previous night's meeting with Brett. Her more senior colleague had suggested they split up, encouraging Kate to build up her confidence and experience going it alone. It wasn't that PC Owen was so far away – he'd popped into the Winter Gardens to let everybody know the local constabulary was out and about – but come Christmas and the new millennium, the sarge had indicated that she'd need to go out alone, if only for the purposes of managing manpower more effectively.

One of the advantages of coming back home to take up a job in the police was that she could keep a better eye on her younger brother. Whilst she was intent on a career in policing, there had been a time when she'd thought Brett might end up on the wrong side of the law. Their father's death had hit them hard, but where she'd risen to the challenge of living alone, Brett had struggled for a while, unable to find his equilibrium. At least he was seventeen when it happened, so there was no question of him being taken into care. Eventually they'd sold their father's house, splitting the proceeds from the sale. Although it had taken a death to bring that money into their orbit, it gave the two of them a head start that many of their age didn't have. Now they both had small properties in the resort.

Her radio crackled. It was just Control checking in;

there was nothing to report and no incidents to attend to. PC Owen's voice came over the radio too, making sure all was well. She could never accuse them of not supporting her, that was for sure.

She couldn't put her finger on why she'd been uncomfortable the night before. It had started with Brett's defensiveness over the woman, who didn't look like the type of person her brother would usually hang out with. She hated herself for even thinking it, but this woman was classy, with poise and a self-assurance that usually came with age. Yet she appeared to be around their age, early to mid-twenties, not the sort who were normally found in Crystal T's.

Sometimes Kate wondered if she was taking the whole detective thing too far. She made no secret of her desire to move into their ranks, and the moment she could make the move to detective constable, she'd snatch at the opportunity to follow in her father's footsteps. Although she'd have to bide her time in uniform first, that was fine with her; she was in no rush.

The music had been too loud in the nightclub and Kate found it difficult to hear what her brother was saying much of the time. Most of his comments were superficial: no, he wasn't seeing that woman from the council anymore; they hadn't been together for some time. Yes, his job at the Maritime Museum in Lancaster was working out fine, but it didn't pay that much, and he was looking for something else.

Then he dropped the bombshell, in the middle of a medley of hit songs from that year that had packed the dance floor; Ricky Martin, Britney Spears and S Club 7 all fighting for her attention. The dance floor was packed, spirits were running high and the DJ was threatening to play Cliff Richard's Millennium Prayer if the crowd didn't all sing along to Livin' La Vida Loca.

'Did you say your flat is up for sale?' she shouted. Her voice was growing hoarse. Next time, she would choose the venue. The Kings was more her type of place; at least they'd be able to hear each other speak in there.

'Yeah, I'm going to stick the money in the bank for a while and try to work out what I want to do with my life. You're lucky, you've always wanted to follow Dad into the police. I'm still not sure what I want to do. But I think it will be somewhere away from this place.'

It was as if he'd just pulled the rug from under her feet. She'd moved back to the resort to be close to him, to keep an eye on her baby brother, just like she always had in the past. She'd been wracked with guilt at leaving him here to complete her police training. But she was back for good now, and this was not what she wanted to hear from Brett.

'It's always a good idea to keep your money in property. Why don't you rent out the flat? That way you can always come back to Morecambe if it doesn't work out.'

The Vengaboys were now playing, all threats of Cliff's millennium song having been withdrawn. The expression on Brett's face was ominous.

'I sold it already,' he said. He was mumbling, but she read his lips. She'd almost guessed it was coming; she could have shaken him. Why the sudden rush? What if he wasn't able to afford to buy another house? That money had been their dad's legacy to them, and they shouldn't squander it.

Kate's radio crackled and she realised she'd been walking through the arcade on autopilot, miles away, absorbed in the events of the previous night. It was PC Owen.

'We've got a purse snatcher, heading your way. I'm in

pursuit from the front of the arcade. Male, white, short cropped hair, red tracksuit bottoms—'

Kate acknowledged the call, her adrenaline kicking in as she forgot the events of the previous night and scanned the arcade, watching out for any movement. The crowd at the slot machine had dispersed now that the old lady had moved on. Then she saw it: a blur of brightly coloured tracksuit, a young lad running through the arcade at speed, no doubt doing his best to avoid PC Owen.

'Got him, he's heading to the rear of the arcade—'

'Wait for me to get there—' came PC Owen's radio response, but she was on her way; the hound had got the scent.

'Oi, watch it sunshine!' came a shout from the far side of the arcade.

'Police, stop!' she shouted. The youth turned to check what was happening, hurled some abuse in her direction, then crashed into a Noddy and Big Ears ride in front of him which he hadn't seen. He went flying over the bright yellow car, cursing loudly as he tried to recover himself. Kate rushed at him, determined to bring him down and immobilise him. She thought she had him for a moment, but he spun round, shoving her away from him. It was not what she'd expected. Kate lost her footing and fell through the side curtain of a Terminator arcade game, stumbling and clipping her forehead against the machine gun which formed part of the console.

There was a small cheer from beyond the curtain and a ripple of half-hearted applause.

'Well done officer, don't mind me if you want to use a bit of police brutality on the waster,' came a voice from the gathered crowd of onlookers.

The public could always be relied upon to offer their

support for the local constabulary, even if they were a little misguided at times.

Kate emerged from inside the arcade game to the sight of PC Owen confidently apprehending the youth, so there was no chance of further escape or violence. He held out a long, cream purse.

'I thought you were supposed to be helping me, not playing arcade games?' he teased.

Although Kate smiled at him, her insides burned with frustration. Sometimes she wondered if she'd ever make it in the police. Colleagues like PC Owen made everything look so simple, yet it was still awkward and unfamiliar to her.

'I'm just teasing you. This little hoodlum is Tommy Andrews, out on one of his regular snatch and grab expeditions from Lancaster. Do you like stealing from little old ladies, Tommy? Does it make you feel good about your life choices?'

Even the way PC Owen spoke to him made a bigger impact. She was too soft; they gave her the run around. Tommy was now subdued, like he'd just been told off by the headmaster. Taking the purse from PC Owen, she recognised it as belonging to the lady who she'd been watching earlier on the slot machine.

As she watched PC Owen, from nowhere, her subconscious mind filled in a gap that had eluded her the previous evening in the heat of the musical onslaught from the nightclub. It was obvious why Brett had sold his house; he was in love with that woman.

CHAPTER SEVEN

'I need to call Lucia; I'll join the briefing shortly.'

Charlotte was moving before she'd even started the sentence. Nigel nodded, and she tucked herself out of the way of the press huddle to avoid interrupting the assembled crowd of police officers and reporters. The rag-tag phone she'd created out of the working parts of two mobile devices appeared to be holding up well. Thank goodness she'd stored Lucia's number in her SIM card; she could never recall it from memory. Lucia answered straight away. That was a first.

'Mum? Are you okay? Dad told me what happened.'

'I'm fine, Lucia, honestly.'

She considered sharing the full truth with her daughter but changed her mind. It wasn't a good idea to terrify her, not when she was coping so well after the traumatic episode at the port the previous year.

'The car's a write-off, but I'm fine. Luckily I knew a man there who could put me up for the night. He's a contact from the newspaper.'

'I fell asleep early last night and only found out when

Dad told me this morning. That's the problem with living in a guest house. There are comings and goings all the time, and I never know who's in or out unless I check the bookings software.'

'I have to ask you a favour, Lucia. The window being smashed has really worried me. Would you go and stay with your brother in Lancaster for a day or two while we get the repair done? I want to get it replaced and see if the police come up with anything—'

'You think it's connected to the parachute jump, don't you?'

She was so tempted to share everything with Lucia. They'd forged a stronger bond after what had happened to them, and she seemed to understand better than Will did.

'Maybe... I can't be certain. But it would help a lot if I didn't have to worry about you. And with this Hollie Wickes woman too, we've a lot going on. It would make me feel a lot better if you were out of the guest house and far away from any trouble that might come our way.'

'Okay. I'll ask Olli and Willow. I can use the sofa bed in their lounge.'

Charlotte couldn't believe it was as easy as that.

'Are you sure? It'll only be for a short time.'

'Sure, it's fine, Mum. I can use the library up at the university campus in town. I bet they'll have more books than our local branch. Besides, they get some decent films at The Dukes, so I can catch up with a few indies while I'm there.'

For the first time in days, something had gone easily for Charlotte. She ended the call and joined the briefing which was now underway.

'Anything new?' she whispered to Nigel. She was relieved that the kids were out of harm's way. It would make life a lot easier if she could stop worrying about them.

'No, it's pretty well what my source told me. Evan was walking his dog alone at dusk last night. He doesn't have a wife – she died one or two years ago – so he wasn't missed overnight. An early morning jogger discovered him. They won't confirm the cause of death yet, but it's fairly obvious, I'd say. Either way, he was murdered. They don't have any leads, but they are linking it to Callie Irwin's re-appearance.'

'Anything about Kate?'

'They won't confirm her name, but DI Comfort did hint that they are seeking someone in connection with the case. It's Kate all right, but they won't reveal it publicly, not unless she's formally made a suspect. Otherwise, there's nothing new. I'm going to be stuck in the office all day final-ising the front page for tomorrow's edition. You're at the wind farm today, aren't you?'

Charlotte had lost track of what day it was.

'Is it Tuesday already?'

'Yes, Tuesday. I've got to get back sharpish and file this story. Will you be okay on your own?'

She would be more than okay; it gave her some space to think things through. She was also keen to check out Dr Maxwell Henderson, an itch she was keen to scratch.

'May I use the car for the wind farm? Will you book it out for me when you get back to the office? Do I need to sign anything at the office or is the insurance sorted now?'

Nigel and Charlotte made their plans while Toni Lawson and DI Comfort wound up the press briefing, having batted off any searching questions. The customary appeal for witnesses was made, but it was clear the police were playing their cards close to their chest on this one.

'I'm going to mention to DI Comfort that we spoke to Evan, if that's okay?' Charlotte suggested. 'We ought to, since we were among the last people to see him alive.'

'Yes, do that,' Nigel answered. 'It might save the police some time if an eyewitness says they saw us with him.'

Charlotte waited for a radio reporter to finish talking to DI Comfort, then caught his attention.

'Before you ask, you can't go to the crime scene and photograph the site—' he began.

'No, it's not about that,' Charlotte said. 'I just wanted you to know that we were speaking to Evan Farrish about his connection with the Irwin case for the paper.'

DI Comfort's eyes lit up, as if she'd just offered to buy him a free lunch.

'Look, I'm heading back to the station. Can you meet me back there and we can do this somewhere more private?'

Charlotte checked the time on her phone. It was just past nine o'clock, but it felt like lunchtime already, with Jed having woken her up so early. She decided to chance her luck and get a head of steam on the day.

'I need to chat to one of your officers at the police station. Can I hitch a lift?'

She couldn't believe her luck when DI Comfort agreed. At this rate, she'd be able to get all the insurance calls out of the way, then pick things up at the wind farm later. And she desperately needed to change into her own clothes; she didn't want everybody talking about her dishevelled appearance. Once she'd brought Nigel up to speed with her plans, she was chatting away to DI Comfort on her way back to Morecambe in no time at all.

She chanced her luck, probing the DI for more information than he'd given at the briefing, but he'd been paying attention at his press training and was resistant to her tricks.

It was worth a shot. He dismissed her information about their encounter with Evan Farrish as being unlikely to give him any leads.

As Charlotte walked with him into the reception area of Morecambe Police Station, she was certain she noticed the officer at the desk rolling his eyes when he saw her. She couldn't be sure if it was just the sight of her again, or a reaction to her sartorial choices. It didn't matter. She gave her statement and received a crime number, which meant she could sort out the insurance.

She walked back from the police station to the guest house, although it was a little further than she'd have liked. The strain of recent events was weighing heavy on her; given the chance, she would probably sleep for a week. A bath would help. She had time for an hour's soak before heading out to the wind farm. It would help to recharge her batteries and think things through.

But that plan went out of the window the moment she walked through the door of the guest house.

She cringed as she walked up the path. The boarded-up window looked terrible; how embarrassing that it would be the first thing the guests saw. Isla and Agnieszka were just about to finish setting up the dining room after breakfast as she arrived.

'Everything all right here?' she asked, trying to sound as casual as possible.

Agnieszka and Isla burst out laughing when they saw her.

'Okay, okay, I know it's not the best I've looked,' she protested, pretending to be offended. Isla and Agnieszka were more concerned about what had happened to her. She reassured them that she was fine, and that the clothes she'd been given to replace her wet ones were causing her more problems than the near miss at Sunderland Point. She kept to her official and edited version of events, sparing them both the full truth.

'Oh, some chap called in about twenty minutes ago,' Isla said as Charlotte was about to leave the dining room. 'His name was Jed. He had something to pass on, from a Kate Allan I think. I put it in an envelope and placed it behind the check-in counter.'

Charlotte had to think twice whenever she heard the name Kate Allan, only ever having known her as DCI Summers. She thanked Isla and found the sealed envelope addressed to her, tearing it open in her eagerness to see what had made Jed call in so soon after dropping her off at Heysham.

Inside the envelope was a damp scrap of paper with a phone number scribbled on it. It looked like Kate's hand had been wet when she'd written it, the ink was so smudged. Kate had scrawled a short note underneath, in haste it would seem. *Call from a phone box only,* it read.

CHAPTER EIGHT

Charlotte didn't recognise it as Kate's regular mobile phone number. But she'd been caught like this already; the text she'd received the day before was supposedly from Kate. That message had taken her to Sunderland Point where somebody had tried to kill her. A shudder ran through her as she realised how exposed she was. If only Kate was still available to confide in as a police officer. She needed the force's help and protection, yet Kate had specifically warned her off. Even as she'd been speaking to DI Comfort in the car on the way back from Heysham, she'd held back a little, just in case he was the rogue officer that Kate had warned her about.

Agnieszka and Isla joined her in the hallway.

'You look shaken, my dear,' Isla said. 'I hope everything is all right. That must have been quite a fright you got out at Sunderland Point. It's terrifying when you get caught out by the tides.'

'I'm fine, Isla, thank you. And you too Agnieszka, thank you both for your concern. I'm going to nip upstairs and have a soak in the bath. That's all I need right now.

Agnieszka, can you cover for me for the next two mornings? I'm going to be rather tied up.'

'Sure thing,' Agnieszka replied. 'We have a short break from seminars this week, so it is a good time for me. How is it you say, make the hay while the sun is shining?'

'Exactly. That's a big help, thank you. And are you okay with everything, Isla? I promise we'll have a staff night out as soon as I get on top of this news story.'

'I'm fine, Charlotte, though I am going to need to talk to you about reducing my hours again soon. Nothing immediate, but I'm beginning to struggle now, especially when we've got a lot of guests in.'

Charlotte never wanted to lose Isla; she'd been a blessing to the entire guest house enterprise from the start. But she'd noticed how tired Isla looked, and with George's health scare and his ongoing monitoring, her friend was long overdue a well-earned retirement.

'Of course, Isla,' she said, touching her arm. 'I'll make sure we get this night out; let's talk then. You deserve more time at home with George and Una.'

Charlotte walked up the stairs, her legs aching. One of the kids had bought her some bath salts for Christmas; they'd been languishing in the bathroom, but this seemed like the ideal opportunity to use them. Everything could wait until she'd dozed in the bath for half an hour.

At least Lucia had left already. That was one less thing to think about. She put Hollie's phone on charge in the kitchen, placing Kate's message and Hollie's SIM card on top to keep everything together. Then she went to the bathroom and ran a piping hot bath. The bath salts were tucked under the sink alongside the bleach and toilet cleaner. The box was damp, and she had to force the crystals apart before tipping them into the hot water.

Before long, the water was several inches deep and the entire room was fogged with steam like a sauna. Charlotte took off the clothes Jed had given her. The shirt and the waist band of the trousers would have swamped even Will. After carefully folding them up, she tested the water by placing one foot gingerly into it, then lowered herself in slowly, allowing her skin to adjust to the heat as she did so. She sank into the water and closed her eyes, almost dozing off.

The only sound was a dripping from the hot tap which she couldn't be bothered to lean over and turn off. This was exactly what she needed. She remained like that for some time, drifting off, thinking about nothing; it was glorious.

Then, from the kitchen, she heard a beep from her mobile phone and her mind reactivated like a newly booted computer. There was no way she was getting out of the bath to check it, but she couldn't afford to fall asleep. She had things to do and important decisions to make.

Rather fittingly, whichever child had bought her the bath salts had opted for the herbal Muscle Soak option. The smell of thyme filled the bathroom and reinvigorated her, and the fog in her head began to clear. As her focus returned, so did her clarity. She had to make a plan; she couldn't allow things to drift any more.

First, Lucia and Olli were out of harm's way. That had been her biggest headache. If Vinnie Mace, or whoever it was, targeted the guest house again, at least they were safe at Olli's place in Lancaster. She'd have time to call the garage and the home insurance people before picking up the company car from The Bay View Weekly in the town centre. The window would be straightforward enough to replace, once she'd got authorisation for the work, and the car would be a write-off. It was an inconvenience, but not the end of the world; they lived centrally, and the buses were reliable.

She sank a little lower into the bath water. It was warm and comforting, so different from the cold and hostile sea water which had been swirling around her in the car like a fearsome enemy which could have taken her life. A wave of anxiety rippled through her body, but she pushed it away, refusing to be taunted by thoughts of what might have happened to her. Kate and Jed had saved her, and now Kate needed her help.

DI Comfort would do anything to get his hands on Kate's telephone number on the scrap of paper. Well, he wasn't going to. Kate had asked for her trust and Charlotte was happy to give it. She'd call the number from a pay phone near the post office, on the way to collect the company vehicle.

Then there was Callie Irwin and her mystery call to Hollie's phone. Was it really Callie Irwin? It seemed unbelievable that Hollie Wickes could somehow be involved in what was going on. Will had warned she was a problematic student, but Charlotte could not even imagine how the two threads might be linked. She'd try calling that number too; it would still be in Hollie's list of received calls. She could extract the information from Hollie's phone if she swapped the SIM cards around again.

The water was cooling now. Charlotte raised her right foot and wrapped her toes around the hot tap, succeeding in turning it on and adding a shot of much needed warm water. She also needed to consider her personal safety. Was it safe for her to be in the guest house? Was she a target? Somebody had knocked her out cold at Sunderland Point, that much was for sure. But was it Vinnie Mace? Vinnie had given her his warning and she and

Nigel had done nothing to antagonise Fabian Armstrong since then.

The details of what had happened at Sunderland Point were hazy. She'd been leaning across the car, backing out, when her attacker struck her from behind. Closing her eyes, she tried to recall everything. If she'd been describing it to the police – which she should have been doing if she wasn't protecting Kate Summers – she'd have said it was cack-handed, not a blow from somebody who was experienced. An attack by Vinnie Mace would have been completely different.

Then she knew, with absolute clarity. She jumped in the bath water, splashing water over the side and onto the vinyl flooring. The person who'd struck her was not a man. She didn't need to have seen their face to know, she'd sensed it. And now she could recall their most striking feature. The person who'd done that to her was tall. Very tall. Just like the person who'd left the package in Callie's room in the ICU when the fire alarms had been set off.

CHAPTER NINE

December 1999

Kate had to attend a briefing first thing that morning. It felt like the entire country was heading for a precipice; the level of planning and preparation for the new millennium was unlike anything she'd ever encountered before. The computer systems had been crawled over by expensive consultants, everything that had a plug on it had been assessed for risk, and planning for policing on the big night had reached fever pitch.

She was glad to be on shift that night, sick of the millennium already. She failed to see how a few digital clocks getting confused about the time could bring the world to an end, although the way everybody was speaking, she half expected the world's nuclear arsenals to launch spontaneously the moment the clocks declared that it was midnight.

A good sleep always helped her to put the previous day's events into perspective. The learning curve was so steep that she sometimes wondered if the work would ever become routine, as it seemed to be to fellow officers like PC Owen. He'd only been a constable for two years longer than she had. She was conscious of letting down her colleagues when she failed to apprehend a runaway or lost control of a situation. PC Owen would mock her at first, then reassure her that she'd get the hang of it if she just kept throwing herself back in the ring.

'Once you get used to dealing with these pricks, you'll see that they're all the same. They've all got more mouth than muscle and it doesn't take much to bring the scrotes to heel.'

If that were the case, her father would still be alive. If Kate had learned one thing from her father, it was that criminals weren't all the same. Many were as PC Owen described, local tow-rags who'd be more at ease if they were still stealing dinner money in a school playground. But having heard her father's stories, she knew better than that; there were some very dangerous people about.

After finishing her morning coffee, Kate put her hair up so it would satisfy the strict guidelines on personal appearance: a plain hair band in keeping with the uniform. She liked the way she always got clear guidance from the police. When she'd worked in the shop, it had been an *anything goes* policy. Shannon and Dawn had expressed their freedom to the extreme, showing far too many curves and more than enough cleavage for a china and knick-knacks shop.

She checked her uniform in the full-length mirror which she'd purchased especially for the hallway in her flat, using a clothes brush to remove specks of dust. Preparing for drills and parades had been a highlight of her training and she saw no need to let those high standards slip now.

Satisfied that she would pass even the closest scrutiny,

she rearranged her clothing so that it was more appropriate for off-duty travel on public transport and put on her coat to seem more like a civilian. She grabbed her bag, locked up her flat and headed out onto Marine Road.

The sight of the sea always invigorated her, whatever the time of year. Today the sky was a beautiful clear blue, affording an unblemished view across the bay towards Cumbria. She walked up to the pedestrian crossing which ran close to The Battery, went across and waited for her bus to take her closer to the station. She'd soon discovered that it was best not to draw attention to herself before she was on shift. It would only encourage the occasional *pigs* comments from the local teenagers and sometimes confuse elderly passengers who'd ask for directions or want to report perceived crimes from the top level of a double-decker bus.

She enjoyed the bustle of the morning shift. When she'd been biding her time in shop work, the day got off to a slow, painful start. They used to gather on the street – come rain or shine – and wait for the owner to open up. Then they'd occupy themselves with boring activities: adjusting displays, dusting showcase items and vacuuming the store. On a weekday, customers would be scarce until after ten o'clock, sometimes as late as eleven, and the high street would die down after three, with a minor surge of annoying teenagers making their way home from school just before closing time.

At Morecambe Police Station, there was always a buzz. Maybe it was an exciting incident the night before, or perhaps a tale of daring and bravery from one of her more senior colleagues. She smiled when she saw her friend Nayeema in the locker area. Their shifts rarely brought them together, but she always enjoyed a catch-up when they did. Nayeema had started at Morecambe the same week as her, so it was always good to hear how she was getting on.

'Hi, Nayeema, are you in for the briefing? I take it you're working on New Year's Eve?'

'Hi, Kate, it seems like ages since we caught up. We must go out on the town one night. Yes, I'm here for the briefing. I don't think anybody's off work that night, are they? I've never seen a panic like it. You'd think it was the end of the world.'

'How's everything going? Are you getting used to it yet?'

Nayeema stopped a moment and checked in the mirror that her tie was properly adjusted.

'I can't believe the racist abuse that I get,' she began. 'I thought the uniform would put a stop to all that, but apparently not.'

She lowered her voice.

'I've experienced a bit of it among our senior colleagues too. Nothing hostile, just hovering in the background. I'm probably being naive, but I didn't expect to face that nonsense here.'

'That's awful, Nayeema. I didn't realise it was such a problem for you. Have you tried speaking to a Sergeant?'

'Would you?'

Kate thought for all of two seconds.

'No, I wouldn't, actually. Look, if you need to get anything off your chest, I'm always here for you. Let's go for that drink sometime.'

'Yes, I'd like that. The rest of the job is fine; it can be exciting at times. I was caught up in a chase across a school field yesterday, with four of us trying to retrieve a dangerous dog that had been snapping at kids in a playground.'

'Wow, that sounds thrilling. I know what you mean, though. No two days are the same. It's the domestics I don't like. At least we get to shut up some of these blokes and give their wives and girlfriends a break. I just worry that they go straight back home and start hitting them all over again.'

Kate checked her own tie, put her jacket on once again and the two PCs scrutinised each other to make sure they'd got their appearance just right.

'I feel like a chimpanzee grooming you,' Kate laughed as she picked a speck of dust off Nayeema's uniform.

There was a flow of junior and senior staff to the briefing room, making it more cramped than Kate had seen it before. She was glad of the chance to look around the room and get a fix on names and ranks; it could be confusing working out who did what.

The briefing began promptly, treated much like a royal visit in the meticulous organisation and assignment of tasks. She observed a larger number of suits in the room than was customary; the new millennium was clearly occupying even those in the most senior ranks.

The officer leading the briefing looked like a man under pressure, more concerned about pacifying those above him than he was about briefing the troops. She smiled at Nayeema as they were allocated their tasks for the night. Kate felt like she'd won the bingo. She'd been assigned to the town centre and promenade, patrolling alone on foot for much of the evening. She took it as a show of confidence in her abilities, having been promised the prospect of solo patrols. Although terrified at the thought, she knew she'd gain in confidence more quickly if she didn't always have someone like PC Owen to pick up after her and take the lead.

'There's a big gathering on the sea front somewhere near The Midland Hotel,' the officer continued, 'and the pubs will be packed to the nines, so let's make sure everybody's aware of a police presence in the area and that they all feel safe. We're expecting the usual trouble in the pubs and clubs and there'll be a lot of fireworks going off at midnight, even more than a regular fireworks night, so that's likely to cause some issues for our fire-fighting colleagues. Those of you on cell duty, expect a busy night. Let's stay alert on the radios and make sure everybody has a good time.'

One of the senior officers piped up from the opposite side of the room. She didn't recognise him; he was an inspector, she thought.

'It's worth mentioning that we're expecting more suicide attempts than usual over this period. We always get a surge over Christmas and New Year, but you more junior team members, speak to a senior officer or a colleague if you need to know more about it.'

There were the usual questions and answers to conclude with, but within the half hour, they were on their way, ready to make a start on a new day, delivering law and order across the resort.

'Sounds fine, doesn't it?' Nayeema said as they walked out of the briefing room together.

'I'm looking forward to it,' Kate said, smiling at her. 'I get to patrol on my own, I'm on my home patch and I'll see the fireworks along the sea front. It sounds like a perfect night of policing to me.'

CHAPTER TEN

Charlotte was still thinking about the identity of the tall woman as Sam Halford's assistant attached her harness for the climb to the top of the wind turbine. This was the second harness she'd been trussed up in the last two days; it was becoming a habit. At least this time she'd be attached to a safety cable which ran the length of the ladder inside the body of the turbine. She wasn't ready to trust in another human being yet, not unless she'd confirmed their identity beforehand.

She was thankful for her long soak in the bath which had reinvigorated her for the rest of the day. Her *To Do* list was already complete, and she'd found the phone box on her walk over to the newspaper offices, but had drawn a blank with the number scrawled on the scrap of paper. She'd try again later.

As she'd expected, the car was a write-off and the insurance was sorted as best as it could be. A cheque would be in the post, apparently. Finally, thanks to Rich at 24/7 *Lightning Glaziers* and an unusually efficient insurance company operator, the window at the front of the guest house would be repaired by the end of the day, so long as there were no complications. Not bad for a morning's work. It would get Will off her back for a short time.

Sam's assistant was a woman called Rebecca. She issued her instructions. 'Okay, gloves, hat and goggles at all times and never remove the clip from the safety cable. I'll do it for you when we reach each of the platforms. Sam will meet us there; he radioed me ten minutes ago to say he's on site.'

Charlotte pulled at the harness and checked the seams and clips. There were no problems, but she wasn't leaving anything to chance. It had been interesting to see the farm house, presumably the place where Fabian and Tiffany had been raised. Now it was a private property. The wind farm offices had been constructed from the original farm buildings.

The two of them looked like they were about to ascend the Empire State Building, with their fluorescent branded overalls and safety gear. They'd even given her a pair of heavy boots, as her lightweight footwear was unsuitable for the climb. One of Rebecca's colleagues took photos of them both on the Hollie's hybrid phone which Charlotte had brought along with her and then they left the small office complex to head over in a 4x4 vehicle and join Sam, who'd entered the wind farm from the far side.

He was waiting for them by one of the nearby turbines. Charlotte could see that the door which gave access to the structure was open already. As they moved closer, she got a much truer sense of scale. Sam looked tiny standing next to the open doorway, yet she'd never considered the turbines to be particularly high.

After exchanging greetings, he started filling her in with the basics she'd need for her article: the number of turbines in the cluster, how much electricity they generated, how high they were and how many homes they powered.

'Ninety metres doesn't sound that high,' Charlotte remarked. 'Do you have any examples of structures at a similar height, so I can give readers an idea of what we have here?'

'It's higher than a cathedral's tower, or if you're familiar with the Blackpool Tower, think of it as roughly the same height as the viewing platform at the top. It's the height of the Statue of Liberty, so not aeroplane altitudes but tall enough to be scary if you don't like heights.'

One of the things she loved about being a reporter was the behind-the-scenes access. People seemed to think nothing of showing reporters around their premises if it achieved some positive PR. Charlotte found it fascinating and a wonderful privilege.

Sam and Rebecca gave her a full safety briefing and warned her that she would not be allowed to take her mobile phone out for photographs as they were making the climb to the top.

'If you drop that thing from a height, it could cause serious damage to somebody at the bottom. So, nothing loose when we make the climb; it's an extremely strict rule.'

They walked up the metal steps and entered the body of the turbine. The wind was cut off and their voices echoed around the vast, open space above them. Charlotte looked up, taking plenty of photographs from all angles before she had to secure Hollie's phone once again.

'That doesn't seem so high,' she said to Rebecca, who chuckled as if she was humouring her.

'That's just the first platform,' she replied. 'There are two more before we get to the top.'

Rebecca went first as Sam explained that they allowed a

specific distance along the ladder for health and safety purposes. Charlotte waited for Rebecca to get some distance up the ladder, then Sam connected her to the safety wire and explained how if she fell, it would hold her. She should await Rebecca's instructions at the platform and not touch the clips that were securing her under any circumstances.

Charlotte put one foot on the bottom rung of the ladder and smiled as Sam took photographs for her newspaper article.

'I'll take plenty of you when you reach each platform and send them over as soon as I get a decent connection,' he said. 'Now, get that phone zipped up in your overalls pocket and you're ready to start the climb.'

She stared up at Rebecca who was some way ahead of her. Already she looked smaller. The sense of scale was difficult to get a grasp of inside the turbines. She'd only ever been up step ladders before, never having even climbed up a house ladder to wash the upstairs windows. Will feared heights, so he didn't even bother keeping a ladder around the house. They paid for window cleaners instead.

The first ten steps were fine, but as she gained some height, she saw how many more it would take to reach just the first platform. Rebecca seemed a ridiculous distance ahead of her already, and even when she made the next ten steps, she didn't seem to be any closer to the top. The ladder itself was narrow and solid, but unlike a house ladder, it didn't slope at all, it went straight up. That made the climb harder for her, hauling her entire body weight upwards with every step.

She cursed the clumsy gloves for making it so difficult to get a secure grip on the curved rungs. The boots were like small blocks of concrete on her feet. Plimsolls or trainers would have been a better choice. She continued the climb, aware that Sam was now beginning his ascent below her, while Rebecca had reached the first platform. She was out of breath already and her legs were growing sore with the constant upwards thrusting from one small step to the next.

Charlotte glanced down, immediately regretting it. In the heart of a vast, steel, cylindrical structure, the height felt stark. At the top of most tall buildings, there was usually something to hang on to. Here, it was straight up and straight down, with no surrounding frames or barriers for safety. There was only a narrow ladder and a safety harness.

She tried to reason it out; if she didn't look up or down, she would be fine taking just one step at a time. But she could hear Sam below her and Rebecca above her, and their sounds gave her a sense of the distance between them. For the first time she wondered if she'd make it to the top.

She kept going, one foot after the other, until Rebecca's voice grew louder.

'Okay, you're almost at the first platform now. You can take a short break here for some photographs. I want you to climb up above the base of the platform, then I'll help you across. Right, up you come.'

Charlotte followed the instructions, watching Rebecca for guidance as she talked her through how to step off the ladder safely and onto the platform. As her boots landed on the metal surface, she was struck by how insubstantial it was, shaking with their weight. She stood back from the ladder and felt the safety of the curved walls against her back. After getting her breath back, she peered upwards at the distance she still had to climb.

'Oh my God, it's so high,' she said to Rebecca. 'It's like a ladder to heaven, going on and on.'

Rebecca was readying herself to help Sam onto the platform. He'd maintained a much better pace than Charlotte and seemed to take the climb in his stride.

'It's much higher than you think, isn't it?' he grinned, as he unzipped his pocket and took out his phone. 'Let's make sure we get lots of photos, so you have plenty for your report.'

As he took pictures from various angles, Charlotte wondered if she had the stomach for the remainder of the climb. She had twice as much height still to cover, possibly more; it was so difficult to get a sense of scale.

Rebecca was readying herself for the second stage of the climb. Charlotte wondered if they'd be annoyed if she ducked out. She'd be teased relentlessly at the newspaper offices if she didn't go through with it.

Rebecca set off on the second part of the ascent, but Sam looked like he had something he wanted to say. He was watching Rebecca make her climb, evidently waiting for her to get out of earshot.

'I wanted to tell you something,' Sam whispered, 'but it has to remain off the record. You can't use me as a source, and I'd deny it if anybody asked. I need this job. But when you were asking me about Tiffany and Fabian the other day, it set me thinking. It's been a long time since the events which resulted in this wind farm being built. Fabian was furious about it at the time; Tiffany had outmanoeuvred him in some way and blocked all his moves to use the land for a more lucrative venture. But something personal was going on, which I think confused things.'

He looked upwards, gauging Rebecca's progress.

'We'd best get you clipped back on to that safety cable.'

He motioned with his hand that Charlotte should step towards the middle of the platform.

'Tiffany was having an affair, despite having a young

family. I never figured out who it was with, but I came across her once, when those offices were still farm buildings. She had guilt written all over her face. And her husband David was nowhere to be seen. I think that was the cause of a lot of what happened on the night they all disappeared.'

CHAPTER ELEVEN

Rebecca had made rapid progress up the ladder, so they couldn't postpone the next stage any longer. Sam made certain that Charlotte was securely clipped to the safety cable before she continued her ascent. The climb was even tougher at this second level; her calves were tight from continually hauling herself upwards. If she'd thought the first section of the wind turbine was high, this mid-section was much worse. It was tempting fate to look down, but she couldn't resist when she heard Sam starting his own ascent below her. Besides, she'd felt the ladder vibrating as he'd confidently placed his weight on the lower rungs. It took her by surprise, making her feel vulnerable for a moment.

The height took her breath away; how could it possibly be so much bigger than it appeared from the outside? Inside the circular, narrowing shell there was nothing to focus on other than how far she'd come and how far she still had to climb. The thick power cables running from top to bottom were of little help in ascertaining how far she'd come, but at least they served as a reminder of the function served by the massive turbines.

The steps seemed endless. Aware of Rebecca reaching the second platform above her, Charlotte was now so scared of the height, she dared not even look up. Instead she stared straight ahead, taking one step at a time, less certain with each move whether she'd be able to find the courage to make the next one.

'You're almost there,' Rebecca shouted from above her. Charlotte looked up, her attention caught by the sudden sound of a voice. As she did, she lost her bearings, forgetting where she was and how precariously she was perched. Her hand loosened on the rung above her head. She tightened it swiftly, but the sharp pang of fear caused her to misjudge where her foot was due to land. Instead of settling on a rung, the toe cap on her boots struck it and she couldn't shift her body weight as she'd expected. She panicked, tightening the grasp of her hands, but not getting a firm enough grip of the rung to her side. Her body slipped away from the ladder, the shock running through her body as if she'd reached out and touched a bare electrical cable. She heard Sam's voice below.

'It's okay, the harness has got you, just go with it—'

She screamed as her whole body dropped like a dead weight. Unlike the parachute jump, there was no resistance. For a fraction of a second, she thought she was in complete free fall, a terrifying sensation. Then, almost as quickly as she'd fallen, the harness tugged around her legs and body as the steel cable took her weight. She closed her eyes, unable to force them open. If she looked down, she would lose her mind.

Sam's boots clanged on the rungs below her, mingling with his shouts as he tried to reassure her. Rebecca too had seen what happened and was in a state of high alert, giving a reminder that the safety gear had got her. For what seemed a lifetime, Charlotte hung there, her body weight supported by the harness, unable to reach the ladder with her arms or legs. She closed her eyes and willed Sam to reach her, as her breathing quickened in frantic gasps of panic. Please, make it end. At last his gloved hands touched her arm.

'It's okay, Charlotte, I'm here. I'm going to take your right arm and guide it over to the closest rung, okay?'

'Just do it, please. Get me back on the ladder.'

Gently, he took her gloved hand and placed it on a rung. Still her eyes were closed.

'Now your left hand,' he said, guiding her over once again.

She opened her eyes momentarily, then shut them again, realising how exposed she was.

'I'm going to guide your boots over to the rungs now. Work with me, don't fight me,' Sam continued, his voice calm and reassuring. As he moved her left foot over to the rung, she put her weight on it, clinging on tightly with her hands. She brought her right foot in without his help and began to breathe normally again.

'Well done. You're safe now; everything's fine. Try to relax a moment, then we'll move up towards Rebecca. Are you okay? Do you hurt anywhere?'

Charlotte scolded herself for such a ridiculous reaction. Sam had told her the harness was secure, yet she'd panicked and made herself look silly.

'My dignity is in tatters,' she replied, opening her eyes. She glanced up again; the height was still terrifying.

'I don't think I can go on,' she said.

'It's easier to keep going upwards,' Sam replied. 'You're almost at the next platform, and the final stage isn't anywhere near as bad. This bit is always the section that scares people the most. Can you carry on? Just one step at a time; take as long as you need.'

Charlotte's heart had stopped thudding in her chest, and the temporary paralysis had subsided.

'I think I can,' she said, as much to herself as to Sam. She moved her left hand up a rung.

'Perfect,' Sam told her. 'Just fifteen more rungs to go and Rebecca will be there to help you onto the platform.'

Charlotte took one rung at a time, making sure she had a firm grasp and secure footing before she took the next move. It was only when she felt Rebecca's hands touching her shoulders from above that she dared open her eyes.

'Just another four steps and you'll be on it. You're doing brilliantly,' Rebecca prompted. 'I was terrified the first time I did this. There's no shame; nothing prepares you for just how high up these things are.'

Rebecca helped her over to the platform and unclipped her harness. Charlotte rushed over to the edge of the turbine and sat down, relieved to feel the cold, solid metal of the shell against her back. Moments later, Sam joined them and made his way over to check that everything was okay.

'I feel really stupid,' Charlotte said.

'It's no problem, honestly, so long as you aren't hurt,' Sam replied. 'Let's take a moment and get our breath back. You're almost there; remember, the last section is nowhere near as high.'

Charlotte glanced upwards and realised he was right. She'd come this far, so she might as well force herself to the top. She would never live it down if she had to go back to the office and admit she'd chickened out.

After almost ten minutes, she was ready to stand up again. She reasoned that if she could only force herself to tackle that last section of the ladder, she'd be at the top and that would be the worst of it. Besides, in her rational mind, the worst had already happened. The safety gear had done its job and the entire incident had been petrifying, but she was safe.

'Are you ready to take more photographs?' Sam asked.

Charlotte nodded and put on a brave face, posing for photographs like nothing had happened. She'd already worked out how she was going to approach this feature when she wrote it up for the newspaper; she'd be truthful about just how scary it was to climb up there. Nobody would have shared that part of the experience before. Most of what she'd read about wind turbines was dry and technical, but her article would paint a much more vivid picture for readers.

'Okay, last section now,' Rebecca said, as she readied herself for the last part of the climb. 'Just take it one rung at a time. There's no rush, Charlotte. Believe me, when you reach the top, you'll be so glad you made yourself do it.'

She was right. It was the last thing on earth that Charlotte wanted to do, but she forced herself back onto that ladder and made her way – more slowly this time – up to the top. This time it didn't involve nearly as many steps, so as long as she didn't look down, she was able to carry on. Finally, she reached the last platform, which unlike the others was rectangular. This had to be the top.

The area resembled an engine room, with more cables than she'd ever seen in her life, all clustered together. She was no engineer, but she could see a large, engine-like contraption at the front which seemed to be linked to the exterior rotors at the front. At the rear, it connected to a generator or some such device, judging from the number of cables running from it. Sam joined them in the upper cabin area and shook her hand.

'See, you made it. Congratulations. I thought you might back out after your stumble, but you recovered well.'

Charlotte was overcome with pride. The sense of achievement had been snatched from her during the tandem parachute jump, but this time it was a personal victory, a triumph over her sense of terror.

'How brave are you feeling now?' Rebecca smiled.

'It depends what you're going to say next,' Charlotte said, grimacing.

'We can open up the doors at the back of the turbine. You'll get an incredible view of the bay from here. Are you game?'

When she'd reached the top of the turbine, Rebecca had promptly fastened her harness onto a new safety track which ran along the top of the structure, even though it seemed much safer up here, almost like being in a small office cabin.

'Ready?' Sam asked.

Charlotte nodded. He took some keys out of his pocket and placed them in a locking mechanism at the rear of the turbine. As he opened the two doors, natural light flooded in. There were three chains clipped across the opening for extra security; Charlotte was pleased about that.

She squinted as her eyes adjusted to the change in lighting. They were right; the views across the bay were spectacular. She may as well have been sitting at the crest of a mountain, the landscape was so remarkable.

'Now that is incredible,' she said, her breath taken away at the sheer scale and beauty of the panorama ahead of her.

'If you look out to sea over there, way off in the distance, you'll see some white structures on the horizon. That's the Barrow, Walney and West Duddon wind farms. We have turbines out there as well. If you think this turbine is high, you should try climbing up one of those things.'

Charlotte struggled to focus on them, so far off in the distance.

'How far away are they from the coast?' she asked. 'They look like they're miles away.'

'Not so far,' Rebecca chipped in. 'Around nine to ten miles out at sea. Barrow Wind Farm is only four miles out.'

'Only four miles,' Charlotte laughed. 'I'm pleased I made it to the top but let me be clear, this is the last time I'm ever climbing up one of these things. And the thought of doing this out at sea? No way. That will never happen.'

CHAPTER TWELVE

December 1999

Kate walked through the doors of the Arndale Centre, scanning the area to get a sense of who was inside. At just after ten o'clock in the morning, it was a wash of blue rinses and walking sticks, the resort's pensioners getting a head start on the day so they could be back in front of their TV by lunchtime. She'd been on the beat long enough to know that school truants were the biggest hazard at this time of day. It was a good opportunity to sneak a look in the shop windows and see if there was anything worth buying when she came off shift.

A tall Christmas tree had been set up in a central area, beautifully decorated with baubles and tinsel and surrounded by gift-wrapped boxes and small plastic likenesses of Santa and his elves. Slade's *Merry Christmas Everybody* had faded out, to be replaced by Wizard's *I Wish It Could Be Christmas Every Day*. She spared a moment to sympathise with the shop assistants who were cursed with endless festive tunes until Christmas Eve, when the retail world would pivot to selling summer holidays. She'd not worked in retail for long after university, but she knew the musical hell that was Christmas.

There was the usual array of chain shops. In retail land it appeared to be the preferred time for tweaking window displays. She watched as a teenage boy awkwardly manoeuvred a pink bra onto a mannequin in the window of Dorothy Perkins, smiling to herself as she thought of the evil female staff who'd set up this hapless school leaver or work experience assistant to humiliate himself in public. Still, it was causing some amusement among the pensioners, who cackled to each other as he placed the two bra cups on the mannequin's shoulder blades, upside down. Kate only hoped he had it all figured out by the time he got a steady girlfriend. Whoever had placed the poor kid in a woman's clothing store must have wanted to punish him for some misdemeanour or other; it seemed a cruel fate for one so young.

As her radio crackled, she tuned in and out of the sounds around her, so she could be alert to messages or calls for assistance from Control. There was a request for officer support over by the promenade. She checked in and offered to assist, but Nayeema was closer, so she got to watch the end of the bra saga. After ten minutes of watching him struggle, two middle-age, female members of staff stepped up into the window display area and put him out of his misery. By this time, he'd managed to position the two cups around the mannequin's head like a pair of pink, lacy goggles. She wanted to tell the lad to defect to Burton's; it would be much more his style.

'Excuse me, constable,' came a voice behind her. 'I wonder if you could show us where the public conveniences are.'

Kate turned round and smiled. Two pensioners were standing there, with identikit perms and beige outfits, their hands firmly clutching the handles of military grade shopping trolleys. She steered them in the right direction.

For her first day out on the streets alone, the more of that sort of query she had to handle, the better. They'd given her and Nayeema easy territory to start with, and the duty Sergeant was keeping in regular contact. She had feared that she might end up as cack-handed as the teenager in the window of Dorothy Perkins, but so far it was going well, and she felt in control.

It was time for her break, so she doubled back on herself and made for a bakery store which also served hot drinks. She checked in with Control, got the all-clear and bought herself a custard doughnut and a cup of coffee. There was a tabloid newspaper on the Formica table, so she picked it up and flicked through the pages. It wasn't even Christmas yet, but millennium preparations were dominating.

The articles revealed much national fretting over the Millennium Dome in London, which had become something of a liability for the UK government. All the newspaper headlines claimed it might not be ready to open its doors on January 1st. Kate turned over the paper to hide the story, sick of hearing about it already. She would be spending the New Year working among the revellers, well out of it as far as hangovers and unwanted midnight kisses were concerned. It was much better that way.

As she looked up from her coffee, she caught sight of a man from behind and did a double take. He was holding a woman's hand; she had two toddlers in a double pram, and one child on foot. It was Brett, and his companion was the same woman she'd spotted him with briefly in the nightclub.

Kate jumped up at her table, keen to let him know she was there, but stopped before she tapped on the window of the bakery to get his attention. What was he doing holding hands in the Arndale Centre with a woman who had three young children? Their ages suggested a husband or partner was on the scene, at least until recently. Happy families weren't Brett's normal thing.

She kept her eyes on them and gulped down her tea. The doughnut was only half-eaten, but she was willing to forgo it in order to figure out what was going on with Brett. She thanked the lady at the bakery counter then walked back out into the covered parade. It was just busy enough to lurk behind them, though Brett probably wouldn't even recognise her in police uniform. He still hadn't got used to her new profession.

Brett and his mystery woman were leaving the Arndale at the Post Office exit. She figured they were heading for the library, seeing as the oldest child was carrying a garishly coloured hard-backed book as if it was some rare and valuable treasure. The bag of books perched at the bottom of the pram section confirmed her theory. They didn't appear to be in any hurry because they were walking the long way round.

Kate held back a little, lurking in the entrance while she watched to see which way they turned. Market Street... yes, it had to be the library. Although she could see they were holding hands, they were being furtive, using their winter coats and gloves to conceal it. They hadn't fooled Kate; she could tell from the body language that these two were close.

She checked in with Control, then turned to go through the doors and follow her brother along Market Street.

'Excuse me dearie, you couldn't help me, could you? I left my walking stick at the till of the shoe shop and now my knees have seized up. You wouldn't fetch it for me, would you?'

'Of course,' Kate replied, wishing the lady had timed things a little better.

She helped the lady onto a nearby bench, then retraced her steps to the first shoe shop she came across. The walking stick was hanging on the lip of one of the till counters. She told the shop assistant what she was doing, then hurried back to the elderly lady who treated her arrival like a knight in shining armour turning up on her doorstep. Kate made sure that she needed no further assistance, then sped along Market Street, frustrated to have lost sight of Brett. Still, how far could they have got? In a race between the elderly lady with her dodgy knees and a lady with a pram and a distracted toddler, it was anybody's guess who would be the slowest.

Once she'd reached the Telephone Exchange on the corner, she hung back, scanning the street for Brett. There was no sign of him, but she could see the woman and her children making their way across the car park to the library. At the sound of raised voices behind her, she turned and saw an altercation going on between two men at the rear gate of the Post Office Delivery Depot. It was Brett, in a tussle with a man she'd never seen before.

As she headed towards them, her radio crackled with an urgent call from Control, asking her to return to the Arndale. There'd been an attempt at snatching someone's cash card while they were drawing out money from a cash machine. She hesitated for a moment as she watched the unknown man grab Brett by the shirt and pull him up close to his face.

'Just back off, you piece of shit, do you hear me? Leave

them alone. You come near my family again and I'll come for you. Got it? Now piss off!'

The man threw Brett through the open gates of the Delivery Depot and stormed off towards the car park, in the direction of the library.

Every instinct told her to run towards her brother and see what he'd got himself into. But her radio crackled again as she moved towards him. Control needed her in the Arndale immediately. Whatever was going on with Brett would have to keep for later.

CHAPTER THIRTEEN

Charlotte was in pain as she walked back towards the company vehicle which she'd parked in the grounds of the former Armstrong farmyard. The descent from the wind turbine had been slow; if there'd been a way of getting down without having to use the ladder, she would have taken it without hesitation.

The prospect of the descent had been at the back of her mind all the time she had been admiring the stunning views across the bay and photographing the gearing and equipment in the contained area behind the blades. Sam had revealed that it was possible to sit on the roof of the upper section, right behind the blades, and appreciate the views from the open air. Charlotte had declined, but he hadn't pushed the issue further, instead borrowing Hollie's phone to climb up himself and take a couple of pictures for her newspaper article.

The backs of her legs were stiff and sore, her calf muscles on fire from the constant motion of taking steps up the seemingly endless ladder then down again. It had been a remarkable experience, but Charlotte was certain it would be a once in a lifetime activity. Even from the safety of the visitor's car park, the turbines seemed smaller and less imposing, a trick of the eyes which she wouldn't fall for again. Even when she'd been climbing the steps of the container lift at Heysham Port, they'd been at an angle, with railings at either side. As she'd just found out from first-hand experience, it made all the difference.

Sam and Rebecca had been sympathetic and kind, but Charlotte knew exactly what had happened inside that turbine. It had scared her out of her wits, bringing back memories of last year's terrifying experiences when she'd tried to rescue Lucia from danger at the port. That had caused another debilitating panic attack of the type she'd not experienced since teaching in Bristol. She resolved to go easier on herself; the last thing she wanted was a return to those difficult days.

Back in the office blocks, she removed the safety clothing and recovered her composure with a hot drink in the staff kitchen. After picking up a press information pack, she said her farewells to Sam and Rebecca, signed out of the visitors book and headed back for the car. Halfway across the tidy asphalt car park, she stopped and took in the scene. It was difficult to imagine this area being a muddy farmyard in a past life, but seeing the distinctive stone house beyond the wooden boundary fence helped to gain a sense of what it might have looked like when it was used for livestock.

This was where Tiffany and Fabian had grown up. Most people would regard it as a rural idyll, so why had things turned out the way they had? For Tiffany, it had led to a life incarcerated in a mental health facility, albeit a comfortable one. And what turned a farmer's son like Fabian into the man he was now, the head of a powerful energy company and a dangerous man too?

She checked the time. It was mid-afternoon, and she wasn't expected back with the car until close of play. She'd already clocked that in the life of a journalist, it was easy to lose a little time during the day. Since they were all driven by deadlines, nobody seemed to mind too much, as long as the agreed word count turned up by the agreed deadline. There was no one breathing down your neck all the time. She liked that; it gave a certain amount of autonomy which she'd never experienced as a teacher.

There was still time to pay a visit to the house owned by Maxwell Henderson, the mystery doctor who appeared to only take on particular patients, notably those who had something to hide. She'd got a rough address and a make of car, so if the car was in the drive, she'd be able to get a sense of who he was and where he lived, at least.

Charlotte got in the car, thankful to give her legs a rest. As the engine fired into life, she thought of the comments Sam had made as they'd been making their ascent. Tiffany and Fabian had been at odds over this land. There was something in their history which had somehow pitted them against each other. Jon Rogers at the library might be able to help with that; there must have been planning meetings and formal applications made at the time. If records were still available, he was the man who could lay his hands on them. It would spare her from getting involved with Fabian too. Her brush – and possibly multiple brushes – with Vinnie were something she was keen to avoid in future.

As she drew out of the car park onto the road, she took a good look at the former farmhouse which had long since been upgraded, extended and given a total makeover. The gardens were mature and well-kept, two very expensive cars were parked in the long, gravel drive, and there was still an aged metal plate on the stone wall which separated the property from the verge. On it were painted a herd of cows and the lettering *Armstrong Herd and Dairy - Holstein Friesian*. She stopped the car in the middle of the empty road and took a photograph, though she wasn't sure why. At the very least it would help Jon Rogers source the location when she found some time to pop over to the library to use his skills once again.

As she drove along the lane, she passed a traditional, red phone box. She'd thought they had long gone, but here was one at a rural crossroads, seemingly in the middle of nowhere. She parked the car on the verge and found the note that Kate Summers had left for her; it was worth another try.

She'd almost forgotten how to use an old-fashioned red phone box. When she'd tried calling Kate via the more modern apparatus outside Morecambe Post Office, she'd felt like an old skill had been wiped from her mind. She messed around finding some change, looking for the coin slot and trying to remember when the call was deemed to have begun. Was it after dialling, or when it was answered at the other end? She keyed in the number, waiting for the line to connect and ring.

There was a click as it connected. Did phones do that anymore? Well, this one did. She let it ring fourteen times, counting each one. She was just about to give up when someone answered.

'Kate?'

There was silence.

'It's Charlotte. I'm calling from a phone box like you asked. Are you okay?'

She could hear a sound in the background, as if somebody, presumably Kate, was walking, or perhaps even running.

'Kate?'

The line went dead. The phone had gobbled her money.

'That was fifty pence!' she shouted at the metal box on the wall. As far as she recalled, it was only supposed to cost ten pence for a quick call like that. She'd used up her change and there was no card facility in the phone box; she couldn't even be certain it was Kate who'd picked up. It would have to wait until later, but she was growing worried. Kate was in trouble, and they needed to talk.

She couldn't get it out of her mind all the way back to Heysham. What would make a person as senior and well-respected as DCI Kate Summers go on the run? She hadn't officially disappeared, but she wasn't making herself available to her colleagues for an interview, that was for sure.

What could cause such a sudden fall from grace? DI Comfort had stayed tight-lipped on the matter during their earlier drive from Heysham, but sure as anything, something serious was going on with Kate.

Charlotte pulled up close to where she thought Maxwell Henderson's house was located. At first, she found a spot on Heysham Road, but she thought better of it, pulling into a side road in case some eagle-eyed staff member from the newspaper spotted the liveried vehicle and later asked her what she'd been reporting on. That was a question she did not want to answer just yet.

She'd been in this area before – twice – firstly with Nigel, trying to get an interview with the local MP, Edward Callow. Then she'd been at the MP's house alone, at night, in terrible danger, with those violent men everywhere.

It didn't take long to locate Henderson's property. Although it was on the next road along from Edward Callow's, the houses were just as big. This would have been perfect for Callow on that night one year ago; if Maxwell Henderson was who she suspected him to be, some dodgy doctor for hire, the proximity of the houses would have been most convenient.

At first, she had no intention of doing anything more than looking around, assessing the scene and trying to get a glimpse of the man. But his house was on a corner plot, meaning it was bordered on two sides by a pavement. A low wall ran around the property, along which ran a wall of Leylandii which had been diligently trimmed. Her legs were stiffening now from the ladder climb, so she sat on the wall, thinking it a natural thing to do. She could kill two birds with one stone, giving her a good reason to survey Maxwell Henderson as well as take the weight off her feet. But as she sat on the wall, she saw there was a break in the hedge, so on a whim, she spun herself around and stepped through, making sure nobody was around to see her.

It took only a couple more steps before she was committed. As she moved away from the Leylandii, it was easy to get cover from a Forsythia that was planted close by. Before she knew it, she was at the side of the house, next to the kitchen window, trying to hear two, low-pitched male voices from the other side of the double-glazing. At least this man was just a doctor. Whatever his involvement with Fabian Armstrong, he wasn't employed in the intimidation end of the business.

At the sound of movement from the kitchen door, Charlotte darted around the corner to seek cover behind the wall. They were coming outside.

She peered around the corner, eager to get a proper look at Henderson. Both men had a cup of something in their hand and they were walking over towards the wooden gazebo at the far end of the garden, chatting and laughing, clearly relaxed in each other's company. Then the telephone rang inside the house. She jumped back as they turned towards the sound.

One of the men cursed, then walked back towards the kitchen door. He must be Doctor Maxwell Henderson. He seemed to be in his early sixties, with grey wavy hair. His skin had given up the struggle to remain supple some years ago. But she wanted to get a closer look at the other man. She couldn't be certain of his identity, not without getting a proper view of his face. He occupied himself in the garden while Henderson answered the phone call, examining the plants and checking his phone. Only when Henderson came out of the house, complaining loudly about a time-wasting sales call, did she get a proper look at the other man. It was Fabian Armstrong.

CHAPTER FOURTEEN

Charlotte had been here before, sneaking around the houses of dangerous men, risking getting caught red-handed, doing things which in her former life as a teacher she'd have thought unimaginable. Yet in real-life, it came one small step at a time. First the gap in the hedge, then the handy shrub cover and after that, the two men chatting away in the gazebo, leaving the kitchen door wide open. She hadn't intended on snooping on Maxwell Henderson in such an intrusive manner, but when the opportunity presented itself to her, she couldn't resist finding out more about this man.

From her hiding place at the side of the house she could see that they were enclosed in the gazebo. This was no backyard gazebo; it belonged to a man who had money in his pockets. It was draped with carefully nurtured plants and equipped with a small bar area. In a moment of madness, she darted inside the house. She might get an insight into this man if she could find his study.

The house was well proportioned and luxuriously decorated. He obviously wasn't the kind of doctor who eked out his living working long hours for the National Health

Service. The kitchen was more like a restaurant, with a coffee machine, smoothie blender, a wine cooler and a juicer lining the granite worktops as well as a rotisserie and wood-fired pizza oven built into the units. The oven was the biggest she had ever seen outside of a catering environment. It certainly put the kitchen in the guest house to shame. There was no way this doctor was earning his living prescribing aspirin and haemorrhoid treatments to Morecambe's ailing pensioners.

A newspaper left on the kitchen island caught her eye; it wasn't local. She scanned the open page as she passed by and realised it was a Preston paper, presumably brought by Fabian Armstrong. She noticed that Steven Terry was touring in the area. She almost shouted with joy when she saw that he was due to appear at Preston Playhouse later that week. That meant he'd be somewhere in the region, perhaps close enough for her to meet up with him.

She moved over to the kitchen window to check that the two men were well out of the way. Their confident, deep voices travelled well across the garden and she could tell that whatever it was they were talking about meant that they were settled for the next five minutes or so. That's all she'd need to move swiftly through the house and then get out before she was discovered.

Charlotte had seen plenty of crime dramas on the TV, so was careful not to touch any surfaces which might leave fingerprints. It wasn't as if she was there to steal anything, but she was cautious, nevertheless. Doctor Henderson's kitchen opened to an ornate dining room so tasteful that it had to have been decorated with the influence of a woman or an interior designer. It was perfect; the colour mix, table settings, artwork and glassware looked like they belonged in a high-class hotel, putting the empty fruit bowl, ketchup stained place mats and stainless steel cutlery in her own home dining area to shame.

She bypassed the lounge, which was every bit as luxurious as the rest of the house, keen to use her time wisely and avoid being too distracted by admiring the decor. As she passed the front door in the wide hallway, she saw that it used an internal locking mechanism, which meant she could leave that way, should the need arise.

At the bottom of the double width staircase, to the right of the front door, was another room. She'd already clocked that the downstairs restroom was on the left, so this could be a study. The door was ajar and opened with a gentle push of her elbow. It was indeed a doctor's study, so traditional that she wouldn't have been surprised if she'd found a screen, sink and examination couch tucked in the corner.

All the furniture was of dark wood, and the shelves were lined with a mixture of medical textbooks and fiction. She was surprised to see that Doctor Maxwell Henderson had an affinity for reading stories with macho leads such as Jack Reacher, John Milton and Joe Hunter. The amateur psychologist in her speculated that he might find working with the likes of Fabian Armstrong exhilarating, a fantasy escape from the precision of the medical profession.

The wall next to the door was covered with framed certificates. He'd qualified at the University of Sheffield and appeared to have held positions on various committees in the past, as well as securing a number of medical specialisms along the way. What was the nature of his current employment and why had he chosen that path?

She grabbed her phone, or rather Hollie Wickes' phone, from her pocket and took photographs, making sure she caught any registration or reference numbers which might be useful in her later research. Much as she was tempted to dig deeper, she already knew that she was chancing her luck; it was time to get out. She scanned the study one last time, searching for anything meaningful, then decided to quit while she was ahead. As she left the study, she walked straight into the cleaner who had come down the stairs carrying the vacuum cleaner. The machine crashed to the floor and Charlotte stood there in shock, looking into the eyes of the Filipino woman, who appeared equally terrified.

Charlotte couldn't think what to say. She almost put out her hand to introduce herself but realised how ridiculous that would be. She heard a voice at the far end of the house. It was Maxwell Henderson; he'd heard the crash and wanted to know what was going on.

'Jessica, what the hell was that? What have you broken now?'

The two women stared at each other. Jessica seemed more fearful of Henderson than she was of Charlotte.

'Okay if I go out the front door?' Charlotte whispered.

'Hurry,' Jessica whispered. 'Don't let that horrible man catch you. I will say nothing.'

Charlotte squeezed her arm.

'Thanks, Jessica. Tell him you tripped over that tuft of carpet that's coming loose on the staircase,' she said, pointing at it. 'That'll panic him; it's his responsibility as an employer to keep you safe from things like that. Good luck!'

She pulled her sleeve down over her hand, grasped the handle and managed to get out just in the nick of time as Henderson's voice came closer, admonishing Jessica for her clumsiness. She could hear the cleaner's attempts at pointing out the rogue carpet on the staircase, followed by the doctor's reply which gave a clear indication of his bullying ways. There was the threat of deportation, a suggestion that any damage would come out of her wages and the obligatory belittling comments for good measure. What drove these people? They had so much affluence in their lives, yet they seemed hellbent on denying even a fraction of it to everybody else.

Fabian's car was parked alongside Henderson's Tesla, looking modest by comparison. Even so, it was a Range Rover of some description, not a cheap run-around. She hurried up the drive, out into the road and along the opposite pavement, only realising how tense she'd been when she started trembling. It was a combination of needing food and the aftermath of the adrenaline rush from what she'd just done.

She walked back to the car, got in and checked Hollie's phone for new messages from her own SIM card inside it. There was nothing except for a confirmation that the photos she'd just taken had been backed up to the cloud. Damn, Hollie had a cloud back-up on her phone. That meant she'd see the photos and realise the phone had been stolen rather than lost.

As she was driving up Heysham Road back into Morecambe, the sight of a mini-supermarket reminded her of her hunger. Two minutes later she had bought a cheese and tomato sandwich, a smoothie and a packet of crisps. She decided to leave the car at the side of the road and walk up the short street behind the shop, which led to the sea front. This was a part of Morecambe she'd never seen before, behind the long-closed Battery pub and away from the main activity of the promenade. The four-storey houses had spectacular views over the bay, though many of them appeared to be flats now rather than guest houses or family homes.

Charlotte found a place to perch and devoured her sandwich in a couple of mouthfuls. As she picked up the smoothie bottle, she remembered Steven Terry, the clairvoyant. She checked her contacts from the SIM card. Yes, his number was there. She dialled it, postponing the prospect of her chilled smoothie for a few minutes more.

'Hello, Steven Terry.'

His distinctive, well-modulated voice was full of showmanship and authority.

'Hello, Steven, it's Charlotte Grayson from Morecambe. Remember me?'

'Charlotte, yes, and your husband Will, how could I forget? I can't recall spending the evening with many couples breaking into an abandoned amusement park then getting apprehended by the police. It was a fun night though, wasn't it?'

Charlotte thought back to the night they'd had, watching Abi performing at the static caravan park and getting a little tipsy with Steven. He was right, it had been fun, even though the local police had spotted their bungled operation minutes after it had begun.

'It was certainly that, Steven. I hear you're in Preston from Thursday night. Where are you now, anywhere near Morecambe?'

'I've been performing at Forum 28 in Barrow-in-Furness this week, and I'm heading to Preston to start a run of performances on Thursday evening. I'm passing by on the M6 on Wednesday. Does that help?'

'Yes, it does. Have you seen the big story in Morecambe?'

'No, should I have? What's going on?'

Charlotte brought him up to speed with what had happened to the Irwin children. She attempted to open her smoothie with one hand whilst talking, but couldn't manage it.

'Would you be able to meet me on the slipway

tomorrow sometime? You might be able to provide some insight for me.'

'It's a long shot, Charlotte, but I'm happy to nip off at the motorway exit on my way to Preston. It will be lovely to see you again. I'll meet you at one o'clock, is that good for you?'

Another call was coming in, from Nigel. She was late back with the company vehicle. Perhaps he was chasing her to see what was up.

'You've got my number; I'll meet you at the RNLI slipway by the Midland Hotel at that time time. Just text me if you're running late. I'll treat you to afternoon tea there, if we have time.'

Steven agreed and said goodbye. Charlotte had missed Nigel, so she rang him back.

'Nigel, hi, I'm just on my way back to the office now. Does somebody need the car?'

'We're heading to Lancaster Infirmary, Charlotte. There's been a major development. Callie Irwin just went missing, and the police haven't got a clue where she is.'

CHAPTER FIFTEEN

December 1999

Sometimes Kate would bump into Brett while out for her morning run on the promenade. She hoped that day would be one of those occasions. He hadn't replied to her text messages and she didn't need a promotion to detective to work out that something serious was going on.

She opened the main door to the flats and took a sharp intake of breath. It was cold, December cold. The path was white with frost, and the remnants of plants in the patch of garden at the front were caught in suspended animation, frozen in time until the healing kiss of Spring. She rubbed her hands together, wondering if it was worth going back for some gloves. Her aim was always to create as little disturbance as possible in the shared hallway, and she was already in and out of her flat at all hours with the erratic nature of her shifts. Some of the cadets in training had disliked the mixed shifts, craving a more 9 to 5 arrangement.

Kate loved the variable nature of it. There was nothing like getting up at some godforsaken time of the morning and feeling like she had the whole world to herself. She also loved the gift of a full day if she was working a late shift. This was a six o'clock run, though she was running a little later than normal because she knew Brett was often late. By the time she reached the town hall, she had a good chance of catching him emerging from his end of the promenade from Thornton Road. They'd always run together after her dad died; she was glad he'd kept up the habit now they were living in their own places.

She took care walking along the path, twisting her trainers to assess how slippery it was as she walked towards The Battery. In place of a warming-up routine, she took a breath and started to jog at a slow but steady pace. Every breath emerged as a white cloud from her mouth, but there was something crisp and sharp about the air that she loved.

The bay was incredible at that time of day. It was still dark, but the streetlights along the promenade gave off sufficient light to mark her way. Christmas illuminations of sorts lined the roadside, though nothing like the glory days she remembered when she and Brett were younger. It had been an annual ritual to attend the big switch-on with their dad, when he wasn't working. She recalled celebrities like Noel Edmonds and Andi Peters coming to enthral the crowds. How she missed those days. Hopefully Morecambe's fortunes would change sometime soon.

After a couple of minutes, she found her pace and her breathing became easier as she acclimatised to the cold. As she passed the occasional dog walker and jogger, she wished them a cheery *good morning*, to reassure them that they weren't about to get mugged as much as anything. She could hear the sea, but it was still too dark to get a proper view across the bay. However, the streetlights from the Cumbrian side marked its course on the far side, so at least the day wasn't going to be foggy.

Kate was in a world of her own as she passed the Midland Hotel on the opposite side of the road, then Woolworths, the Winter Gardens and the RNLI, each landmark punctuating the progress of her run, like seeing a friend on a daily walk. Brett tended to mix up his routes more than she did, so he was unpredictable, but at least some part of his run usually involved the promenade. It was like Morecambe's best kept secret; whatever blows and indignities the resort suffered economically, the locals loved the sea view.

A car passed her with its beams on full, catching the reflective tabs on a jogger's trainers up ahead of her. There was a good chance it was Brett; he liked to keep himself in decent running gear. The problem was, he was the better runner and he had a good lead on her. The bitterly cold air in her lungs made it difficult for her to maintain anything other than a steady pace, so it was clear she would struggle to make up the distance between them.

Kate took a deep breath, then upped her pace, levelling up with where she'd spotted the reflective strips. Now and then she caught a glimpse of somebody, and she pushed herself harder, determined to catch her brother. Soon she was in shouting distance, so she ventured a call.

'Brett! Stop!'

He hadn't heard her, so she pushed on. Then he stopped dead and moved over to the railings along the promenade to take a rest. He saw her approaching as he perched on one of the railings and raised his hand in a greeting.

'There's a bench... over that way... shall we talk?'

Kate was struggling for breath, but she was pleased

she'd caught him. For a moment she'd doubted her ability to keep up.

'Morning sis, it's freezing, isn't it?'

He stood up and walked over to the bench. She joined him, wincing as she sat on the icy cold wooden seating. If only she'd worn tracksuit bottoms instead of shorts.

'What made you... what made you stop?'

'Just a twinge in my leg. I had a bad fall yesterday.'

'I can see,' Kate replied, studying his forehead. 'You've scraped yourself too, by the look of it.'

'You know how it is at this time of year. I wasn't concentrating, and I slipped and fell. The council should do a better job of gritting the pavements.'

They stared out at the bay in silence. It was slowly becoming lighter, revealing the beach and sea beyond.

'So, you've been avoiding my calls. Any reason for that?'

Brett hesitated.

'Just busy with the house sale. Solicitors, removal vans, address redirections... it's endless.'

'I saw you yesterday—'

'What?'

'In town. With that woman again. And that man who pushed you to the ground. That's where the scratch came from. And I'm guessing that's why your leg hurts this morning.'

'Jesus, Kate, am I under surveillance or something? I'm your kid brother, not some dodgy criminal. Maybe this is one of the reasons I want to get away from here.'

'That's not fair—'

'It is fair, Kate. I can't do anything around here without you finding out about it. Maybe it's time we both had some privacy.'

'I'm worried about you, Brett. Something's off here.'

'Well, you're not a detective yet, so you might want to keep your theories to yourself for a while.'

Kate let his words hang in the air. Brett was all she had left now their father was dead, and the last thing she wanted was to push him away. But if somebody was yelling at him in the street, he must be in trouble.

'Who's the woman, Brett? Is she married?'

'Kate!'

'Come on, Brett. You were walking together in the Arndale Centre; it's obvious something's going on.'

'You've been following me? For Christ's sake, Kate!'

'No, I was on the beat and I just happened to see what went on while I was taking a break.'

'Then you'll know David Irwin is a bit of a head case—'

He stopped, mid-sentence. Kate could tell he'd slipped, but it was all she needed. A name, a lead, a crumb, was all it took. And now he'd given it to her.

'I didn't mean to say that,' Brett continued. 'Ignore me, I'm talking rubbish.'

'Is that his wife you're seeing? Are those his kids? Come on, Brett, if you're having an affair with a married woman, what else do you expect? Can't you stick with women your own age?'

'She is my age, Kate. Not everybody waits until their mid-thirties to start a family.'

'So, you admit you are a couple?'

'I don't want to talk about it, Kate. Seriously, it's none of your business.'

Another silence. She could tell the signs; he was pissed off with her. She gave it one last push.

'Why are you talking about moving from Morecambe if you're seeing this woman? She's got three young kids; she can't just hop on a train and come and see you on a whim—'

The penny dropped as she spoke the words.

'My God, you're planning to run away together. Hell, Brett, please tell me you're not planning to run off with her and the kids?'

'That's enough, Kate! Unless you missed it, I used to have a mother, but now she's dead. And you didn't replace her, right? That's not your role here. So, I'd be grateful if you minded your own business and left me to get on with my own life. Okay?'

He stood up. She could see his leg was troubling him, but he set off towards his house, at a half-jog, half-limp. For a moment, she considered going after him. But she knew the signs; Brett needed some cool-off time, and he'd come round sooner or later. She'd leave him for a day or two, then try again. Besides, she had a name. David Irwin. He sure as hell was getting checked out at the earliest opportunity.

CHAPTER SIXTEEN

Charlotte picked up the debris from her impromptu snack and jogged back to the car. A traffic warden was standing in front of the vehicle with his camera, just about to take a photo for evidence.

'Hi, I'm the owner of this car. Have I done something wrong?' she asked.

'This is a residents' parking bay; you're supposed to display a disc here.'

'Oh,' was all Charlotte could say. She found parking regulations an ordeal. By the time she'd worked out the hours of operation and if it was residents only or not, she'd almost given up the will to live.

'I see you're from the local paper,' the traffic warden continued. 'Are you working on a story?'

Charlotte tried to figure out if she was dealing with a jobsworth or if engaging this man in some casual banter might result in a stay of execution. She opted for a positive outlook.

'You could say that,' she replied, making her best attempt at a cheery smile.

'I've been working on the story of the lady who was found at the slipway. In fact, I'm just about to shoot off to Lancaster now. There's been a big development—'

'Anything you can share?'

'Well, between you and me, the girl involved has just disappeared from hospital.'

'Really?'

The traffic warden put the camera in his pocket. Had he taken any incriminating photos yet? She couldn't tell, but it was looking promising.

'Yes, I'm just about to pick up Nigel Davies now so we can get the latest news for the paper.'

'Nigel Davies, you say? He's a bit of a celebrity around here. If there's ever something going on in Morecambe, you can bet your life Nigel will be reporting on it. Tell him I sent my regards, will you? Warren Sellars is my name, and I was patrolling that bit of the promenade the morning they found that girl.'

'Did you see anything interesting?' she asked.

'Only that I can tell you she walked there. She wasn't in a car and she wasn't dropped off; she was on her own. I think she may have been sleeping on the beach, I'm not sure. But I saw her from a distance before she collapsed at the slipway. She seemed to be drunk.'

'She has diabetes. I think she may have been in desperate need of insulin by then. It was bad enough to put her in a coma, that's for certain. Can I take your details? This is very interesting information.'

That was the money shot. Warren saw fame and fortune awaiting him as a news source for the local paper. She could tell she'd escaped a ticket when he placed his electronic unit on the car roof in order to pull a bundle of business cards from his pocket. Goodness knows why a traffic warden would have a business card. Warren handed one to her and she studied it for a moment. It turned out he had good cause to carry them with him; he also ran a mobile DJ service around the resort.

Morecambe (Sound) Waves Mobile DJ - Sounds of the 60s, 70s & 80s - Weddings, parties, special events - Also karaoke and compère - Great value!

'I own the Lakes View Guest House round by the Town Hall,' Charlotte said, still studying the card. 'I may be able to use your services from time to time. It's great to meet you, Warren.'

Warren couldn't have looked more pleased with himself if he'd just secured a multi-million-pound business deal. She could imagine him adding a new line to his business cards as soon as he got home: *Trusted adviser to The Bay View Weekly.*

Still, she was grateful for the snippet of information about Callie Irwin and she was serious about trying him out the next time they had an event at the guest house. The last time she'd taken a chance on some young lad, he'd turned up with a mobile phone, an amplifier and a UV light. The event was for a local branch of the Women's Institute. He hadn't played one piece of music that the middle-aged to elderly audience had recognised all night, and the amplification was too much for a sit-down meal followed by speeches from committee members. To top it all, as the WI members walked over to complain to the DJ, the UV light showed up their dandruff and false teeth, so all he could do was grin at them as they admonished him. Warren sounded like he might be just the ticket, a more mature DJ who stuck with the songs that got everybody over the age of 40 tapping their toes.

To cement the deal, Charlotte shook his hand, then got

in the car and drove off before he could remember what he'd been in the middle of doing. That was a close escape; it would have been embarrassing to come back with a parking ticket on her first day out in the company car.

Nigel was waiting for her in the reception area of the newspaper offices. He jumped up when he spotted her pulling up at the kerb outside.

'How was the turbine?' he grinned as he slipped into the passenger seat beside her.

'Terrifying!' she replied, driving off the moment his door closed.

Nigel laughed.

'I didn't want to say beforehand. When I went up one of those things, I couldn't get further than the first platform—'

'You're kidding?'

'No, I was terrified. I can honestly say it's one of the scariest experiences of my reporting career. Did you get to the top?'

'Yes, I did, driven on by the fact that I thought you'd done it too.'

'No, I chickened out. I never told the guys in the office, but the lady who took me up left me cowering on the first platform, grabbed my phone and took lots of photos for me. You're the only person who knows that. You have power over me now.'

'I wish I'd known beforehand; I'd have given up at the same point.'

'You have my admiration,' Nigel replied. 'Pull over here.'

Charlotte stopped at the side of the road, outside a 24/7 store.

'Got the munchies?'

'No, we're going to see Simone in the hospital CCTV office again, and I want to go bearing gifts.'

Nigel was out of the car and back again within two minutes, looking as if he was about to attend a confectionery convention. He must have run his hand along the shelves, picking up one of every popular chocolate brand: Curly Wurly, Mars, Snickers, Flake, Freddo, Fudge... they were all present.

'This is the way to Simone's heart. We'll top up her chocolate drawer and she won't be able to resist us,' he said, stuffing the haul of snacks into the side pocket of the door.

Nigel had planned it well. They couldn't get any useful information out of the police officers in attendance when they arrived. DI Comfort was on hand, as they'd expected, looking like a man who was in trouble with his superiors. The hapless PC who they'd met on their previous encounter had been replaced with two officers, a man and a woman. Callie had been moved from the ICU into a private room since the last time they were there. Yet she'd still eluded the police officers and hospital staff.

'What happened?' Nigel asked DI Comfort as they found Callie's new room in the labyrinth of corridors that was Lancaster Infirmary.

'She's gone, that's all I can tell you.'

'Was she snatched, or did she run off of her own accord? Are you sure she's left the hospital?' Charlotte asked.

'We'll brief the press tomorrow. We're more concerned about locating Ms Irwin in connection with our enquiries surrounding the disappearance of four persons in the year 2000.'

Charlotte knew they were done for the moment he

started communicating in police-speak. The shutters were down, DI Comfort had egg all over his face, and the press would have to wait for whatever scraps he was willing to give them. The thought of DI Comfort having to recount how a key witness in a cold case from two decades ago had walked out from under their noses was not something she would like to do.

'Chocolate it is,' Nigel said, once DI Comfort was out of earshot.

They retraced their steps back to the ICU and from there were able to locate Simone's office. Charlotte tapped at the door, hopeful that Simone would remember them. She clocked the chocolate first, then gave a beaming smile as she recognised them. Charlotte suspected it was the haul of confectionery rather than the sight of two reporters from the local paper, but Simone did her best to hide her personal preferences.

'How nice to see you again,' she said. 'And bringing gifts too, I see.'

Nigel handed over his haul and Simone placed it in her chocolate drawer, except for the Curly Wurly, which she opened straight away. She had the same expression as Gollum when he had the ring secured between his fingers.

'How can I help you?'

'We're after some footage from earlier today—'

Simone took a break from working her way through her first bite of the Curly Wurly to interrupt Nigel before he'd got into full flow.

'No. I got a dressing-down the other day and had to do an online refresher on the hospital's security protocols. I can't show you any footage, I'm afraid. Besides, the police have already run off a copy.'

'Were you there when they did it, Simone?' Nigel asked.

'Yes, I saw the footage, it was me who ran off the copy for the police officer. I can't show it to you, but I can tell you something about it. That girl they were supposed to be watching, she left here on her own. And she took a load of diabetes medication from her room when she left.'

CHAPTER SEVENTEEN

'What the hell is Callie playing at?' Nigel asked, as he unwrapped the Freddo bar that Simone had offered him.

'I have to tell you something,' Charlotte replied, chewing on the orange creme sweet that she'd taken from Simone's drawer. 'I feel like I just squashed a week's worth of life into 24 hours. Don't ask me how I came by it, but this phone is not my own. It belongs to a student called Hollie Wickes who's been making a nuisance of herself with Will at the university. Callie Irwin was trying to call this phone first thing this morning.'

Nigel stopped dead in the hospital corridor and faced Charlotte.

'Careful!' warned a porter, almost running into the two of them. He and a colleague were wheeling an elderly lady in a bed. Whatever drugs they'd given her, she appeared to be enjoying the ride.

'Hello dearies, don't mind us!' she called.

'You've got a contact number for Callie Irwin?'

'Yes, but I can't raise her. How would she get a phone in hospital, though?'

'I assume she'll have had one when they found her,' came Nigel's instant reply.

'But wouldn't the police want to examine it?'

'Why? She's not a murder suspect, she's a missing person. They can't arrest her or charge her with anything. She's a person of interest, that's all. Maybe the phone was locked. Who knows? Either way, you've got the phone number of someone who claims to be Callie Irwin. Try the number again, will you?'

Charlotte took the phone out of her pocket and navigated to the call log. The number started to ring, so she placed it on speaker phone. Just as she was about to give up, there was a click. Someone had answered, but it was silent at the other end. All Charlotte could hear was traffic noise in the distance.

'Callie?' she asked.

Silence.

'My name is Charlotte Grayson; I work for the local paper. You can talk to me, Callie, I won't tell the police—'

The call ended.

'Damn it,' Nigel cursed. 'Try again, will you?'

Charlotte dialled, but the call tone continued until the phone clicked to voicemail. There was no personal message, just the default from the automated voice.

'What's the time?' Nigel asked, suddenly distracted.

'Quarter past five,' Charlotte replied, checking the phone. 'Why?'

'I forgot to tell you, I arranged to meet a guy at Forton Services in half an hour. Are you okay to tag along? He's involved in the fracking protests in Lancashire, and he was keen to talk to me in person. I think he's one of those paranoid types, convinced his phones are being tapped and his emails monitored.'

'Who by?'

'Fabian Armstrong, according to him. It's very unlikely; it's hard enough for the police to get permission to do it. But he's a veteran of protesting against Fabian's projects and he saw my web updates online. He's keen to speak.'

Charlotte thought through what lay ahead that evening. Will was out, the kids were safe and the staff were taking care of the guest house. She'd thought about staying off the premises, bearing in mind the events of the past 24 hours. It seemed safer. The longer she was away from home, the harder it would be to find her. That seemed like a good option, at least until she got a better grasp of what was going on and who had wanted to leave her stranded at Sunderland Point like that.

'I'm up for it,' she replied. She'd eat her evening meal at Forton too, if Nigel was willing to hang on that long.

They cut it fine, with Lancaster's impregnable snake of city centre traffic moving even slower than usual. Even though they didn't have to pass through the apex of hell and cross the city's bridges, every slow driver and bad parker seemed to be out on the side streets as they attempted to cut across the city. Nigel took the wheel, giving Charlotte the opportunity to think.

It seemed strange to be passing the university where Will would be spending his evening. As the campus passed by on her left-hand side, it struck her that she and Will might stay at a B&B in Lancaster that night. It made sense. She was annoyed to find that she couldn't use her usual apps as the phone was set up the way Hollie liked it, so she texted Will, rather than messaging him. After she sent the text, she wondered if Will would see it was from her, or whether it would seem like it had been sent by Hollie.

His reply came swiftly.

Hey, Hollie, how's things?

Will, this is Charlotte writing the message. It's a long story as to why I have a different phone, I'll tell you later.

Why had he answered a text like that when he thought it was Hollie? Wasn't she supposed to be stalking him? A surge of nausea rose up. No way, not Will. He was just being professional and friendly. So why hadn't he blocked her number?

Fancy staying at the Travelodge in town tonight? It'll save you a late bus journey and I'm in Lancaster right now.

Sure, great idea. Why the hell have you got Hollie's phone? This is Charlotte, isn't it?

She wondered how willing she'd be to accept a message like that from someone who was supposed to be stalking him.

Stirling Travelodge. 1998. Cleaner walking in. It's Charlotte all right :-)

She smiled to herself as she wrote the text. It was a little secret of theirs, an embarrassing one at that, and one they'd never shared with anyone else, but which still made her wince. They'd been on a romantic weekend away. That poor cleaner got the shock of her life when she walked in on them.

Will's message came back.

Hi Charlotte :-) I'll see you later, it might be after midnight. Text me the room number, I'll tap quietly at the door x

Could be the cleaner, out for revenge :-) See you later x

No, there was no way Will would cheat on her. They'd been together so long, neither of them could remember what it was like to be with another person.

'Here we are,' Nigel announced. 'I hope he's not in too much of a hurry.'

Charlotte peered through the window. The spaceship-like tower of Forton Service Station was up ahead, and Nigel was pulling over into the slip lane. They parked up and headed for the Costa coffee area. Nigel was relieved that his man was still there. He'd been very cloak and dagger, insisting that he place a copy of a Dan Brown book on his table so they could identify him. Charlotte immediately clocked him as the conspiracy theory type.

The introductions were made, and, to her surprise, Nigel's contact turned out to be of sound mind and credible. He knew his stuff too. Neil Harris had been campaigning against fracking in Lancashire since he'd first feared his property was about to be shaken to the ground in 2011 when the first controversial earth tremors were felt in Lancashire.

'It was a red event,' Neil explained. 'That means you can't ignore it.'

Since that time, Neil had teamed together with other concerned Lancastrians and become mobilised as a formidable force of householders hellbent only on making sure some big corporation didn't inadvertently reduce their houses to rubble. Charlotte realised it was a much more complex issue than that, and she'd never formed a view on the topic before, since it didn't seem to affect her. But Neil's allegations of the conflict of interests between the various parties were fascinating. She couldn't believe that she lived in the same county as Neil, yet had missed out on this entire conflict.

But it was when Neil talked about an old school friend from his village – a local farmer – that he became even more impassioned, if that were possible.

'This man you want to know about – Fabian Armstrong – I'm telling you, that man is the devil himself. He was putting my mate Henry under tremendous pressure to start exploratory drilling on his land, but Henry wouldn't countenance the idea. He told Armstrong to get lost. Then one day, Armstrong suddenly has all the permissions he needs, signatures and all. And my friend Henry is found dead in his car, parked up in an old barn, the engine still running, a suicide note at his side—'

'Wait, isn't that how Tiffany Irwin was found at the slipway back in 2000, Nigel?'

Nigel watched her over the top of his coffee as he finished taking a sip.

'Yes, that's exactly what happened to Fabian's sister. It had all the hallmarks of an attempted suicide, the same as Neil's friend. He seems to have a strange affinity for carbon monoxide poisoning.'

CHAPTER EIGHTEEN

December 1999

Although she lived in Morecambe, Kate preferred to use the Salt Ayre Leisure Centre near Lancaster for her gym work. Located between the two communities, it was the ideal place to work on her strength training and it allowed her to steer well clear of anybody she might have had an altercation with on the local streets. She seemed to be invisible to most people when she was out of uniform, but still, it was reassuring that she could sweat profusely without fear of running into someone she knew.

Besides, the leisure centre hadn't been open that long and it was state-of-the-art. Most gyms in the seaside resort were in small, back-street venues, many of them doubling-up as boxing clubs. She preferred the mixed sexes at Salt Ayre, and it was a lot less intimidating when she wasn't being eyed up by the six-pack boys every time she flexed her muscles.

She and Nayeema had decided to go for a pre-Christmas workout in the hope that the cellulite gods would have mercy on them when it came to the festive season. As they put on their sports gear in the changing rooms, they exchanged notes about how the job was working out.

'I had to apprehend a flasher yesterday.' Nayeema laughed as she struggled into her sports bra. 'Here, give me a hand with this will you. It's all very well containing your boobs in these things, but you need to be an escapologist to get them on and off.'

Kate helped Nayeema into her sports bra. She was right, it was more like medieval torture equipment than clothing designed with comfort and ease in mind.

'How embarrassing,' Kate said, once they'd performed the delicate operation. 'Did you see him doing it or was it called in on the radio?'

'I caught him at it red-handed. He had the tiniest thingy I've ever seen. Not that I'm an expert, you understand. He was wearing flasher pants—'

'Yeah, that's what the other guys call them,' Kate said with a laugh. 'Jogging bottoms. They wear them because they can pull them out fast and give people a flash. They don't bother wearing underwear either.'

'Yuk!' Nayeema replied, making an exaggerated face in mock disgust. 'God, there are some weirdos around. I always knew people could be odd, but we meet all sorts in our line of work.'

'Right, I'm on weights,' Kate said. 'What about you?'

'Trying my luck on the running machines today. I'm not as disciplined as you,' Nayeema answered, shrugging. 'I can't even drag my butt out of bed to go for a jog along the prom every day. Shall we meet up at the sweetie machine afterwards?'

They made their plans and headed off to the respective areas in the leisure centre. It being a Sunday morning, the weights were quiet, and Kate had the run of the place. She started simple and began with a set of dumbbells which wouldn't give her a problem. Another guy walked over and made straight for the heavier weights. She watched him as he surveyed his flexed muscles in the mirror, grunting at every strain.

As she moved away from him into an area that gave her more space, she looked up. Through the glass wall of the weights room, she could see a family making their way along the corridor. The man was the one who'd pushed Brett to the ground, and he was with the same three children and the woman. One of the children was ambling along with a large rubber ring in her hands. The younger children were in the double pram and buggy, both sides of which were loaded up with swimming paraphernalia. This is what it took to take a young family for an hour's swim. They looked like American settlers on the hunt for a brand-new home.

'You've got great muscle tone,' the man said. She was surprised he'd stopped watching his own reflection long enough to notice. 'Do you work out here often? I haven't seen you around before.'

This went with the territory, it was fair enough that the guys hit on her when she worked out, so long as they took no for an answer. She figured being a narcissist must be a lonely life at times.

'Thanks, I'm just trying to keep in shape after the kids —' she began.

He left to return to his lifting, obviously the sort of guy who preferred picking up weights to lifting toddlers and changing bags. It was a white lie, but it did the job. Some of the more experienced WPCs had suggested wearing a wedding ring on the job was useful for fending off the uniform fetishists. She hadn't suffered enough suggestive comments yet to motivate her sufficiently, but it was always at the back of her mind when the come-ons became too wearing.

Once she'd seen off the guy without making a big thing of it, she left the weights area and walked into the corridor. The family created a whirlwind of sound and confusion as they made their way into the family changing rooms up ahead. Kate stood there, motionless, wondering whether to pry. This was the perfect opportunity to get a handle on what was going on in Brett's life.

She gave them a few minutes to get themselves organised, then followed behind them. They'd got a family cubicle by the time she entered, so she took a seat on a nearby bench and listened in to the conversation. The woman was taking the lead; the man seemed short-tempered and annoyed.

'You promised you'd come with us today. Please can you help keep Rowan safe on the changing table?'

'I told you I was busy today—'

'It's one day, Dave. That's not too much to ask, is it?'

A mobile phone rang. She heard the man's voice.

'I've got to take this, Tiff, it's important.'

Kate heard the cubicle lock sliding across. The man dashed out into the changing rooms and the cubicle door was locked behind him. The woman started muttering.

'Of course, you've got to do something else... Callie, don't deflate your rubber ring!'

The man looked in her direction as he made for the door to leave the changing area. He hesitated for a moment, as if he recognised her. Had he spotted her the day she'd been following Brett? She'd been too concerned about her brother to notice.

Kate wondered if it was too risky following him. If he had clocked her, it might land her in trouble with her superiors. She went after him anyway.

He'd taken a seat by the confectionery machines and was engaged in a phone call. He didn't see her following him, so she took cover behind two young families who'd ventured out for a Sunday swim. Two of the four youngsters were tired and fractious; Kate didn't envy their parents. They had no chance whatsoever of getting a nice, relaxing Sunday at home before the start of a new week.

She took a table round the corner where she could listen in, near the hot drinks machine. Two kids who appeared to be on their own were feeding money into it, trying to figure out which drink they were going for. The machine started gurgling and clunking just as the man's conversation was becoming more interesting. She caught enough snippets to get the gist of it.

'...now the old man's dead, it should be easy to sort out... that bloody wind farm idea of hers, I told you, she's a damn hippy. Look, you take care of the legals, I'll make sure Tiff plays ball—'

Brett had described him as a head case. It wasn't a convincing description, but he did appear to be tangled up in some venture or other in which his wife was causing an obstruction. One of the youngsters cautiously removed a steaming hot plastic cup of chicken soup from the machine. It smelled amazing, even though Kate knew it would be a mixture of semi-boiled water and half dissolved powder.

'Any more about that kid? Do you know who he is yet?'

The machine rattled and spluttered again as the second child selected his hot drink. This time there was foam, and the machine made a sound so loud it seemed like it might lift off into orbit. She leaned over in an attempt to catch more of the exchange.

'Just sort the little bugger out, that's all.'

She caught the tail end of it, but that was all she needed to hear to know that Brett had placed himself somewhere he wasn't wanted. And it wasn't just an angry husband tussling with her brother in the street. Now he was asking some friend to get involved. Every policing instinct in her body was screaming at her.

'Excuse me, would you mind not listening in to my call?'

He'd spotted her. She focused on the youngster reaching for his hot drink, trying to appear casual about it.

'I wasn't. I was just looking around—'

'You've been listening to my call. What were you doing in that changing room? Are you following us? What are you, some bloody private detective or something?'

Kate stood up. The man was moving into her space, his body language aggressive. She could handle herself, thanks to her police training, but she had no wish to get caught up in an incident.

'Please calm down. I was just sitting here taking a break. Honestly, I didn't hear anything; it's none of my concern what you were talking about—'

He faced Kate head on and stared at her.

'I recognise you. You're that copper who was hanging around near the Arndale Centre. Who are you? What the hell are you up to?'

'It doesn't necessarily mean Fabian was behind the death,' Charlotte ventured, half-heartedly. Her distance learning course had made much of impartiality and scepticism when talking to interviewees, so she felt duty-bound to at least challenge the theory.

'Poisoning by carbon monoxide is the ideal way to make it seem like suicide. All you do is find a secluded spot, and hang around until your victim is out cold. There are no bruises, cuts or wounds left behind as evidence. What's more, you can even leave some half-arsed suicide note which was knocked out on a word processor. And because of the remote location, there are no CCTV cameras.'

Neil was deadly earnest as he spoke. Yet it all seemed too far-fetched; besides, Fabian wouldn't have risked prison for a falling-out over some land. Would he?

'It still feels like a weak link to me,' Charlotte said. 'Besides, Tiffany Irwin was found on the slipway right next to the Midland Hotel. That doesn't sound very secluded to me.'

'The hotel was derelict then,' Nigel reminded her. 'In

1999, on the eve of the new millennium, it was an excellent place to kill someone.'

'Well, Henry isn't the only one to die that way,' Neil continued. 'Another landowner, Felicity Worthington, was also found dead at the back of her barn, inside some old Land Rover that had been left there for years. She'd also put up a resistance to Fabian Armstrong, though in the interests of fairness, he wasn't the only one after that land.'

'They only want test drilling though,' Nigel chipped in. 'It's not as if they're building a massive housing estate on somebody's pasture lands, is it?'

'The problem is it splits the community right down the middle. I wouldn't want to be a landowner for all the money in the world. You get hate mail and bricks through your window from both sides of the argument.'

Neil was warming to his theme now. He looked like a man confident of his facts.

'Some people want to take the blood money and get the new village hall or a massive donation for the local school. There's good money on offer too, so with all the funding cuts, a Parish Council wouldn't turn their noses up at it.'

He paused a moment to survey his audience. They were both listening intently.

'Then you have those who don't want the heavy vehicles or the disturbance. Most of us are scared of the tremors and what they're doing to our properties. It's a bloody mess, I can tell you, but there's big money involved.'

He looked like he was about to finish, then added a final thought.

'Shale gas is cheaper, it creates less pollution and it stops us relying on Russia and the like for our energy. If it hadn't shaken my house like that, I might be all for it.'

Charlotte was riveted. This was a new world for her.

'I get that the stakes are high,' she said, addressing both Nigel and Neil, 'but these are big companies, not cowboy outfits. Big companies don't go around killing off people who object to their plans. We have planning and appeals processes to deal with them, don't we?'

She was starting to doubt her own line of reasoning now. Massive corporations had done some heinous things in the past, but this still seemed preposterous to her. Besides, the police would investigate. It could backfire and bite them in the behind.

'Fabian Armstrong started small-scale,' Neil continued. 'He was a farmer with his own land right at the beginning. Correction. He was a farmer with shared land. Look what he did to his own sister—'

'Do you know something about that?' Nigel asked.

'Not much. Only that he locked her up in an untenable situation over some land deal which was all very nasty. He showed in court that she was mentally incompetent, something like that. Can you imagine doing that to your own sister? Still, she got the better of him in the end. She went behind his back and leased out the land to a wind farm company.'

'Really?' Charlotte asked. 'Is that common knowledge?'

'The lease and its timing are a matter of public record; the fact she stitched him up is conjecture. But Fabian didn't want wind turbines on that land. He had it earmarked for nuclear or chemical use. Let's put it this way, you won't see any fan posters of Greta Thunberg on Armstrong's office wall. You're more likely to find them on his dart board.'

'I'll ask Jon Rogers at the library about that. I'll bet he can help.'

This was an interesting new twist; had Tiffany managed

to thwart her brother? Is that why he seemed so vindictive towards her?

They finished the conversation, but Neil had no more nuggets hidden away. However, after he'd gone, Nigel and Charlotte agreed they were much better clued up on the high stakes in the energy industry. Fabian Armstrong was clearly the kind of man who liked to get his own way, at whatever cost and risk.

Nigel was in a rush to get back home for his evening meal, so was reluctant to delay any longer when Charlotte suggested eating at the service station. Instead, he agreed to drop her in the centre of Lancaster where she would check into the Travelodge for the night. She was checked in by seven o'clock and back on the streets prowling for fast food five minutes later.

Lancaster had changed since she and Will had been students here, but she recalled a KFC just a short walk along the road. Will and she had gone there years ago, as broke teenagers, and all they'd been able to afford was a bag of chips. The staff had taken pity and given them a plastic cup filled with water, rather than insisting on them purchasing a soda drink. They'd made that bag of chips last for over an hour. That's how they rolled back in the eighties; they could entertain themselves with a brown paper bag if it came to it.

She was famished, despite the earlier cheese sandwich. It must be nervous energy. From the day she'd just had, it was a wonder she hadn't lost half her body weight with anxiety. She ordered her food and took it over to a quiet seat in the window, almost where she and Will had sat all those years ago. He would never risk what they had with such a clichéd affair, not with a woman who wasn't much older than his daughter. They had too much history.

She took out Hollie's phone and felt an instant pang of guilt. However she tried to justify her actions, it was a stolen phone. This would be terrible for Will if it ever came out. What if Hollie was innocent? Panic took over. What had she been thinking of, taking it? She was torn for a moment; she'd planned on checking out Hollie's pictures and contacts, but now, in the cold light of day, she could see it was a massive intrusion on this young woman's privacy. Her fingers were covered in the grease from her chicken portions and chips, so she had a few moments to think through what to do next. She could replace Hollie's SIM card and drop the phone off at the library. Hollie would be none the wiser.

Then she winced at what she'd said to Callie Irwin when she'd picked up the phone; she'd given her name. She couldn't believe how stupid she'd been. At the time, she'd meant to offer reassurance; instead, she'd identified herself as the thief. Dishonesty and subterfuge didn't come easily to Charlotte, and she couldn't shake the sense of guilt that hung over her.

She finished her food, cleaned her fingers on the serviettes and decided that the phone had to go back to Hollie. She'd send it with Will the next day, and he could drop it off at the university library when he went to work. Hopefully, Hollie would be so relieved at being reunited with her phone, she might get away with the call to Callie.

She took Hollie's SIM card out of her pocket and placed it back in the phone, then wrapped up her own SIM card for safe storage. Would she be able to get a cheap replacement phone in Lancaster at that time of night? As the SIM card picked up Hollie's operating service, messages popped up on the home screen, much of it trivia from student friends. But at the top of the latest notifications were three messages from Will, sent shortly before Charlotte had first called Will herself from Hollie's phone, using her own SIM.

Are we still meeting tonight?

I'm clear after 9pm. We can talk then.

It's time to get this out in the open. Pls reply so I know you're still coming.

CHAPTER TWENTY

Will didn't get back to the Travelodge that night. When Charlotte woke up, she was curled up at one side of the double bed on her own. Where was Will? Her first reaction was to assume he'd missed the last bus back from the campus, which was located well beyond the city centre. Perhaps he'd slept at a friend's house. He hadn't messaged her, even on Hollie's phone.

After getting dressed, she walked downstairs to buy five copies of The Bay View Weekly from the 24-hour store below the Travelodge. She figured she could never have enough copies to hold on to as keepsakes and to distribute among the wider family. She still felt detached from the publication process, aware that Nigel was constantly filing updates to the website and developing longer articles for the special edition of the paper.

The last she'd seen of her article about Yasmin Utworth was when she'd emailed it over late on Sunday evening, and she had very little idea of what happened to it as it passed through the production line and ended up in print. She wasn't even certain if they printed the paper locally any more.

Charlotte walked along the road to a pub which was serving breakfasts, eager to pull open the pages and check out the newspaper coverage about Callie Irwin. She ordered bacon and eggs at the bar, took a seat and laid out the papers in front of her.

'I take it you enjoy reading the local newspapers?' a middle-aged man said as she scanned the front page. 'Reading it one time is enough for most people. Five times is overly keen.'

He laughed at his own joke and his wife smiled politely. Charlotte was relieved when their breakfasts arrived and the couple were distracted by their food. She wasn't in the mood for making small talk with strangers.

There was a certain element of anti-climax in reading the front pages when she knew the details of the news story already. Nigel's name was highlighted in bold and she was in awe at how he'd managed to produce so much coherent editorial while spending a lot of time running around in the car investigating. A pang of inferiority struck her for one moment until she turned the page and saw her own article staring up at her.

They'd given her a full name check and used her photograph. She wondered where they'd got the picture from, until she remembered that it was the one she used on her press card, the one which made her look more like a criminal mastermind than a reporter.

She scanned her words, at once embarrassed at her work being so publicly available and incredibly proud that her feature had made it to such a prominent position. As far as she could tell, it hadn't been revised or edited; it seemed to be as she'd submitted it, word for word. Nigel had warned her that it might be hacked down in the editing process, but Teddy had been as good as his word; she must have done a good job.

Her first instinct was to phone Will. Will, who hadn't turned up at the Travelodge as they'd arranged. Will, who hadn't picked up his phone when she'd called him. She'd even stayed true to her conscience, resisting the temptation to re-insert her SIM into Hollie's mobile phone, and risking the expense of using the hotel phone in her room instead. It didn't matter, Will hadn't answered it anyway.

She refused to allow the thought of an affair to creep up behind her and sabotage her sanity. Besides, the way Will snored and had to run to the bathroom at least twice every night, there was no way a woman as young as Hollie could have a romantic interest in him. Not one that lasted more than one night with him at her side, at least. If she managed to raise him, she'd listen to his account of events.

Charlotte devoured her breakfast as soon as it arrived, unable to believe how much she was eating. She seemed to be on constant alert since her first altercation with Vinnie Mace the previous Saturday. She counted the days. No wonder she felt drained, having operated at 100 miles an hour for almost a week now, and she was still jittery after the attempt to drown her at Sunderland Point. It was the first time she'd thought of it like that. *Somebody had tried to kill her at Sunderland Point.* And she hadn't even reported it to the police. Would they try it again?

Charlotte manoeuvred her last forkful of bacon through the runny yolk of her fried egg, making sure it was fully coated before placing it in her mouth and chewing it slowly, like it was the last piece of bacon on earth. She was certain the person who'd struck her was the tall woman who'd helped to set off the smoke detectors in the infirmary. She didn't seem to be a professional killer, not like Vinnie Mace who'd deployed his military skills to deliver a fright during the tandem skydive. So, although she needed to be on her guard, she shouldn't need to worry about any assassination attempt from some grassy knoll, should one be available in Lancaster or Morecambe.

If she stayed in public, made sure Will was around in the guest house, and didn't go on wild goose chases on her own to remote locations, she wouldn't be particularly vulnerable. And as far as Fabian Armstrong was concerned, she and Nigel had backed off since receiving their warnings. He had no idea she'd been within spitting distance of him at the doctor's house.

The paper was packed with details about the Irwin family. As she moved on to pages 5 and 6, it provided plenty of background information, gleaned from previous editions dating back to 2000, which she hadn't seen so far from her library microfiche printouts. The information was the same, but a half-page montage of images showed articles of the people who'd gone missing at that time: Brett, Morgan, Tiffany and the Irwin family. She began to cry when she saw Evan Farrish's photograph in the by-line of the newspaper copies. Until that point, she hadn't realised how she'd suppressed her emotions around that incident. The thought of him being killed like that was terrifying; the whole thing was spiralling out of control.

She closed the pages of the newspapers and checked the clock behind the bar. There was time to freshen up in the hotel room, get checked out and catch a Morecambe bus at the station. With any luck she'd be in the office by nine o'clock for the weekly debrief and prospects meeting. It appeared to be something news outlets were obsessed with. They never seemed to stop reviewing news prospects, then raking over the coals of what they'd done. She'd heard one of the older hacks mumbling *Same old shit every week* under his breath at one meeting and she had to agree until the Irwin case. How much planning did it require to coordinate lost dog stories and presentations of giant, cardboard cheques? But she'd changed her mind since Callie Irwin had been found at the slipway; a story of that size was almost like a police operation for a local newspaper.

Charlotte finished her breakfast then walked back to the Travelodge, wishing that she'd bought a plastic bag for the newspapers. Would she get away with wearing the same clothes two days in a row? She hadn't thought it through when she'd suggested to Will that they stay in the hotel overnight. She decided to risk it. The soap in the hotel room was highly perfumed, so her body was clean even if her underwear wasn't. She could nip back to the guest house after the meeting and put things right. Besides, how bad could it be compared to turning up to a press conference in Heysham the day before, wearing Jed's clothes and looking like a poorly dressed scarecrow?

Charlotte was delighted to see a Morecambe-bound bus waiting in the bay at the bus station when she arrived. She got on it and paid for her ticket. Another trick she'd learnt about journalistic work was to wear trousers with pockets. A phone, pen, small notepad, cash card and 10-pound note were all that she required to survive out in the wild. With those objects, she was unstoppable.

As the bus revved its engine and the beeping sound at the rear of the vehicle gave its warning that they were now in motion, Charlotte realised that she would have to get over her conscience issues and use Hollie's phone once again. The 24/7 store hadn't had any throwaway mobiles, and she'd been too tired the night before to go hunting for one.

But they'd had a cheap USB lead, so at least the phone was fully charged now. She activated the screen, still incredulous that Hollie hadn't locked it with a password. But then she'd seen how Ollie and Lucia operated. Their phones were such a part of their bodies, it would have been like password-protecting their hands to them.

She activated Hollie's screen and checked the battery. Yes, it was on full charge. Still feeling guilty, she was compelled to check the new notifications. Perhaps they might hold a clue to what had happened to Will. She almost dropped the phone when she saw what was sitting at the top of the notifications. There was nothing more from Will. But sent first thing that morning was a text message from another phone.

READ THIS, THIEF! I know you have my phone. I know you were in my room. I know what you did.

CHAPTER TWENTY-ONE

December 1999

'Look, it's true, I am a police constable, and I did see what happened the other day—'

'I knew it.'

David Irwin looked like a man vindicated in his paranoia.

'But I saw what you did to my brother. I was only running after him to say hello. How was I to know I'd see you beating him up?'

'The piece of shit deserves it—'

A woman who'd just sat at one of the tables with her two daughters shushed him. For one moment, Kate thought he was going to give her a mouthful, but he fell quiet. She could fill in the blanks for what he really wanted to say to her. It was obvious that David Irwin was a nasty little man.

'I was within my rights to apprehend you,' Kate reminded him. She wasn't so sure about taking that line, particularly as she was off duty. But now he'd seen her in her police uniform, a gentle shot across the bows might just help Brett.

'And what would you arrest me for?' he scoffed. 'For telling your brother to back off from my wife and family? Good luck with that!'

Kate didn't like the way this was going.

'Are you okay?'

It was the guy who'd been lifting weights earlier. Assistance sometimes came from the most unexpected of sources, though Kate still suspected the altercation wasn't over yet. She watched as David Irwin checked out the guy's muscles. He gave them a little flex too, just for good measure. It worked; David Irwin decided to back off.

He walked away, back towards the changing rooms.

'He looked like a waste of space,' the guy with the muscles said.

'You can say that again,' Kate replied. 'Thanks for stepping in, I think that might have escalated if you hadn't come along. He must have thought you were my husband or something.'

'Well, play your cards right—' the man tried his luck.

Kate gave him a gentle tap on the arm.

'God loves a chancer,' she smiled, not wanting to give him a hard snub. Perhaps she'd judged him too hastily; he seemed like a nice enough person.

'He should watch his language around young children,' the woman at the table grumbled.

The man with the muscles took the hint and headed back to the weights room.

'Hope to see you again some time,' he said. 'We need more ladies lifting weights, otherwise it gets full of people like me.'

She had mis-judged him. Next time she saw him, she'd be a little less dismissive.

David Irwin breezed past her again as if he was about to ignore her, then turned at the last minute.

'Has your boyfriend gone now? Let me be clear. Cop or no cop, your brother is out of order. If you're his sister, have a quiet word in his ear. If he doesn't back off... let's just put it this way: warn him not to take a shit in my back yard or there'll be consequences.'

'Language, please!' the lady admonished.

'Get stuffed!' David cursed at her, storming towards the exit of the leisure centre.

The lady looked stunned.

'I'm sorry,' Kate said, as if she were personally responsible. 'Let me treat your girls to something from the machines. I'm sorry he spoiled your visit.'

The restorative powers of a packet of salt and vinegar crisps and a toffee bar were astonishing. The two girls' excited chattering had soon distracted the mother and Kate returned to the changing room. Tiffany was still there, wrestling the children, the door to the family cubicle now wide open. She'd managed to change into her own swimming costume, and the two older children were also ready and playing a game with their armbands and rubber rings, but the baby was wriggling on the changing mat and showing no signs of co-operating. Kate wondered if this was what life was like with young children, with everything taking five times as long as usual to achieve.

One of the girls ran into the changing room, chasing her rubber ring which she'd rolled away.

'Callie! Callie, please come back where I can see you.'

Tiffany looked up and Kate could see she'd been crying.

'I've got her,' she called over, picking up the rubber ring and taking Callie's tiny hand.

'Come on cheeky,' she beamed at Callie, 'let's get you back to your mum.'

'Thank you,' Tiffany said, wiping her eyes.

'Is everything okay?' Kate asked. 'You seem to have your hands full. Can I help?'

'Do you have kids?' Tiffany asked.

'No. Not yet. Maybe never.'

'I love them to bits, but they can be such hard work sometimes. There are only three of them but sometimes I swear they multiply behind my back while I'm not looking. Have you ever seen that Gremlins film? Welcome to my world.'

Kate laughed and picked up a set of arm bands.

'Come along gorgeous, let's get you ready for the pool,' she said to the baby.

'That's Jane, this is Rowan and you just rescued Callie. Thanks, by the way. I'm Tiffany... Tiff. Better not shake hands; I've just changed Rowan's nappy and I haven't been able to wash my hands yet.'

'How about I watch Rowan and sort out these arm bands and you go and wash your hands?'

'Would you? Thank you so much.'

The way she said it, you'd have thought Kate had just handed her the keys to a new house. Kate finished wrestling the arm bands onto the two girls and tidied up the kids' clothes into the bag that was sitting in the corner.

'This is a lot to be managing on your own,' Kate ventured when Tiffany returned. The break of two minutes seemed to have revived her.

'My husband was meant to be coming with us, but he got called away for work. I should have expected this when he insisted on coming in the second car. He really wasn't committed to this from the outset. Sorry, I shouldn't have said that.'

'It's fine. You're entitled to get things off your chest if you need to. I'm guessing the kids don't do much listening?'

Tiffany laughed.

'You can say that again. I really appreciate your help. You're a natural with the kids. Don't rule out having a family. I know it looks like mayhem from the outside, but it's not that bad, and it won't be like this forever. Maybe just space them out a little better than I did.'

'How old is the baby? He can't be more than a few months, can he?'

'Nine months old. I'll be honest with you, that one was a surprise. David, my husband, was never so keen on having his own children. I think that's why he finds it all too much sometimes. He was struggling with just the girls.'

Tiffany's eyes welled up and Kate put an arm around her shoulders.

'I'm so sorry,' Tiffany said. 'I don't usually get upset like this.'

'Is Mummy sad?' Callie asked.

'Mummy's okay, Callie, she'll be ready to go swimming in a moment.'

Tiffany steadied herself. It looked like she was accustomed to doing that. The woman she'd seen walking with her brother had seemed relaxed and at ease. They'd been laughing and chatting, and the children were comfortable with the situation.

'I hope you don't mind,' Kate began, not entirely sure where the sentence was heading, 'but I sort of know you already.'

Tiffany tensed up and pulled away, forcing Kate to move her comforting arm away from the woman's shoulders.

'Who are you?' she asked. Her hackles went up, taking Kate by surprise.

'I saw you with my brother the other day. He's called Brett, Brett Allan. That was me in Crystal T's nightclub, Brett didn't introduce me before you left.'

'Jesus, who are you, are you one of Fabian's cronies? Are you some private detective or something?'

'No, no, it's nothing like that—'

'Just piss off and leave me and my children alone, okay? Just go away!'

'Tiffany, it's not like that, I'm just a friend. I saw you with my brother. Brett. Ask him about me, he'll tell you.'

The children had picked up on the change in atmosphere. Rowan was now crying, Jane was about to follow suit and Callie was tapping on her mother's leg, demanding attention.

'I don't know who to trust any more. I want you to leave us alone. Please go. And if Fabian sent you, tell him to get lost and respect my position. He's not getting his damn chemical plant or whatever it is he wants, and I won't be intimidated by him.'

Kate was desperate to explain herself, but Tiffany was growing more distressed and the children were picking up on it. Another family had just come out of the pool via the foot bath and the man and the woman had homed in on what was going on.

'Look, I'm sorry,' she began, 'I didn't mean to spook you. I just wanted to help with the kids.'

She spoke gently and calmly, remembering the technique from her training. She hated role play, but now she was glad they'd chosen her to act out that particular scenario in front of the other cadets.

Tiffany said nothing. She looked like she was about to explode into a cascade of tears. Kate turned around to see the couple. They seemed to be on the cusp of deciding whether to intervene or not. She had to put her career first; she couldn't risk this flaring up.

'I'm sorry, Tiffany, honestly I am. But please ask Brett. I'm Kate, his sister. I only want to help. Your children are lovely. I'm sorry if I scared you.'

Kate walked out of the changing room and along the corridor, towards the vending machines. Nayeema was there already, just showered and sitting at a table with a coffee, her sports bag at her side. And sitting opposite her, looking like he'd known her all his life, was the man with the muscles.

CHAPTER TWENTY-TWO

The last thing any of them expected was a petrol bomb being hurled through the front window of the newspaper office. But that was how the fire was started, resulting in a full evacuation.

Charlotte made good time from the hotel, arriving at the office ten minutes before the morning meeting began. She even had time to make a useful round of phone calls using her own SIM in Hollie's phone. Hollie knew she'd got the phone now, so that cat was well and truly out of the bag.

Isla and George were well on top of the guest house. Every time she checked in after another absence, she'd grit her teeth, expecting Isla to say she'd had enough and that she'd have to get on with it on her own. She deserved it; the guest house had become somewhat of an afterthought. It was paying the bills though, so she couldn't afford for that to happen.

Still, the activity around the Irwins diverted her attention. She and Will needed a serious talk about the future of the Lakes View Guest House. She resolved to check in on Rex Emery and ask him how his compensation claim was progressing. It would be the best outcome for everybody if he bought it back from them and re-started his life.

Isla even had some good news; the window had been fixed first thing. Fortunately, the weather was still, or else they'd have had a gale blowing through the lounge. As it was, the guests saw it all as a novelty, Isla had reassured her.

There was nothing from Will. He hadn't texted Hollie via her mobile number, nor had he got in touch with Charlotte via hers. That was unusual. Will always told Charlotte what he was up to. That was why she was certain he wasn't having an affair. He was like his own GPS signal, telling her every detail of his movements, and this current behaviour was completely out of character.

She thought about how the Loose Women on TV might regard her thought processes if she were explaining the story to them. They'd have Will tarred and feathered already; they'd reckon it was a slam-dunk of an affair. But she knew her husband. Hollie Wickes wasn't even his type of woman. He disliked facial piercings too, though he did his best to accept them, understanding people did it to express themselves. If he was guilty of anything with Hollie Wickes, it would be that he was too naive and helpful and the student might have read it the wrong way, being so young.

For a moment, Charlotte doubted herself. Was she being an idiot? No, she was certain she wasn't. However, she did want to speak to her husband as soon as possible.

She even had time to check in on Lucia who'd been drinking in Lancaster with Ollie and Willow. She was annoyed with herself for falling asleep in the hotel room. If she'd thought about it, she could have joined the kids for a night out.

By the time she walked into the office, she was feeling

happier. She'd even had time to catch the market traders and buy some new socks and knickers, which she'd changed into in the staff toilets. Although she'd got the order of events the wrong way round, she was now showered and wearing fresh underwear, albeit they had only cost her £4 for four pairs and the elastic might not last the length of the day. Besides, the patterns on them were ghastly. She would have to destroy all traces of them when she got home. She'd opted for the best of a bad lot, a pattern with green striped tigers. If Will or the kids ever saw them, she'd never live it down.

'Good morning, Charlotte. Did you and Will have a pleasant evening in Lancaster?' Nigel asked.

'Yes, fine thanks,' she answered, not yet ready to share the details of Will's absence.

The small team assembled in the newsroom, cups of tea and coffees in hand, some eating cereal and others munching hot sandwiches packed with sausages, bacon and other culinary delights. Several people complimented her on the article, telling her it was great writing and that it had moved them to tears.

Teddy arrived and called the meeting to as much order as these newsroom get-togethers ever achieved.

'Good morning everyone and thank you for showing your faces; it is appreciated. Before we get started, let's have a round of applause for our newest intern, Charlotte Grayson, who provided that excellent feature on missing people for this week's edition.

There was an enthusiastic round of applause and a few shouts of *hear, hear!*

'Some of you might want to speak to Charlotte for a refresher. That's the best piece of writing I've seen for some time. Congratulations.'

Charlotte felt the heat rising in her cheeks. She liked a pat on the back, but she didn't relish being set up as a shining example. The regular reporters had to bang out stories day-in, day-out and keep it fresh. She'd written what was, essentially, a passion piece. She wondered if she'd be able to maintain that standard after a couple of years of writing about smashed shop windows and local council meetings.

Teddy began mapping out the intended course of the Irwin story, but Charlotte was distracted by a shriek from downstairs. Nobody else seemed to notice it, but her ears tuned in straight away. A phone rang at Teddy's side and he ignored it whilst in full flow. Shouts could be heard from the open window to the side of the office, then the fire alarm sounded.

'What the hell is going on?' Teddy asked. 'It's not alarm testing day, is it?'

He picked up the phone.

'What's happening down there?' he barked.

Reagan in reception was screeching down the phone, and Charlotte was close enough to hear it all.

'Oh my God, someone threw summat through the window. There's fire and everything down 'ere. You all need to get out.'

Teddy was calm and in control. Fortunately, he wasn't taking his lead from Reagan.

'Okay, Reagan, I want you to put the phones on out-of-office and wait for us at the fire assembly point. Remember to bring the staff list with you and phone the fire brigade from your mobile phone if you haven't alerted them already.'

The staff were grabbing mobile phones from their desks, and some were retrieving coats and wallets.

'Come on everybody,' Teddy began. 'You know the drill. We've got a fire in reception, so leave your belongings and make your way out via the fire escape at the far corner.'

'What about me, boss? We're not going to use that bloody evac chair, are we?'

The man speaking to Teddy was Geoff, who used a frame to walk. He was okay using the stairs when there was no rush, but he wouldn't be able to get out quickly. Charlotte and Nigel hung back, waiting to see if their help was needed.

The sound of breaking glass was coming from outside the office window and they could see plumes of dark smoke. Charlotte detected the lingering odour of petrol.

'It's up to you Geoff, we can either get you down the stairs in that contraption, or you can wait in the rescue area—'

Another reporter shouted to them from the other side of the room. 'The fire exit is blocked, boss. Somebody's left a load of photocopier paper in front of the door. We'll be faster going down the stairs.'

'For God's sake, who put the copier paper there?'

Teddy seemed agitated now, like a man with a plan who'd been sabotaged by his staff.

'Beth, you're a fire warden; grab one of those fire extinguishers and head down the staircase. I'll take the other one. Nigel and Charlotte, can you take Geoff to the refuge area and then come straight down? You do all these bloody fire drills, but when the shit hits the fan, see what happens!'

Charlotte had never heard Teddy cuss like that. He was normally such a gentleman, but bearing in mind the present situation, she couldn't blame him. Fire engine sirens were blaring in the distance. A snaking line of staff followed Teddy and Beth, who were taking their roles so seriously, they could have been extras in the film Towering Inferno. Charlotte and Nigel accompanied Geoff to the refuge area at the top of the stairs.

'Are you sure you're okay here, Geoff? The evacuation chair is just over there; I'm sure me and Charlotte can figure it out between us.'

'I'll take my chances with the fire brigade,' Geoff replied. 'Those chairs make me feel like an invalid. I'd rather come out the building walking than be carried in one of those things.'

'So long as you're sure? We can stay with you if you want,' Charlotte offered.

'No, go,' Geoff replied. 'The fire chaps are here now; they'll have it sorted in no time. If anybody asks, my last words were *Screw the Bay View Weekly pension scheme!*'

Both Charlotte and Nigel laughed at that one. The pension scheme was a tricky topic in the office, not that it concerned Charlotte. It was massively under-funded, and they'd be lucky if any of them got to see their pensions the way things were going at the newspaper.

Nigel and Charlotte made a last check on Geoff and then started down the stairs. They reached a small landing half-way down, and when they turned the corner, they could see the flames beyond the fire door at the bottom of the stairwell.

'Oh hell,' said Nigel, 'That doesn't look good. I don't fancy our chances going that way, do you? I hadn't expected it to be as bad as that.'

CHAPTER TWENTY-THREE

'We can't leave Geoff to his own devices up there. We need to go back upstairs and shift the blockage at the fire exit.'

Nigel and Charlotte began to run back up the staircase. Beyond the fire door and the entrance to reception, they could hear the fire engines arriving. The flashes from their emergency lights made their way through the flames like a spectral presence.

'Change of plan, Geoff!' Nigel called out. 'We're going out the rear fire exit now. I hope you're up to moving a couple of reams of copy paper?'

Geoff seemed relieved to have some company, even if it meant that the most direct exit was also blocked. He followed Nigel and Charlotte into the office and towards the upper fire exit in the far corner.

'Which idiot put all this paper here?' Nigel groaned as he saw the extent to which the fire door was blocked. 'Okay, Charlotte, can you see if there's a trolley anywhere on this level? I'm sure I've seen one somewhere for moving delivery parcels, but I can't think for the life of me where it's kept.'

Charlotte nodded and rushed off. Being unfamiliar with

the nooks and crannies of the building, she darted into cupboards and side rooms; it would have been useful if they'd included this in an induction day rather than as part of an emergency escape plan. She found the four-wheeled trolley in a store cupboard which she didn't even know existed. It insisted on going in the opposite direction to which she was pushing it. The loud squeaking would give Nigel and Geoff plenty of notice that she was on her way.

'Can you believe this?' Nigel began as she came round the corner, 'There's a note attached to this box of paper apologising for leaving it in front of the fire exit and saying it'll be moved first thing this morning. Stupid things like this turn me into a clipboard-carrying health and safety fanatic.'

Charlotte pushed the trolley over to the fire door and the three of them started loading the boxes of paper onto it.

'It's the same with my disabled parking space out the back. People are always nipping in for five minutes, never thinking I might need it. Pricks.'

Although Charlotte didn't share their passion for these topics of conversation, she was eager to get out of the building and they both had a point, although she'd rather have discussed it after the fire exit was clear.

'Are you going down in the evac chair, or do you want to walk it?' Nigel asked.

'At least somebody hasn't used the evac chair as a go kart,' Charlotte chipped in, keen to break the tension if only for the sake of her own nerves.

Geoff snorted.

'I wouldn't put it past the buggers. No, I'll walk down, Nigel. I'd like to preserve some dignity in front of my colleagues. The fire is at the front of the building, so I don't think we'll be in much danger.'

After they'd moved three trolley-loads of hastily stacked

copier paper to a desk in the main office, the door was clear enough. Nigel pushed it open; if they walked sideways, they could squeeze out onto the metal platform of the emergency staircase. Firefighters were there already, assessing the situation and poised to enter the building at the rear using their axes.

'Any more unaccounted for?' one of the firefighters asked through his breathing gear.

'No, I'm certain that's everybody out now, provided everybody who went ahead of us got out okay,' Charlotte replied.

'I was rather hoping for a fireman's lift,' she ventured, but the firefighters seemed more intent on securing the building than engaging in flirtatious banter.

Nigel was walking down the metal staircase with Geoff, his arm held outwards ready to steady him if needed.

Once Geoff reached the bottom, the senior firefighter suggested they make their way along the side alley, away from the newspaper premises, and join their colleagues for a roll call in the designated meeting place. There was a small cheer and some half-hearted clapping as the three of them emerged from the alleyway and the assembled team of staff saw that their colleagues were out safely.

'It's not exactly *Backdraft*, Nigel, but I guess rescuing Geoff from the flames makes you like Kurt Russell,' said one of the reporters. Laughter rippled through the group and Teddy added their names to the register.

'That's everybody out,' he said. 'But whoever left that paper in front of the fire exit needs to call into my office, if there's anything left of it after all this, and have a quiet word. Needless to say, that was not the cleverest thing I've seen all week.'

The atmosphere became serious for a moment until

Teddy walked over to the firefighter in charge to hand over the list of names.

'I blame management,' came the voice of the witty reporter, 'they'll do anything they can to block the doors and stop us going home at night.'

There was more laughter and then people moved into huddles to start up their own conversations.

'The damage only looks superficial to me,' Nigel commented, glancing across the road at the front door to the office.

'Are you all right, Reagan?' Charlotte asked. She'd just noticed that the normally chirpy receptionist appeared frightened out of her wits.

'It were terrifying,' she said, her voice shrill. 'It were a bottle filled with petrol or summat like that. The flames went all over the door, it were 'orrible.'

'You did a great job getting everybody out,' Charlotte told her. She always felt guilty dismissing Reagan because of the way she spoke, but she was a nice kid; she was just in need of some guidance. The girl began to cry.

'Oh Reagan, what's the matter?' Charlotte said. 'It's okay now, we're all safe, and the fire is out. There's not too much damage, just some burning to the main window and entrance. They'll soon patch it up.'

'It were my fault that paper was left near the door,' she continued, keeping her voice low. 'I asked them buggers where to put it and all they did was take the piss. So, I told the delivery guy to put it there out of the way. I didn't mean to mess up.'

'It's okay, Reagan, anybody can make a mistake. I'll come with you to speak to Teddy and we can explain it together. He'll understand.'

'I'm scared,' Reagan said, sobbing.

'Nigel, I'm going to take Reagan for a coffee at the shop around the corner, it's all been too much for her. Will you tell Teddy that's where we are, if anybody needs us?'

'Sure,' Nigel answered, breaking off from a conversation with Geoff.

Charlotte guided Reagan away from the crowd, taking a short walk up the street to the nearest coffee shop.

'Grab a table, I'll get the drinks in. And how about a cake, too?'

That seemed to cheer Reagan up. Charlotte placed the orders and joined her young companion.

'So, what happened?' she asked.

'I was minding my own business, filing my nails, when there was this smashing sound. I didn't know what it was at first, but then I could smell something, like petrol. Then I saw them flames and I screamed.'

The shop owner brought the cakes over. Charlotte had opted for sweet and sticky, and from the expression on her face, it seemed that it was just what Reagan needed. She took a massive bite from her cake, devouring almost half of it in one go.

'How did the others get out?' Charlotte asked.

'I used the fire extinguishing thingy and managed to get the door open. The flames had spread along the carpet into reception, and I was so scared, I nearly shat myself.'

'You sound like the hero of the hour,' Charlotte reassured her, though she couldn't recall Kurt Russell using similar words to describe the drama in the Backdraft film.

'Teddy will be fine. When he hears how you saved everyone, he'll forgive you about the printer paper. Expect some extra fire safety training, but believe me, that'll be all that happens. I'm certain of it.'

It seemed that Reagan was suitably reassured by her

words, because the second bite of cake disappeared into her mouth seconds after the first piece was swallowed.

'Did you get a look at who threw that bottle of petrol or whatever it was?' Charlotte chanced.

'Yeah, I'm surprised no one has asked me yet. I got a good view of her. She wasn't the type you'd expect to be hurling things like that around. The thing I noticed about her was that she was very tall. You don't often see women that tall.'

CHAPTER TWENTY-FOUR

December 1999

As she walked along the promenade that weekend, Kate noticed that most people seemed to have finished their Christmas shopping and were now getting into holiday mode. With the festivities taking place over the following weekend, the final buying frenzy had taken place. There was another week at work, then the fun would begin. Kate was happy to be on shift over Christmas and New Year, preferring to stay busy. Despite their altercation earlier in the week, Brett had kept their pre-existing Sunday lunch appointment, and they were now walking it off along the promenade.

'Do you think they'll ever re-open this place again?' Brett asked.

They were walking past the Midland Hotel. It was boarded up and secured, and the vandals had got to it with their spray cans.

'Who knows? You'd think somebody could make a go of it. It's in a lovely position but it's such an eyesore. All it needs is a developer to come in and restore it to its former glory. Morecambe needs some love from somebody, but it's hard to see where it'll come from. I guess if you're planning to move on, now is not such a bad time. I sometimes wonder how long this place can survive.'

Brett walked alongside her in silence. She hadn't broached the Tiffany issue yet, letting it slide during lunch, making Brett laugh with tales of amusing policing encounters instead. They'd get to it eventually, but she was enjoying his company and didn't want to rock the boat.

'Jeez, it's so damn cold today; there's a biting wind coming off that bay. How do you live on the front?'

'It's not so bad,' Kate replied. 'Fancy a walk to Happy Mount Park? I bet it's all festive at this time of year.'

'Okay. If you don't mind though, I'll turn off home after that, rather than walk with you all the way back up to your place. Things to do, places to go...'

Happy Mount Park appeared to be busy most of the year round, with an endless supply of young children content to spend their time there, whatever the weather. It was a nice time to be out too; everybody was dressed in scarves, gloves and hats, amid an air of Christmas excitement. If the ground had been covered in a crisp white snowfall, it would have looked like a modern-day Christmas card.

'So, what are your plans for Christmas Day?' Kate asked as they idly watched the kids on the swings. 'I told you I'm working, didn't I? I'm meeting with two friends from the police station on Boxing Day, so we're having a late Christmas dinner then.'

'I'm going to have a quiet one,' Brett replied, glancing around. 'Don't make a big fuss, but I'm going to start walking down the path. Just follow me without making a big deal of it.'

Kate's instant reaction was to turn round, but Brett grasped her arm and gave it a squeeze.

'I said don't look,' he complained. 'Some detective you'll make, if you can't keep a low profile.'

Kate followed his lead and they moved over towards the far end of the play area, away from the main flow of people.

'What was all that about?' Kate asked, hoping it was safe to glance around.

'It's nothing,' Brett mumbled. 'Just somebody I didn't want to run into.'

Kate surveyed the park to see if she recognised anybody, but it was hard to pick anybody out from the sea of bobble hats, mittens, winter coats and scarves.

'That wasn't her, was it?' Kate ventured. If Brett was going straight home after the visit to Happy Mount Park, she didn't have long to broach the topic.

'I'm not sure,' he replied. 'I didn't get a close enough look. But it was certainly him.'

'David Irwin?'

'Yes.'

'I was shocked when I saw what happened between you two earlier in the week?'

Brett said nothing, walking on.

'He was pretty angry with you. Are you having an affair with his wife?'

More silence.

'I'm not here to give you a hard time about it. I just want to know what's going on. More than anything, I want to be sure you're safe.'

Brett walked over to a vacant bench and took a seat. Kate sat beside him and waited.

'Look, I was going to tell you. It's just that I wasn't sure in my own mind what we were doing. You found out about us before I was ready to talk about it.'

'Are you ready now?' Kate asked.

'Some of it,' he replied. 'I can't tell you everything now. But my head is bursting. I have to speak to somebody about it.'

'How about starting by telling me who she is? That would be a good start.'

Brett shuffled on the bench as if he was settling in.

'Her name is Tiffany. Tiffany Irwin. Most people call her Tiff. She's 24 years old and has three kids. And yes, she's married. To David Irwin. He's not very nice to her. She wants to leave him.'

'Damn it, Brett, there's a lot to unpack even in that information. Are you in love?'

'Yes, and I know what you're going to say about her seeing me as an easy way out of an unhappy marriage. But we are in love. I've never felt this way about anyone before.'

'And the kids?'

Kate had never heard her brother speak like this. At one point in his teenage years she'd wondered if he might be gay, such was his disinterest in women. As it turned out, his hormones were just lethargic. As soon as they kicked in, he more than made up for what he'd been missing. But it had all been fun and games until this.

'That's what makes this so difficult. She desperately wants to leave him, but how do you make a clean break with three children?'

'One of them is a newborn too. The marital problems must be relatively recent.'

Brett said nothing.

'So, what's the plan?' she asked, hoping that he'd keep talking.

'We want to be together. And yes, that means the kids too. You're probably going to tell me I'm too young, but Tiff is young too. We can make it work.'

'I sense there's a *but* coming?'

Kate knew better than to challenge her brother on his decisions. He had money from the house, and it wasn't as if he was an 18-year-old.

'Yes, we've got a problem. Tiff's family owns farmland, a lot of it too. Her father died recently and there's a lot of tension over how everything will be carved up. She has an ambitious brother who wants to offer the land up for nuclear or chemical use, but Tiff doesn't want that. David and her brother are ganging up on her, and she's under a lot of pressure—'

'So, taking his three children from him is going to be the least of her problems?'

'Yes. Tiff's facing a big enough mess with her father's estate, let alone a relationship breakdown. She's desperate to leave him, but the timing is terrible. She hates him; there's no love between them anymore—'

'Does he hurt her?'

Kate had already intervened in more domestic assaults than she would have liked in her short policing career, and it was a topic about which she became incensed.

'Not yet, at least not physically. But he runs her down all the time, making her feel useless, like she can't make a sensible decision. I want her to leave him, but she says she has to hang on until she works out the money. If she messes that up, it might make things difficult for the kids.'

'You're leaving soon, aren't you? This isn't some far away plan. It's happening imminently, isn't it?'

Brett waited several seconds before answering.

'Yes.'

'That's why you sold the house. You're getting all your ducks in a row. And you're just going to run for it, aren't you?'

'How else can we get away? How do you break off a relationship with three young kids in tow? We've talked and talked about it, but we can't think of any other way. As soon as Tiffany makes sure her father's estate is all tied up, we're going.'

'Are you going to tell me where?'

She got her answer from his silence.

'I won't tell anyone, Brett. Not if you're sure this is what you want.'

More silence.

'When are you going?'

It appeared Brett had finished sharing, but she could fill in the gaps herself.

'Jesus Christ, Brett, you're going over Christmas, aren't you?'

'Kate, keep your voice down.'

A passing family were watching them as if they were a couple having a row.

'If I hadn't asked you, you'd have just disappeared and you wouldn't have even told me. Bloody hell, Brett, does it count for nothing, all that time I spent taking care of things after Dad died?'

'I couldn't tell you, Kate. We have to make a clean break of it.'

'This might have been the last time I got to see you. Was that our last supper, Brett? Is that why you kept our lunch date today?'

'Be quiet, Kate, they're coming this way. Keep your head down, don't talk to me.'

Kate glanced to the side, then down at the ground. She

had every good reason not to catch his eye; it was David Irwin, out in the park with his three children. No wonder Brett had wanted to make himself scarce earlier. They sat in silence while the family group passed by. To her relief, no one noticed them; she had no desire for a re-run of the events at the leisure centre.

'Speak of the devil,' Kate murmured. 'That was a close call. Did Tiffany see you?'

'He wasn't with Tiffany,' Brett replied.

Kate checked again. She'd assumed it was Tiffany, but with her head down, she hadn't got a proper view. Now it was obvious; it couldn't possibly be Tiffany. The woman accompanying David Irwin was far too tall.

CHAPTER TWENTY-FIVE

'We're all going to have to use the rear door while they get the front of the building patched up,' Teddy explained to the assembled staff. 'If you can work at home, please do so for today, otherwise come and speak to me and we'll make other arrangements. Only the management team are allowed back in the building until we've had the all-clear.'

Charlotte and Reagan just got back from the tea shop in time to catch the tail end of Teddy's update.

'Did I miss anything?' Charlotte asked Nigel once she'd found him in the small crowd of people.

'Not much. The officer in charge has confirmed that the fire was caused by a bottle of accelerant thrown at the front of the building. By accelerant he means petrol. It hasn't caused structural damage; much of the burning is superficial, but they'll need to get the carpenters in to sort out the doorway. They couldn't have chosen a better day to do it, bearing in mind this week's paper is out now. Speaking of which, what did you think of your story?'

'I was so proud when I saw it this morning. I bought five

copies: they're sitting on my desk upstairs. Does the thrill ever wear off?'

'You get used to it, but no, it's still a buzz for me when I write a really good piece and then I see it in the paper. I guess it's like the excitement an author feels when they see their book in print.'

Charlotte thought over what he'd just told her about the fire.

'Do they have any idea who it was? It wasn't the *Bring Back Mr Blobby to Happy Mount Park* campaign group was it?'

Nigel laughed.

'No, they're not sure what it was about yet. It could be somebody with a grudge who didn't like their court case being reported in the paper.'

'Reagan told me she saw who threw it. She couldn't name her, but she described her as a tall woman. Ring any bells?'

'Really?'

Nigel's eyes lit up.

'I'll mention it to one of the attending officers. I'm not sure it gets us any further forward, but I'd like to find out who this woman is. Could it be Jane Irwin, do you think? With Callie disappearing like that and the fire alarms going off at the hospital, do you think it's all connected?'

Charlotte nodded.

'I don't have a clue how it's all linked, but I'm sure as hell it is. Even the police don't know yet, or if they do, they're not telling us. I bet there's some heat on DI Comfort. How embarrassing for him, her slipping away like that.'

'Well, Callie's not a murder suspect, but she is right at the heart of a missing person case. They probably didn't expect her to be a flight risk. I wonder where she is. Simone told us she'd taken her diabetes medication when she ran, so it doesn't sound like she's planning on coming back any time soon.'

'I've just had a thought,' Charlotte said after a brief pause. 'I bet she's not even known as Callie Irwin anymore. But if those kids are still alive, someone must have raised them. They must have gone to the doctor, the dentist, to school or university. Whatever happened to them after they disappeared, they'll have new identities. Which means they'll slip under the police radar.'

'It'll be more difficult for Callie now they know what she looks like, but you're right. They could even still be living in Morecambe. Who could even tell—'

'Damn, what's the time?'

With all the excitement, Charlotte had lost track of the day.

'Five minutes to one. Why?'

'I'm supposed to be meeting a contact by the slipway at one o'clock. I've got to go. No one's expecting me back in the office now, are they?'

'No, let's catch up tomorrow. I'll make sure I speak to DI Comfort about this mysterious tall woman and I'll tell you if there are any further developments.'

Charlotte was in so much of a rush that she only caught the tail end of what he said. It wasn't far to the slipway, so she jogged it. Trying to ignore her stiff body, she pushed through it, putting it down to the challenges of the past few days. As she crossed the road opposite the RNLI building, she saw Steven Terry waiting at a distance. There was something about him, a presence, even when he was away from a floodlit stage. He was the sort of man you'd pick out in a crowd.

Charlotte was out of breath by the time she reached him.

'Steven... sorry I'm late... just give me a minute, will you?'

'Charlotte, how lovely to see you,' he said, embracing her. His assured, measured voice made her feel that she was in safe hands. He gave her a while to recover.

'I do love this town,' he said. 'That's Barrow across the bay, isn't it? It's such a lovely drive from that area.'

'Well, the last time I saw you, we were breaking into the old leisure park along the sea front. I don't have anything as exciting for you today, I'm afraid.'

'I had a lot of fun that night. How is Abi? Have you seen her recently?'

It was a strange turn of events that had linked them all together. Steven had met Abi on the entertainment circuit and she in turn had brought Steven into their lives. His insights into their previous problems had been remarkable. She was hoping for some of that magic at the slipway, as she suggested they take a nearby bench while she brought him up to speed with her news. He was fascinated by the story of the Irwin children.

'You do have a habit of getting caught up with some fascinating news stories,' he said, having had time to process all her updates from the past week. 'I'll do what I can to help you, but I can't promise you anything. There's very little for me to grasp here, no person or building to pick up any echoes from, and thousands of people pass by here every week. It's unlikely I'll be able to help, I'm afraid.'

'I understand,' Charlotte replied, a little disappointed that he seemed so doubtful. However, she knew enough about Steven Terry to appreciate that his insights often came out of left field.

'I can tell you one thing for starters,' Steven began, standing up and walking towards the slipway, 'you have an extraordinarily strong emotional connection to this spot. Something very frightening happened to you here.'

'You can say that again,' Charlotte said. 'You see the stone jetty over there? That last bit of trouble I got mixed up in involved them tying my son to the front of that jetty while the sea was coming in. I had to rescue him. We almost lost our lives.'

Steven turned towards her with the grave expression that he used so well when performing on stage.

'Let me tell you something now as a friend, rather than a clairvoyant.'

'What?'

'Take more care of yourself, Charlotte. I mean it. You shouldn't be getting tangled up in events like this.'

Charlotte thought it might be too late for that, but she kept it to herself.

'Where was the girl found?'

'Somewhere around that area,' Charlotte said, pointing. 'I think the family car was a little closer to the slipway back in 1999.'

She left Steven to do his thing. He ambled around the area that she'd pointed out, much like a water diviner without a stick, occasionally stopping to put his hand on his forehead, like he was starring in an advert for headache tablets. She left him like that for over five minutes, then could contain her curiosity no longer.

'Are you getting anything?' she asked. 'This place must be full of ghosts.'

He wrinkled his face and looked around.

'There are so many echoes here, and from so many years ago. I thought I caught something of your lady – Callie, was it? – but it was momentary and confusing. Imagine what it would be like for you to walk into a big theatre when the entire audience is speaking and you're trying to focus on just one voice. That's how difficult it is in a place like this.'

'So, you think you caught something from Callie? What was it? A memory, a glimpse into the past?'

Steven shook his head.

'It was momentary, Charlotte. I can't even be certain it was your woman, though the echo was recent, and it was strong. You need to take what I say with a large pinch of salt. It's really not reliable.'

Charlotte felt a pang of desperation. He always did this to her, whether on stage or in person. She just wanted him to tell her straight.

'What is it, Steven? What are you getting from Callie?'

'That she was very confused and scared. She was seeking something here. She was burning up with anger, too.'

CHAPTER TWENTY-SIX

If Steven Terry had been performing a show on the promenade, at that very moment the spotlight would have been shut off as the stage curtain closed and a gasp of suspense would have rippled through the enraptured audience. As it was, Charlotte just stared at him, wondering how he did it.

'I can see you're intrigued by what I just said, Charlotte, but please remember, it doesn't come with the Steven Terry guarantee of authenticity this time around. I believe it's Callie's echoes I can feel here, but I might be mistaken. Is there anywhere we could go that might be easier for me to get a fix on a specific person?'

Charlotte thought about it for a moment.

'The stone graves at Heysham. Sunderland Point, perhaps?' she suggested.

'I'm not familiar with those places. Are they far from here?'

'What time do you have to be on stage this evening?'

'I need to be in Preston by five o'clock for the sound

check. If we're no more than two hours away, I can do it. What happened at the stone graves?'

He'd started walking back to his car already, so Charlotte followed and brought him up to speed.

'I stand a very good chance of picking up something at the stone graves. It's recent and it involves this Evan Farrish and one or maybe two other people around the time of his death. Sunderland Point may be a little more problematic. Can we get into the old pillbox, do you think?'

Charlotte explained the connection between the two locations and the news story she was investigating, and Steven appeared more hopeful. She was mindful of time and grateful that they hadn't got caught up with school or home-from-work traffic; she didn't want to be responsible for making Steven late for his technical run-through.

The journey to Heysham seemed to take no time at all. Before she knew it, they were passing by St Peter's Church and stepping among the ruined stone walls of the old chapel further along the path, with the cliffs below them and the grey, choppy sea ahead of them.

'This is breathtaking,' Steven said. 'What an incredible place. I've seen Heysham marked on the road signs so many times, but I wasn't aware it was so dramatic.'

Charlotte was eager to get him to the stone graves, but he was intent on wandering through the ruins of the old chapel and taking in the wonderful view.

'There was an argument within the walls of this ruined chapel,' he said, without warning. 'These people knew each other, but they were not friends.'

Charlotte realised it was better not to say anything when he was in full flow. So she stood and watched while Steven walked up to the stone graves. What happened to him when he was having a vision was a mystery. Will was sceptical about his talents, even though he'd been on the receiving end of them. Steven Terry challenged Charlotte's rational thinking, but his ability to reveal insights was uncanny.

'Oh yes, this is strong,' he said, when they reached the graves. 'It was this one, this one here.'

He pointed to the larger stone grave. Charlotte nodded unnecessarily; Steven was telling her, not asking her.

'It happened suddenly. This person hadn't come to kill—'

'How many were there?' Charlotte asked.

'There were two of them here, one of them a woman. He was not scared of this person; his death came as a surprise. It was sudden, caused by a turn of events and a panic. This was some sort of reunion, and Evan Farrish was not their prey.'

Steven went quiet as he walked around the carved-out shapes in the stone, each one resembling a human form.

'This woman did not mean to kill him. It was a moment of rage, of sudden and intense panic. Evan was going to reveal something; he was threatening to tell somebody something very important.'

'Do you have any idea what it was? We'd only just met him; he didn't seem to be a man hiding secrets when we walked along the cliff edge with him.'

'I pick up echoes of emotions, Charlotte. I can't grasp conversations or words. But it's intense here, as I would expect it to be. There was an overwhelming rage in his killer. Was there a dog here?'

'How do you know that? That's incredible.'

'There's an innocence about animals which is easy to sense among signs of powerful emotions. It might be a child or a pet; in this case it's most likely to be a dog. But yes, I can tell an animal was here.'

Being close to Steven Terry always left Charlotte mildly stunned, even though she wasn't a big believer in what he did.

Steven checked his watch.

'If you want to get to Sunderland Point, we'd better move on. I can tell by the look on your face that you derived something useful from that.'

'You can say that again,' Charlotte replied, leading the way back down the hill towards his car.

As they drove off towards Sunderland Point, Charlotte asked why the police didn't ever call upon Steven's services.

'Most of them regard me much like your husband did when we met: an oddity, a novelty, but not a credible source of information. Sometimes they call in people like me when they're desperate, but you must have been around the police long enough now to know how cynical they are. They see the darkest side of humanity, so it's hard for them to open up their minds and let in something which they consider to be supernatural.'

'Is it supernatural, though? I never hear you talking about ghosts and ghouls. What you do seems to be... almost scientific.'

'Ah, now Charlotte, that's why you're a believer. It's nothing to do with ghosts and spirits, you're right. I talked about dogs earlier when we were at the graves. If you've ever been around those lovely creatures, you'll realise that they see and sense things that we don't. That's what happens with me. If you could free your mind enough, you'd experience the same things as I do, a frequency I'm tuned into. I've always been very receptive to it, but most other people are too distracted and of closed mind to see what's in front of them.'

He was a spell-binding storyteller. She could listen to his voice all day.

'But yes, it's science, not spooks. The tabloids prefer to portray it otherwise, because it sounds better. But people who see ghosts are experiencing echoes. They don't actually exist, but what they're seeing is real. It's like they picked up a radio signal that nobody else can receive.'

Charlotte got a flashback to when she was a small child, sitting on the story carpet at school, listening to the teacher transport her to a faraway land with the help of a story book. That summed up her feelings when she listened to Steven Terry.

She said nothing as they drove across the causeway to Sunderland Point. Will's voice was in the back of her head all the time, advising her to be wary of Steven Terry. *You just fill in the gaps. He doesn't actually tell you anything, you make it up yourself. His expertise is in reading emotions; he's no better than a fortune teller at Blackpool Beach.*

His voice was loud and clear, warning her to be cautious. But when she saw how Steven slowed the car at the precise point where she'd been left to drown, she knew he'd picked up something.

As they parked up at the end of the causeway, she heard the heavy throttling of jet-ski engines in the distance, sounding like a swarm of agitated mosquitoes heading their way. It shattered the peace of the place and she could see why Jed had bemoaned the presence of these two young men in the community. She looked out for him on the shingle, but he was nowhere to be seen.

Steven loved the location and vowed to return when he had more time. Charlotte was relieved to see they were well clear of the high tide. Perhaps that was what Steven had picked up on as they'd driven along the causeway, her sense of panic and trepidation about being there again.

They would have to focus if he was going to get away in time, so she directed him to the small path which led to the far side of the peninsula. Soon they were laughing, much like they had as they'd scrambled over the security fence of the abandoned leisure park the year before. They had to climb up the muddy bank to reach the pillbox, and after that there was a barbed wire fence to tackle and an electric fence to step over. Even the cows in the field seemed drawn by Steven's presence; it wasn't long before the pillbox was surrounded by the animals.

As they stepped into the dark, ruined structure, they turned on their phone flashlights to get a better view. Charlotte sensed the area had been disturbed, but she couldn't work out how. Some Ginsters sandwich packs had been discarded in the corner. She checked the dates; they were recent. Perhaps it was some kids picnicking, or more likely teenagers making out.

'Anything here?' she asked hopefully.

'Very little, I'm afraid,' Steven said at last. 'To be honest with you, I've been distracted since we crossed that causeway. Something shook me as we were driving across it and I can't get it out of my mind.'

Charlotte turned around to face him. She was right, he had sensed something.

'Everything is being crowded out by you, Charlotte. You have known extreme fear in this place, am I right?'

She was going to nod but had Will's voice bouncing around in her head. *Don't give him any clues.*

'I have to be clear about this, Charlotte, and you must listen to me. You have experienced terrible danger in this place once before, somewhere on that causeway. But that's not why I'm so concerned. You escaped from whatever it was, or you wouldn't be here now.'

This was why she'd wanted to speak to him again. He always came up with something that nobody else could see.

'Your life could end in this place, Charlotte. Please listen to me; I'm deadly serious about this. You are in danger of losing your life here.'

CHAPTER TWENTY-SEVEN

December 1999

After the near miss with David Irwin and Brett's revelation, there was no way Kate was going home.

'I have to get packed up so I'm ready,' Brett protested.

'I'm not letting you do a runner without saying goodbye. I hate to play the older sister card, but I insist—'

'Come on, Kate.'

'Brett!'

That tone always worked. She'd finished raising him on her own until he was eighteen years old. When push came to shove, Brett would always defer to her.

'Help me pack up then, and we can talk while we're working.'

Brett's home was not so far away from Happy Mount Park. She could sense his defensiveness as they walked along the path.

'I don't want you to try to talk me out of it, Kate. We're in love; we both want this.'

'But does it have to be so drastic? Why do you want to

leave the area? It'll be awkward at first, but it'll settle down. Besides, he has rights as the father of the children.'

She got the feeling Brett wasn't telling her everything.

'We have to go, and it has to be this way, Kate. David Irwin would do everything in his power to stop Tiff if he caught a whiff of what we're planning. And believe me, if you think what you saw the other day was rough handling, that's the least of it—'

'Is he threatening Tiffany? If he is, you must go to the police. I'm sure someone at the station will help.'

'He's not hurting her in that way. Not with his fists or anything like that. But he controls her, so she doesn't know whether she's coming or going. She has to lie to leave the house on her own, and she's losing her grasp on what's real and what isn't. All she wants is to get away from him.'

They'd come to his house now, so the distraction of him finding his key and letting them in created a useful break in their conversation.

'No For Sale board?' she observed.

'What do you think?' Brett shrugged.

They took off their shoes, coats and gloves and Kate rushed to the radiator in the lounge to warm her hands. Brett always ran a warm house, choosing to wear boxers and T-shirts most of the time, rather than put on a shirt or a jumper. She was grateful for it now that the winter chill had worked its way through her gloves. The room was filled with packing boxes.

'Don't bite my head off, Brett, but I have to ask you this question. Could she be using you to help her get away? If she feels trapped in her marriage, she might just see you as a free ticket out of it. Even more so if you have the means to buy a house for cash.'

If it had been close to a frost outside, it was nothing

compared to the sudden drop in temperature in Brett's lounge.

'I don't want to discuss this again. Tiff and I are in love. We intend to take the children and get away. We'll talk to David Irwin when we're settled, but we have no intention of discussing it with him beforehand.'

She'd raised the question, and her duty as a stand-in parent was executed. She wasn't convinced about his answer, but she trusted Brett. His heart had always been in the right place since he was a kid.

Something caught Kate's eye at the top of one of the open packing boxes. It was a picture of their father, receiving a commendation medal, proud and impressive in his immaculate uniform. She thought she was in control of her emotions where her father was concerned, but she choked up seeing him like that, wishing he were here to advise them now.

'I didn't know you had that picture. Will you make me a copy when you get wherever you're going? That's how I always remember Dad. He must have been the proudest police officer in Morecambe. I hope I can live up to that one day.'

Brett had moved through to the kitchen to put the kettle on.

'I take it you'll have a hot drink?' he called through. 'And yes, I will send you a copy. But only if you make yourself useful and start packing up those books on the shelf.'

Kate's hands were warm now, so she prised herself off the radiator and knelt by the bookshelf to remove the books one by one, checking out their titles. Brett came through with the drinks and placed them on two mats above the gas fire. He stopped at Kate's side and took some books off the shelf from the opposite end. This was just as they'd been as children, happy in each other's company, content to be busy together, not needing to speak. Kate wanted it to last a while longer. If this was going to be the last time she saw Brett for goodness knows how long, she had to cherish these final moments.

They worked alongside each other for over ten minutes, without saying a word. Then, from nowhere, Brett began to cry. She spotted a tear drop onto a book first, then saw that he was trying to stifle his sobs. She said nothing, shuffling over to him and putting her arms around him for a while.

'What is it, Brett? Please tell me. I want to help you.'

'I can't, Kate. You mustn't get involved in this. It's something me and Tiff have to work through on our own.'

'Brett, I can help. I'm a police officer now.'

'A fat lot of good it did Dad! I'm sorry, but being a copper doesn't solve every problem in the world. They couldn't help Dad when he needed it, and it won't help here. Some things have to be taken care of by the people involved. Getting the police in will only make things worse.'

'Then talk to me, Brett. Forget the police, talk to me as your sister. You know I'll do what I can to help.'

Brett was still sobbing. She'd never seen him so scared, vulnerable and upset since their father died.

'I think he might kill us if he finds out—' he said, cutting through the tears with a steady voice. 'I've seen what Fabian Armstrong and David Irwin are doing to Tiffany. One of them will kill us if they find out what we're planning.'

Kate let that sink in for a moment. Normally she'd take those words as a figure of speech, but there had been something hateful about David Irwin's body language when he was challenging Brett in the town centre that made her certain her brother meant it literally.

'Has he threatened either of you directly?'

'No, you saw how it was the other day—'

'So, what makes you think they'd harm you physically if you tried to run away with Tiffany?'

'Something is going on with the land they inherited. Tiffany needs to make sure she retains her share of it, but Fabian is trying all sorts of tactics to get what he wants. And he and David are working together, trying to run rings around Tiff. He's her brother, for Christ's sake. It would be like you trying to steal everything from me after Dad died. Who even does that?'

'Who was that woman we saw David Irwin with earlier? The tall one. How is she involved?'

'That's Joanne Taylor. She's the nanny. Only I reckon she's more than that.'

'They're having an affair?'

'Yes, we're certain of it. But he won't want anything to happen in their marriage until the money is all tied up. A nanny's job is the ideal cover. If anybody spots them out in the park like that, he has the perfect excuse.'

Kate wished her brother hadn't got caught up in this. She couldn't see how it would end well. Even if both parties wanted the split, the division of property and money sounded like it was a powder keg ready to go off.

'So why do you think you're in danger, Brett? I can see they might be angry, but threatening your safety? That's a different thing altogether.'

'Because you didn't see everything when you saw David Irwin and me in the town centre the other day. He told me as much. He kicked me in the stomach and told me that if I don't leave his wife and family alone, I'll be found with my throat cut in a back alley somewhere. And once he's done that, Tiff will be joining me.'

CHAPTER TWENTY-EIGHT

However much Charlotte pushed Steven Terry for more information, it wasn't forthcoming. He always did this, and it was what brought out any morsel of scepticism which lurked in her mind. He was driving them back to Lancaster so he could join the motorway to head for Preston. Charlotte decided that she'd catch up with Will after work and they could travel on the bus together back to Morecambe. That's if she could find out where he was. They needed to speak; events were slipping away from them.

'Can the event you warned me about be a thing that happened in the past?' she asked, hoping she was over the worst already. She'd already escaped death once at Sunderland Point.

'I can't be certain,' Steven replied.

She'd told him about her earlier experience on the causeway but had omitted the details of Kate's involvement in the rescue attempt. But Steven was unable to confirm if that was the incident he was sensing, or if it was something that lay in the future.

'I just have to warn you to be careful. Though I seem to

remember I've given you a warning like that before and you ignored me.'

He smiled when he said it, so she was relieved he wasn't scolding her.

'I didn't ignore you, Steven. It's just that sometimes... well, events are set in motion and you can't do much to stop them.'

'I'm worried for you, Charlotte. Though I was worried for you last time and you seemed to be able to take care of yourself.'

'Can we change our path in life?' Charlotte asked. 'You're telling me I'm going to encounter terrible danger at Sunderland Point. What if I decided never to go there again; could I avoid it that way?'

'It's possible,' Steven replied after a while. 'But it's more likely that what I told you will play out regardless. The die is already cast; events will lead you to that place again, whatever happens.'

Charlotte struggled with his logic. Surely it was possible to avert fate if you had warning of it? She had no intention of returning to Sunderland Point again, not unless it was for a day trip with the family, and that wasn't happening for some time, because the car was a write-off.

'Well, I want to be able to sleep at night, so I'm going to assume you were getting a bad signal out there and that what you saw was the attempt to kill me on the causeway—'

She stopped as the words stuck in her throat. She was talking about it like it was an everyday event. Somebody had tried to kill her, possibly the tall woman who was showing up everywhere. She had to find out who this woman was and what she wanted. If only Kate hadn't warned her off speaking to the police; it made things almost impossible. Perhaps Toni Lawson was the right woman to confide in as a half-way house; they'd hit it off, and she wasn't a police officer. She resolved to contact her as soon as possible.

They'd hit the snake of traffic at the edge of Lancaster. Charlotte was miles away in thought.

'Where shall I drop you?' Steven asked.

'Somewhere central, please, by the Dukes Playhouse or Dalton Square, somewhere like that. Will we see you again, Steven? Socially, I mean. It would be lovely to meet up for another night out with Will and Abi, like we did last time. I promise I won't get you detained by the police this time. We'll just have a pleasant evening.'

'I'm not back in Morecambe until Christmas,' Steven answered, as he checked his mirrors before pulling in at the side of the road. 'I'm filming a TV special at The Park Hotel and we've timed it to coincide with a short run at the Winter Gardens again—'

'The Park Hotel?'

'Yes, it's got a long history of ghostly goings on. They want me to join up with a couple of other minor TV celebrities to record a show for some satellite TV channel. It pays well and it'll be fun. Maybe we can meet again then?'

Charlotte leaned over and gave Steven a peck on the cheek.

'Thanks for coming, Steven, I do appreciate it. And I promise I'll stay safe. Nothing's going to get in the way of me and a Christmas night out with good friends. I'll see you in December!'

She got out of the car, gave Steven a final wave and watched as he re-joined the traffic moving through town. Dalton Square was a good place to find a seat and contact Will. She found a bench and took out Hollie's phone. There was just one message from Nigel, telling her to use the back entrance the next day, as the front of the newspaper building was boarded up while they repaired the door. She texted back, keen to find out if the police had any leads yet. The reply came back straight away: *Nothing yet!*

Charlotte texted Will. Since he'd started work at the university, she was never sure whether or not he was taking a class, so she avoided calling him.

I'm in Lancaster - again! What happened to you last night, did you stay with a friend? :-) Do you want to catch the bus home this evening and go out for food and a catch-up? Let me know when you're leaving work and I'll meet you in town or we can eat in Morecambe xxx

She pressed *Send* on the message. Moments later, it came back as a failed delivery. She checked her phone signal, then made sure she hadn't got the wrong number. Taking more care this time, she re-typed the message and sent it again. It was returned. Her immediate instinct was to use Facebook Messenger as her back-up. She opened the app, then remembered this was Hollie's phone. Damn it, she couldn't remember her own Facebook login details. She would get a new phone while she was in town. Then she could try Will again. She texted Lucia, thinking of a workaround.

Hi L! Please will you forward this text to your dad, I can't raise him. Send it by Facebook too. Technical issues. Don't ask :-) Mum xxx

That text was sent successfully. That was odd. Lucia was straight back to her.

Can't raise Dad. Weird. Is his phone okay? Btw you know you asked me to do some digging on that news story? I found out something about Kate's brother from an old article in the Lancaster newspaper. He used to work at the Maritime Museum in Lancaster. Worth checking out?

Now that was excellent timing. She'd sort out a new

phone, visit the Maritime Museum and meet up with Will, if she was able to contact him.

Pls email, text and Facebook your dad and if he gets the message, tell him I'll meet him for food at 5pm at Pizza Margherita. You & Olli can join us if you want?

Lucia confirmed that she'd sent on the messages, then declined Charlotte's invitation.

Soz Mum, we're off to see a play tonight. Evening of culture :-) Luc x

Charlotte checked the phone and removed any traces of her own messages and outward calls. As she saw the stream of messages from Callie Irwin, each one trying to raise Hollie to see what she wanted, Charlotte remembered she needed to contact her. Borrowing a pen from a passing office worker, she copied Callie's number onto the scrap of paper in her pocket, then took her SIM card out of Hollie's phone and replaced it with the student's own SIM from the paper parcel she'd put together earlier. She'd give the phone to Will when she saw him. It would be a relief to be rid of it. Besides, the battery was almost dead, and she had no way of charging it until she could access an electrical socket and get it plugged in. All she could hope was that he'd receive the meet-up information via Lucia and they could catch up over an evening meal in the restaurant.

The Argos store across the road was the best place to buy a phone without a lot of fuss. She bought a contract-free model with her payment card and sat in a coffee shop while she put it all together. It was a waterproof model which came with a secure carry case. With her recent track record, it was probably the best thing. Before long, her old SIM was installed and the phone was charging, thanks to a seat with a free charging point. She sat with a hot chocolate and muffin, thinking through the events of the day. As she munched on the marshmallows sprinkled on top of her hot drink, she watched the world passing by outside.

She was worried about Will. Had his phone malfunctioned? It was unusual that he hadn't made it back to the Travelodge the night before, but he might have stayed with an academic colleague in town if they'd gone on for drinks. What with the fire at the office and her meeting with Steven Terry, she'd been distracted.

And she had to talk to Will about the guest house, too. She'd been an absent owner lately, and Isla was too old to keep on covering for her. It was unfair to take advantage of her good nature. As soon as things were resolved, she'd take Isla and George out for the evening and come up with a better plan.

Her new phone let out a loud, melodic ringtone and she felt her cheeks colouring with embarrassment. She should change it to something more socially acceptable. She checked the message; it was Lucia again. At least everything was working, and her SIM and network contract were playing ball. The message didn't offer any relief.

No reply from Dad. That's unusual. Not even sure the text message got delivered. Let me know when you hear from him. Worried! Luc x

CHAPTER TWENTY-NINE

The Maritime Museum was along St George's Quay. Charlotte knew enough basic local history to realise that the quay area of the city went hand-in-hand with Sunderland Point's maritime past, both places being located at different points along the River Lune. Even if she drew a blank with information about Brett, she'd get better understanding of the area inside the museum and that was bound to come in useful in her reporting work.

The walk through the centre would be a welcome distraction from Will and everything else that was preying on her mind. So, Brett Allan had worked at the Maritime Museum, but that was two decades ago. People tended to stay around in jobs like that. Jon Rogers at Morecambe Library was an excellent example; she might even strike gold and find out more about him, if any of his former colleagues still worked there.

As she passed the George and Dragon pub, she smiled to herself, remembering a romantic night out she and Will had shared inside it, not long after their return to the city from working the holiday camp at Middleton Sands for the summer. She'd had a little too much to drink and shot out of the pub door, intent on going for a swim in the river opposite. She couldn't swim to save her life then; the notion was ridiculous. It had been all Will could do to restrain her from stripping off and jumping in. It wasn't her proudest moment, but the memory provided some light relief in the day.

She walked through the entrance of the Maritime Museum and smiled at the man serving at the kiosk. The afternoon was drawing on; they might be closing soon.

'Hello, what time do you close?'

'You've got just under an hour, we close at four o'clock,' the man replied.

'That's fine; I'll have a ticket please.'

'Are you aware of anybody here who might have known a Brett Allan? He worked here twenty years ago. I know it's a long shot.'

The man laughed.

'I was only four years old, so I'm afraid I can't help you. Keep an eye open for Marjorie; she's worked here for longer than that. She's floor-walking at the moment. You can't miss her. She must have been working at the same time as... what was his name?'

'Brett,' Charlotte replied. That was a better response than she'd hoped for. If Marjorie could give her an idea of what Brett was like, it might help to fill in some of the gaps which Kate was so reluctant to talk about.

She thanked the man at the kiosk and entered the exhibition area. The museum itself was in its afternoon lull, that time between the school parties departing and staff closing up for the day. She almost had the entire place to herself, as if someone had given her VIP access to the exhibits.

Her one and only visit to this museum had been years

ago, presumably with Will since she'd spent most of her life with him. It was interesting to peruse the displays and get a better sense of the area's maritime past. She was mindful of the time though, and keen to rush through the building to locate Marjorie.

She hovered at the Sunderland Point exhibition, finally getting to see what she'd missed at Sambo's grave and discovering what was beyond the peninsula, out in the bay. There were incredible photographs of the wind turbines that Sam Halford had described. They looked even bigger than the one she'd climbed up; she shuddered at the thought of going inside one of those.

Someone caught her eye as she marvelled at the size of the turbines. It was a grey-haired woman, tidying up the interactive exhibits.

'You must be Marjorie?' Charlotte said, taking the lady by surprise.

'Yes, do we know each other?'

Charlotte held out her hand.

'I'm Charlotte Grayson, I work for The Bay View Weekly, but I wanted to talk to you on a personal matter. The gentleman at the ticket kiosk told me to watch out for you.'

Marjorie seemed relieved by that snippet of information. Her expression relaxed, as if she'd expected Charlotte to start selling her double-glazing at any moment.

'How can I help you?' Marjorie asked.

'I hear you've worked here for a long time. Did you know a man called Brett Allan, twenty or so years back?'

Marjorie looked as if a ghost from her past had just walked through the room.

'Oh... that's the last thing I expected you to say.'

Charlotte could see that Marjorie was shaken.

'Shall we take one of those chairs over there?' she asked, leading the way. Marjorie followed, without saying a word.

'I take it from your reaction that you knew him?' Charlotte asked, after they'd settled in the seats.

Marjorie swallowed hard.

'Yes, I knew Brett. He was about the same age as young Brandon on the reception desk. In fact, he sometimes reminds me of Brett in his manner. It's funny you should want to speak about Brett. I've been thinking a lot about him recently.'

'That's interesting,' Charlotte said. 'Why's that?'

'I'm retiring in a couple of weeks,' Marjorie continued. 'Not that I want to, but I've been struggling with breast cancer for some years now and it's finally got the better of me. You'd think a double mastectomy in my fifties would have seen the disease off, but it's been lying in wait until my sixties, ready to strike again. I don't have the same energy I had ten years ago; I think it's going to finish me this time—'

'Oh, I'm so sorry,' Charlotte said. She'd known so many women who'd had to deal with the blow of breast cancer. Barely a day went by when she didn't check in the shower, fearful of finding a lump. She rested her hand on Marjorie's arm, immediately sympathetic for the journey she'd had to take and the deadly one yet to come.

'I'd hoped to retire of old age rather than with health issues, but I'm sixty-four now, so that's not bad for a second chance.'

They waited while a middle-aged man made his way through that part of the exhibition, appearing to be on the lookout for something specific. Once he'd passed by, Marjorie carried on.

'I'm rather pleased you're here,' she said, smiling at Charlotte. 'Brett was a lovely lad. He had a sister who was local, and he was enormously proud of her. She went to work for the police, if I remember correctly. He was in awe of her, I think. I got on well with him; he was one of those nice young lads who are happy chatting to women old enough to be their mothers. His own parents were dead; he was working here when that terrible business happened with his father. His father was in the police too, you know.'

'You said that you were pleased I was here,' Charlotte prompted. 'It sounded like you wanted to say something about Brett.'

'Yes, I do. I don't want to go to my grave carrying this secret, if that's where I'm heading. After all these years, I'm not sure who I can tell. I doubt the police would even be interested after all this time—'

'What is it?' Charlotte encouraged her. 'It's not about his disappearance, is it?'

'Yes, it is. What else would it be about where Brett is concerned? My God, I cried for that boy when they said he'd probably committed suicide. I couldn't believe it, not that lovely boy. I knew something was up that Christmas. He was distracted, and he told me he'd sold his house in Morecambe. But I didn't think things were that bad, not so terrible that he'd end his life.'

'What happened? What have you been keeping to yourself all these years?'

'It was the strangest of things. We'd grieved for him, shared our stories and memories of him, and all we hoped for was that one day, they'd find his body and we'd all be able to understand what happened to him. But there's something I never told anybody at the time, because I swore I never would. And that's what I want to pass on to you now, seeing as you seem to know all about Brett. Three weeks after he was supposed to have taken his own life, I received a letter from him.'

CHAPTER THIRTY

December 1999

Kate slept badly, troubled by what Brett had told her about David Irwin. She was on an early shift the next day too, so she was almost grateful when the alarm clock sounded at five and she could at last stop tossing and turning and start a new day. As she poured out a bowl of breakfast cereal which she had little appetite to eat, she wondered what she could do to help Brett without messing up his plans.

She'd seen enough of police life already to realise that she had to take care who she confided in. Her first port of call would normally be Nayeema, but this matter required experience and seniority, someone who could offer sound advice or perhaps practical police support. As Kate allowed the steaming hot shower water to cascade over her body in a blanket of warmth, she considered her options. By the time she was heading along the promenade on the first bus of the day, she'd resolved to take action. She couldn't allow Brett to run off like that; she wanted him in her life. As far as she could tell, it was threats and intimidation that were making him and Tiffany take such extreme action.

The Sergeant on shift that morning was Amanda Pickering. Although formidable with the male officers, she'd shown her nurturing side to Kate and Nayeema, so she seemed like a good person to start with. As Kate tuned out the banter in the locker area and checked her uniform was in order, she psyched herself up for the encounter, working out how she'd frame it when she spoke to her Sergeant.

She'd drawn the long straw in terms of her beat area for that Monday morning, on solo patrol within the radius of the police station, so it provided the ideal window to talk in confidence. The criminal fraternity had obliged them all by having an early night on Sunday and a lie-in on Monday, so all was quiet, just as they liked it when saddled with an early shift to start a new week.

'Mind if I have a quick word, Sergeant Pickering?' she asked, as the teams went about their duties for that day.

'That's what I like about you new recruits,' Pickering said with a smile. 'There's none of this *sarge* lark. It's the only place I get any respect.'

Kate knew that wasn't the case. Sergeant Pickering was feared and respected in equal measure. She was a formidable force at Morecambe Police Station, and whatever they said in jest, she was the type of police officer who'd get immediate back-up in a heartbeat, if it were ever needed.

'May we use an office?' Kate asked.

Sergeant Pickering motioned with her arm towards a vacant meeting room and they made their way over. Kate closed the door behind them.

'How's it going, WPC Allan? In general, and with the

solo patrols? Are you up for the New Year? You don't feel out of your depth, do you?'

'My colleagues have got my back, so yes, I'm fine. I've dealt with a range of problems now – more domestics than I ever thought I'd see – but my biggest challenge is working out what sort of police officer I want to be. Tough, compassionate, no-nonsense… I'm still finding my style of policing, I think.'

Sergeant Pickering nodded.

'It's one of the hardest things about starting in the force,' she began, taking a seat. 'You'll have guys telling you to treat them all like shits, you'll hear older bobbies who behave like they just walked off the set of a sixties cop show and think little has changed since then, and you'll have the voices of your training officers ringing in your ears with the latest initiatives and policing trends. I remember it well. Let me offer you some advice though, WPC Allan. To get through this job with your sanity and your integrity intact, you just have to be true to yourself. Remember who you are and why you joined the police force. That part of you will be challenged time and time again, but if you hold fast to your values and ignore everybody else, you'll get through this just fine.'

'That's good advice,' Kate replied, 'thank you, I'll keep that in mind.'

'It should be good advice. Do you know who gave it to me, when I was a young officer like you are now?'

Kate stared at her. She couldn't work out what the sergeant was talking about.

'Your father told me that. Did you know we served together? You don't need to flatter me by telling me I don't look old enough. Yes, it was your father who gave me that advice. I never met a more honest copper; the police force lost one of its finest the day he lost his life. You should be proud of him. Trust that you'll do the right thing.'

Kate hadn't expected her emotions to be hi-jacked. She'd prepared herself for a different conversation. Now she was choking up, her father's words coming back from beyond the grave to guide her even now.

'What did you want to speak to me about, Allan? You need to be quick; I'm attending another briefing in five minutes.'

'It won't take long.'

Kate steadied herself and worked up to her question. Sergeant Pickering's firm stare didn't help. She tried to see beyond the uniform and the rank, to the person behind it.

'I need some advice. If I knew someone who was in trouble – let's say they were being threatened or intimidated by someone – what should I do now I'm a police officer?'

'I hope this person isn't you?'

'No, Sergeant Pickering. It's a friend – an associate. Something has been brought to my attention, and I'm just not sure how to deal with it.'

'I think this takes us back to your father's words, doesn't it? What do you think you should do?'

'I feel duty-bound to help. Only it involves someone who's influential in the town, which makes life difficult. And it's a deeply private matter. I have a personal stake in this. I just want to do the right thing, as a police officer and a friend.'

Sergeant Pickering's expression showed Kate this was a situation she recognised well.

'I don't want to get all philosophical on you, WPC Allan, but this goes to the heart of all policing. What do you do if you find out a friend is breaking the law? Do you report them, or do you have a quiet word with them? What happens if somebody you know is involved in something serious, like an assault or a rape? Do you keep quiet and secretly hope your colleagues find them? Or do you provide an anonymous tip-off? Your policing life is going to be filled with dilemmas like this. All I can suggest is that you be guided by your conscience. If it's something minor, treat a friend the same way you'd treat a member of the public: advise them and give them a push in the right direction. If it's something more serious, the law tells us what we have to do. I believe it's our duty to do it. Does that help?'

Kate wasn't so sure that it did. What she wanted to do was blurt out the truth about what was going on with Brett and get somebody to lean on David Irwin and tell him to back off. But even before speaking to Sergeant Pickering, she'd realised that it wasn't an option.

If Brett and Tiffany planned to run off with the children, that was abduction – wasn't it? But she didn't have a clue how to solve the issue. What she wanted was for Brett to see some sense, and for him and Tiffany to break up the marriage in the normal way. They'd stay local, and David would get access to the children, making it a relationship breakdown, not an abduction. She had her answer. That was the right thing to do.

But if Brett fled the area, the police would get involved and it would get messy. What if David Irwin seemed serious about carrying out his threat of violence? Brett would have to report that to the police. It was his only way through this.

'Thank you, Sergeant Pickering, I think that helps. I know what I need to do now.'

'Be sure to check in with me again if I can be of any further help. I trust you'll do the right thing, WPC Allan; you have an excellent policing pedigree.'

Kate was dismissed. She had to make Brett see sense; it was her only option. She headed back to the lockers to retrieve a radio from the charging dock and collect the rest of her things. It was raining outside, drops of water beating hard against the windows.

She clocked that her locker door was ajar the moment she turned the corner; it was very slightly protruding from the neat row. She would never have forgotten to lock it. That was one of the basic tenets of personal security. She rushed up to check, cursing her carelessness so early in her policing career. As she opened the door, eager to check the locking mechanism for a fault, she noticed a plain, brown envelope had been placed inside. She snatched at it and tore it open.

The contents were the last thing on earth she would have expected to see: two photographs, taken surreptitiously as far as she could tell from the picture quality. One showed Brett and Tiffany, holding hands at a table in some pub which she couldn't recognise.

The other showed David Irwin and the tall woman who she'd seen in the park with Brett. Joanne Taylor, he'd said. She and David were without the children, sitting on a park bench. In the photo they were kissing. Not a peck on the cheek or something superficial between colleagues or friends. Even though this was only a photograph, it was perfectly clear; this was a kiss between lovers.

CHAPTER THIRTY-ONE

'But Brett's supposed to be dead. Suicide, they said. Are you telling me he's been alive all this time?'

Charlotte had read thrillers with fewer twists and turns than the events surrounding the disappearance of the Irwin family. What Marjorie was telling her now turned everything on its head.

'That's why I want to tell you about it. I've carried this burden for twenty years. He swore me to absolute secrecy and told me his life was in danger if I told anyone. But I can't go to my grave without sharing the truth with somebody. The real story will die with me. I was going to write it in a letter to leave with my will, but now you're here and you know about Brett, I can pass it on to you.'

'Why are you still working, Marjorie? If you think this is the end for you, why carry on here?'

Charlotte was acutely aware that for Marjorie, this conversation was almost a last wish, a personal epitaph. She didn't even know this woman, yet here she was, passing on a secret which she'd carried for two decades.

'How would you spend your last days if you knew you were going to die? Moping in a chair waiting for it to happen? I'm divorced from my husband, we never had kids and I've always loved this job. This is where I want to be until I go in for my next course of treatment. When I leave this place, a light is switched off. I can't let Brett's secret fade.'

'Does his sister know?' Charlotte asked. She had to decide what to think about Kate and her part in all of this.

'I have no idea,' Marjorie replied. 'I just know that Brett needed me to do something for him. That's why he wrote to me.'

Charlotte waited, wanting to reach out and hug Marjorie, desperately sorry for her lack of family support. She hoped she had good friends.

'Can you remember what his letter said?'

'I can remember every word, I've read it so often. Not many people were using email back then; we were still sending letters to each other. It came by Air Mail, so it took a while to reach me.

Charlotte thought back to the distinctive Air Mail letters, written on lightweight paper to keep the postage costs down. She hadn't seen one for years, yet at one time they were commonplace if you had relatives abroad or pen friends. So, Brett was abroad somewhere. If he truly was still alive, that made sense.

'He began with an apology. That was typical of Brett, he was such a thoughtful young boy. I was going through the menopause when we worked together, and he would often get me a glass of water without being prompted or pull up a chair for me. Sometimes, he'd cover for me if I was having a hot sweat so I could sort myself out in the bathroom. He was only in his early twenties; what sort of boy would think to do that for a woman who was old enough to be his mother?'

Charlotte thought about her own family. Whenever she had a hot flush, all she got from her own family was teasing. *Mum's about to boil over again,* Olli would say. Cheeky thing. She'd have threatened to stop his pocket money if they still gave him it. So yes, Brett was unusual in his attentiveness.

'He apologised for taking my bank card—'

'He stole from you?'

'Not quite. Unknown to me, he'd set up a payment to my bank account. It was a lot of money, bearing in mind it was the year 2000. He'd transferred the proceeds from his house sale to me, £29,500 in all. He must have planned it well, because the payment was delayed until nine days after he went missing—'

'I don't understand. Why was he apologising for stealing from you?'

If Kate Summers knew about this and had withheld the information when her brother disappeared, no wonder she was in trouble.

'He'd taken the card from my purse and copied my bank details so he could make the transfer. But he put it back; he didn't steal any money. Still, he apologised for taking it in the first place.'

'Why did he give you all that money?'

'He didn't. He wanted me to send it to an Australian bank account. He said he had to delay it until he found out his bank details. He'd taken a chance with his money because he could trust me.'

'So, you transferred it to his new bank account? But you didn't tell the police?'

'No. That's why I'm telling you now. I still think I did

the right thing. Brett was no criminal; he just had to make a fresh start. I transferred the money, and that was the last of it.'

Charlotte paused to think. She wasn't sure how matters of estate were handled, but she assumed Kate would get power of attorney over what Brett left behind. So she must have known he was alive.

'What else did he say in the letter?' Charlotte asked.

'Not much. Just the apology about the bank card. And for making us think he'd died like that and putting us through all that grief. He said that he didn't have any choice and that he'd got caught up in a terrible problem. He was fleeing for his own safety and would have to stay away from the country.'

'That was it?'

'Yes, and that I should never tell anybody about it. So I didn't. They all thought he'd killed himself, and he wasn't wanted for any crimes, so I let him have his peace. But I have to pass on the information, in case something happens. I can't take that secret with me to the grave.'

Charlotte could scarcely believe it. Everybody had assumed that Brett was dead. But they'd never recovered a body. Until now, she hadn't even considered the possibility of him being alive. And now it had become crystal clear why Kate had been so evasive.

'Marjorie, I'm so grateful for you sharing this information with me. I must go now, but I just want to thank you for sharing that with me. I assure you I'll use it to help Brett if I can. And I hope your treatment goes well. You deserve to see out your days here until your proper retirement.'

She could see from Marjorie's face that she already knew it wouldn't happen, but it seemed cruel to speak to her as if that was it.

'I'll try to call in again before you go, to see how you are.'

'Thank you, I appreciate it.'

This time Marjorie took her hand and gave it a small squeeze. Charlotte didn't want to get any more choked up than she already was, so she headed back towards the town centre. With some time to kill before her meeting with Will, she made her way to the city library. She wasn't sure whether she was allowed to use the mains sockets to charge her new phone, but she found one that was tucked out of the way and concealed the cable with a copy of the Daily Mail newspaper, which somebody had left open on a nearby table. There were still no messages from Will, but Lucia had sent one to confirm that she hadn't heard from him either.

As she idly flicked through the newspaper, whiling away the minutes, she tried her best to stem a rising sense of panic. If Will didn't turn up at five o'clock or get back to her with a phone message, she'd have to assume that something serious had happened. And if that was the case, she'd have no option but to confide in somebody at the police station, however dangerous Kate Summers had warned her that would be.

CHAPTER THIRTY-TWO

Will didn't turn up. She knew in her gut that he wouldn't before she even walked up to the pizza restaurant, but she went anyway. She wanted to scream. Where the hell was he? She wished the university wasn't so far out of the city centre, if she had access to a car and it wasn't past everything closing up for the day, she'd have gone to hunt him down there and then.

Her rational mind, which was having a hard time making itself heard, reminded her that his phone might be lost, damaged or discharged. Then her irrational thoughts would roar back at her, asking why he hadn't replied to her messages. If his phone was out of action, surely he would have got word to her somehow? Especially after not coming back to the Travelodge the previous night. All the while, she forced back the dark, ugly thought that was plaguing her most; was he having an affair with Hollie Wickes? Was he going to leave her?

She refused to entertain the idea, but it was becoming more compelling all the time, however much she tried to deny it. In a fit of half-temper, half-righteousness, she took

Hollie's phone out of her pocket again. Screw Hollie Wickes and her right to privacy, she'd search the whole damn phone for evidence if she had to. The phone was dead. It was probably just as well. In a moment of madness she had been ready to violate every safe space on that phone: photos, emails, the lot.

Back at the guest house it was the busy time of the evening. The shifts were covered, as far as she could recall, but the business was becoming an annoyance.

There was something about reporting that gripped and compelled her; she'd never experienced anything like it in her life. Every time she found out new information, she wanted more. It was as if she couldn't stop until she knew the truth.

She phoned the guest house, feeling wretched that she was about to drop Isla and George in it once again. Agnieszka picked up the phone.

'Oh, hi, Mrs Grayson. Are you all right? We are surprised not to be seeing you this evening.'

'Hello, Agnieszka. Is everything under control? I'm so sorry, but I've got caught up in something personal that can't wait. I promise I'll make it up to you. Earlier on, I worked through the online bookings on my phone, and we seem quiet now.'

So much of their business came in online, via international booking websites. Many hoteliers who had been in the game for years hated their reliance on these services. But for Charlotte, it was a dream, allowing her to be hands-off as much as possible. The bookings came in automatically and the payments were administered by the websites, so they seldom took cash or cheques, and the entire check-in process had been simplified and fast-tracked. They'd budgeted for the percentage these websites took from their income from the outset, so their entire business model was built on this process. Many of her guest house colleagues in the resort hated these changes, but Charlotte had never known anything else.

'We are running out of gammon tonight, so we have to take it off the menu. And the delivery guys only bring in half the lettuce we need, but I buy a few from the supermarket and we are okay.'

'You'll make a brilliant manager, Agnieszka. That's excellent, thank you. If you go into the family accommodation and check the small chest freezer, you'll find some gammon steaks. And are you still okay to work tomorrow morning and evening?'

'Yes, that's okay for me—'

'You haven't seen Will, have you?'

Charlotte had lost interest in the guest house again, wondering if Agnieszka had run into Will on the university campus or perhaps on the bus back to Morecambe.

'I see no Will for a day or two. Is he okay? He does not reply to my texts.'

'Thanks, Agnieszka, I'm not sure where he is, but I'm getting concerned about him. You haven't seen him with anybody on campus, have you? Somebody he's been spending a lot of time with, perhaps?'

As a former escort, she knew Agnieszka would be expert at keeping her mouth shut. However, she claimed not to have noticed anything different about Will. Charlotte asked to speak to Isla, but George came to the phone.

'Hello, Charlotte. Isla's busy in the kitchen now, but I can guess why you're calling.'

If it had been anybody else but George, that might have been a barbed comment. But it was said with an acceptance of who she was, and without judgement.

'I'm so sorry, George, but I need you to stand in again. I've got caught up in something that needs my attention so it's doubtful I'll be home again this evening—'

'Charlotte, it's fine, of course it is. Isla and I rather enjoy staying in the guest house overnight. At our age, it almost counts as a holiday. And Una is happy up here; she treats this place like a second home. We rarely get disturbed by the guests. We had a request for an extra pillow last night and somebody needed letting in after midnight who'd forgotten to take their key. Otherwise, it's all fine. Just get to the cash-and-carry if you can; we're running a bit low on some of the staples.'

'George, you know I can't ever repay you and Isla. I'm so grateful. I promise I'll make it up to you. Just bear with me while I sort things out. I'm going to stay in Lancaster tonight, but I'll let you know my movements and get back as soon as I can. Oh, and I'll sort out an online order to come first thing tomorrow morning.'

They finished the call. It couldn't continue like this; she and Will had to discuss the future of the guest house. It had served its purpose in her life, however briefly.

She began to walk back towards the Travelodge, keen to stay away from the guest house while she was getting a firmer grasp on what was going on. The tall lady appeared to be an even greater threat than Vinnie Mace, whose presence hadn't been felt since the parachute jump. It was all more confusing than ever, and Will's disappearance wasn't helping.

As Lancaster Town Hall appeared up ahead, she passed a double phone box, half-concealed behind a tree. She searched her pocket and brought out a 50p, a 10p and a 2p. It would have to do.

She tried the first phone box, but it stank of urine and

the phone receiver had been pulled off the hook. The second kiosk was in better condition. She'd seen people cleaning them, something which she was sure they never did in the old days. The drunks and vandals had stolen a lead on them with that first booth.

She found Kate's number scrawled on the paper in her pocket. It was getting screwed up and damaged. If she didn't write it down somewhere safe, she'd lose the lifeline with Kate. She dialled the number, not expecting it to be answered. She was wrong. There was a click and a hesitant pause.

'Charlotte?' came a tentative voice.

'Kate, thank God. Are you safe? What the hell is going on?'

She could hear a distinctive noise in the background, not loud enough to obscure Kate's voice, but Charlotte couldn't place it.

'Charlotte, I'm so pleased you're okay—'

The coin that Charlotte had placed in the phone dropped into the belly of the machine and the display flashed.

'Damn, I haven't any money Kate. I'm going to get cut off—'

'I need to tell you something then—'

'Be quick please, before we lose the line. I'll call you back later when I've got some more money—'

'I need you to do something for me, Charlotte. You have to go to my house, it's too dangerous for me—'

'Where do you live?'

'We're at Hest Bank, before the level crossing turn-off as you approach from Morecambe. Bright red door, cherry tree in the front garden. Go through the neighbour's garden; I'm sure my house is being watched, either by the police or perhaps by Fabian Armstrong's people. My neighbour is deaf and partially sighted, so you won't have any problems. You'll find a key to the back door under the water butt at the back. Go into the bedroom with model aeroplanes hanging from the ceiling. Inside the Monopoly box in the toy cupboard is a brown envelope. Take it and hide it somewhere where nobody will ever think of searching for it. And please stay safe—'

'Where are you Kate? Can I do anything to help? Are you safe?'

The call ended; she was out of money. The last thing she heard was that distinctive sound. Where the hell was that coming from? She was as sure as she could be that she'd heard it before.

CHAPTER THIRTY-THREE

December 1999

Kate was wound up enough to beat down Brett's door that night. The moment her shift finished, she stormed round to his house, even though she suspected he would still be at work. The scene that greeted her didn't help to calm her temper. A removal van was parked outside on the street. The heavy work had been done and the removal team was just taking the last items from the garden. Brett ducked inside the door the moment he spotted her, but she'd seen him. He wasn't escaping that easily.

'What the hell is this?' she shouted at him, not bothering to tap at the open front door or explain her presence to the removal men. She held up the pictures she'd found in her locker.

'Thirteen months! Thirteen months the date on this picture says you've been with this woman. At least. When were you going to tell me, Brett? How long have you been keeping this a secret?'

He was like a rabbit caught in the headlights of a car

about to run it over. The house was completely bare. Ghostly shadows created by years of dust were the only sign that he'd had pictures on the wall. Indentations in the carpets showed where his furniture had once been. She was surprised at how quickly the personality had been stripped from his home.

'Where did you get that?' he asked.

'Somebody dropped it into my locker anonymously. Who the hell would be doing that, Brett? Who knows about you and Tiffany? Who would care about it?'

Brett shrugged.

'And what about this one?'

Kate held up the photograph of David Irwin and Joanne. Brett was visibly surprised by that one.

'Okay, where did you get that? Are you spying on us all? You're a copper, Kate, not some private investigator—'

'I didn't take these photos, Brett, somebody gave them to me. Who would care enough about this to bring it to my attention? What's going on? When your domestic life starts screwing with my job, your love life becomes a big problem for me.'

Brett nodded.

'I think that's us done, guv. You happy for us to take it straight over to the storage units?'

Brett's expression changed to one of friendly geniality. He handed a key and a slip of paper to the removal man.

'I'll call round to settle the bill tomorrow and pick up that key from you then. Thanks very much Davey. Here's something for you and the boys.'

He handed over four ten-pound notes.

'That's kind of you,' the removal man said. 'I'll leave this with Morwenna on the reception desk. You know where we are, on White Lund, yes?'

Brett nodded and the man left. Soon after, the removal van roared into action. As it moved away from outside the lounge window, light flooded into the room.

'You didn't bother telling me that today was your removal day,' Kate said. 'Did it not occur to you to mention it when I was helping you pack yesterday?'

'Look, Kate, I'm trying not to involve you in all of this. The less you know about it, the better, okay? Me and Tiff are navigating a difficult situation. It's delicate. Not everything works to a regimented shift pattern.'

Kate took a deep breath to calm herself.

'I'm worried about you, Brett. Really worried. If you take those children without David Irwin's consent and deny him access, it's like a kidnapping. Has Tiffany considered that?'

'Yes, she has. There's no easy way to do this, Kate. If I were you, I'd turn a blind eye and leave us to it. That way you won't get caught up in it and we won't cause any problems for your work.'

Kate watched him, remembering how close they'd always been. It was why the deceit was so hurtful.

'I don't care about any of that. All I care about is you, Brett, and I don't want you to go—'

She began to sob. He moved up to her and put his arms around her.

'I don't want to go either, Kate,' he said gently. 'But I feel trapped, and I can't see another way. If it was any other man, we might be able to do it amicably. But Tiff has tried that. It won't work.'

Kate pulled away from him and held up the picture of David and Joanne.

'What is this, Brett? They're having an affair, aren't they?'

Brett waited a moment before answering, as if weighing up what he should tell her.

'That's been going on for a long time, well before I met Tiff. That's what she's had to put up with. Every time she challenges him about it, he denies it. Joanne came in to take care of the kids before Rowan was born, because Tiff had had some problems with postnatal depression in the past. She reckons they were already having an affair and moving Joanne in just made things more convenient for them. These days they don't even try to hide it. You saw them in the park yesterday. He tells everyone she's the kids' nanny, but everyone knows the truth.'

'Why don't they just divorce and put each other out of their misery?'

'Why do you think, Kate? Money. Money, land and property. Do you have any idea how much money that land would go for, sitting alongside the bay like that? Imagine if a chemical company got it or the nuclear power plant doubled in size. It's worth a fortune, Kate. But Tiffany wants to honour her parents' legacy and keep it as working farmland. Fabian and David don't give a stuff about that. They want to sell to the highest bidder. Tiff's compromised; she says she'll allow a wind farm on the site so long as they can continue grazing there. But David and Fabian will have none of it.'

Kate pondered that information, trying to sift through its implications.

'But if Tiffany divorced David, it wouldn't be any of his business, would it?'

'Exactly! He won't allow Tiff to leave until she agrees to sell off the land to the highest bidder. He'll also make life difficult over custody of the children. He was objectionable before he discovered I was on the scene. If you thought that was nasty, it's heated up even more since then.'

'I still don't understand. Isn't it up to Tiffany and Fabian to sort it out?'

'David has power of attorney over Tiffany's affairs. She was in such a bad way with postnatal depression, they committed her. The power of attorney remains in place. She didn't even know about it until after Jane was born, by which time it had become a way of threatening her. She's getting it overturned. It'll happen any day now—'

'This all sounds like a legal nightmare,' Kate observed.

'It is, believe me. The moment we get the go-ahead from the solicitors, we're leaving. He can't overrule her then. She's got the all-clear on her mental health issues, so David can't challenge the ending of the power of attorney once it's completed. The only way he can get to her is through the children. And Fabian can't do anything without her joint signature. Which makes it checkmate.'

Kate couldn't process it all. Her head was in danger of exploding at any moment with all the permutations whirring around inside it.

'Okay, I'll take your word for all that. So, who cares enough about your love lives to be taking photos like those? Why would anyone else care?'

'I take it you've heard of Edward Callow, the local MP?'

'Yes, of course I have. He always strikes me as a bit of weasel.'

'You know he's involved in a lot of big property deals?'

'I didn't, but I do now. So what?'

'Edward Callow is part of a big consortium waiting to do all the construction work on that land, but only if the deal goes through. There's a lot of money at stake.'

'Okay, but how does that make a difference to you?'

'Edward Callow wields a lot of influence in the bay area. The guy is minted. He has a copper on his team; I bet you're familiar with him. He's called Harvey Turnbull.'

'Turnbull? Yes, I'm aware of him, but I don't know him personally.'

'I'll bet he was the guy who slipped those photos into your locker.'

'Jesus, Brett, he's not threatening you or anything is he?'

'No, no, nothing like that. But he's a copper, and because he's connected with Edward Callow's outfit, he keeps his eyes and ears open. It'll be Turnbull or one of his lackeys who took those pictures. But in case you were about to have a heart attack, no, he's not done anything wrong. That's my hunch, anyway.'

'When does this power of attorney get revoked? I take it everything depends on that?'

'Basically, yes. The timing could be better but it should be sorted by New Year. I'll be staying at a local guest house while we wait it out. The minute Tiff's out of his clutches, we're on our way.'

Earlier that day, Sergeant Pickering had advised her to follow her judgement in tricky personal matters which challenged her position as a police officer. She'd made her decision; Brett had told her enough now.

She'd seen David Irwin's hateful body language when he was attacking her brother in the street, so she couldn't even begin to contemplate how defenceless Tiffany must feel with a bullying husband who had a power of attorney at his fingertips. Her mind was made up. The sergeant was right; she knew what she had to do now.

'Okay, Brett, you've convinced me. Now tell me what I can do to help you.'

CHAPTER THIRTY-FOUR

Charlotte woke up feeling refreshed. She hadn't realised how exhausted she was, but the ten-hour stretch of uninterrupted slumber told its own story. Her plan had been to call Kate Summers again, having taken out some notes at the cash machine. She'd bought another pack of underwear from the store that was closest to the Travelodge, but she hadn't found anywhere to purchase a fresh top. It felt like she was turning into a tramp.

She rolled over on the bed and checked her new phone which was fully charged. She pulled out the cable, retrieved her discarded jeans from the floor and pulled Hollie's phone from the pocket to charge it. If she'd woken up during the night, both phones could have been fully charged by now. That was the 20th century equivalent of having every chamber full in a six-shooter. Now she could cope with whatever the day threw at her.

Last night she'd slept naked under the sheets, not wanting to crumple her clothes too much. She rolled off the bed and took a shower; at least her body was clean, even if her clothing would be better off in the wash basket. By seven, she was showered and ready to take on the day. She would check in at the newspaper office, catch up with Nigel and book out the car. Her life was restricted with her own vehicle off the road, and if she was going to get to Kate's house, the simplest course of action was to use one of the newspaper vehicles. At a push, she could class what she was about to do as investigative work.

Worried that Will still hadn't contacted her, Charlotte searched a sample of missing person websites on her phone. She'd always thought there was a delay between someone going missing and being able to report them, but all the websites told her she could report her husband's absence to the police immediately. But that wasn't the best thing to do. They would ask the usual questions. Was he depressed? Had you argued? Is he having an affair? Has he done this before?

She'd have to admit that he'd been out at an event and that she had some spurious evidence suggesting he might be having an affair. They would then dismiss her concerns and tell her to wait a bit longer. Perhaps they'd promise to keep a lookout for him, but with the police being so stretched, they wouldn't concern themselves about it for some time.

All she could do was hold steady and trust her husband. He would contact her the moment he could. If he was in trouble... she shivered at the thought. They could do the same to him as they'd tried to do to her, but why would they? She'd been causing the problems, not Will.

So she had to wait, even though every bone in her body wanted to know where he was and whether he was safe. She would talk to Toni Lawson, the press officer, as soon as possible. That was the safest way to move things on.

Charlotte passed by McDonalds on the way over to the bus station and balanced her breakfast on her knees as she headed back to Morecambe on the bus. For a moment she considered calling in at the guest house, but it was all in hand and she'd placed an online food order on her phone before falling asleep the night before.

Her priority was to secure the package that Kate was so desperate for her to retrieve. Kate needed to prove her innocence, and she had to figure out what was going on with Callie, Evan's death and Will's disappearance. Then the whole episode would get cleaned up and they could go back to normal. Reporting on cats getting stuck up trees was looking very appealing.

She phoned the guest house en route to see if Will had appeared, but there was still no sign of him. George even ran up the stairs to check the family accommodation, but there were no messages. At least the internet order had arrived and the guest house was operating well in her absence. Charlotte thanked her lucky stars that she had employed such a great team as she got off at her stop further along the promenade.

Thankfully she had time to catch the market and buy a new sweatshirt and pair of cheap jeans before going into the office. She even found a five-pack of socks for £1. The only place to change was the disabled facility in the market hall, every minute filling her with guilt. It was the only way to avoid the walk of shame jokes if she changed at the office.

By nine o'clock, she was working her way up the metal staircase at the rear of The Bay View Weekly offices, the same staircase they'd escaped down the previous day. On the top level of the building, there was no sign of a fire having even happened.

'Good morning,' Nigel said, doing a double take. 'Did you realise there's a price tag hanging off the side of your sweatshirt?'

'Oh hell, I thought I'd got them all,' Charlotte cursed. 'Would you pull it off for me?'

'Did you dress in a rush this morning?' Nigel asked, leaning over to remove the tag. 'Got it!'

He threw it in the bin as the assembled staff settled down for Teddy's update.

'Everything okay?' he whispered.

'Yes, sort of,' she replied. 'It's a long story, but nothing I can't handle. Any news on Callie yet? Anything from the police?'

'Nothing. It's a dead end. We could do with a fresh development—'

'Good morning everybody, thanks for being prompt today.'

Teddy launched into the morning briefing. Everybody was all ears after the fire, desperate to hear the latest.

'We'll be using the rear entrance for the next week, I'm afraid, but the contractors have assured us the new frontage will be ready by next Wednesday at the latest,' he began. 'I want to thank Charlotte and Nigel for staying behind to take care of Geoff yesterday. Due to the access difficulties at the rear of the building, Geoff is working from home until he can get into the building from the front—'

There was a small ripple of applause. Charlotte squirmed at the attention; they were hardly super-heroes. She looked around for Reagan, but she wasn't present. She panicked, wondering if Teddy had disciplined her before she could leap to her defence, as she'd promised.

'Reagan is taking the day off because she was shaken by what happened, as you'd expect. She gave the police an excellent description of the person thought to be responsible for throwing the bottle of petrol at the front door.'

'Any idea why they did it, boss?'

Charlotte tried to see who'd asked the question. She didn't recognise the voice.

'The police think it's someone with a grudge, perhaps a person who didn't like our reporting of the Irwin story in yesterday's paper. Although this is more dangerous than we're used to, you know the score. We're a media operation, so threats and hoaxes go with the territory. But I would ask you to be extra vigilant, because it was a particularly nasty attack. Why couldn't they just use the letters page like everyone else?'

There was a roar of laughter, helping to ease the tension in the office. It was one of the things she loved about working as a reporter. They'd all just been smoked out of their office building, yet here was Teddy making jokes about it, scarcely twenty-four hours afterwards.

The meeting went on for another ten minutes or so, then Teddy dismissed everybody and it was back to business as usual. In a 24/7 rolling media operation, having your own front door set alight was just one more event in an endless procession of news stories.

'I'd like to take a car out today, if that's okay?' Charlotte asked, as she took her seat opposite Nigel.

'What are you working on?' he asked. 'Anything interesting?'

'I've got a hunch about something and I just wanted to check it out. Is that all right?'

Nigel peered at her, searching her face for clues. Charlotte knew he could smell something on her but couldn't make out what it was. She hoped he wouldn't push her; she didn't want to lie to him.

'Yes, go for it,' he answered. 'Once you start doing this job, you don't get a lot of time for investigative work. Make the most of it. Until DI Comfort turns up something in the Irwin case, we're in the hands of the police.'

Charlotte took the car keys from Nigel's desk, checked her pockets to make sure she had what she needed to get by for the day, and left. Her next stop was Kate Summer's house; she was going to find out what was so important that she needed to sneak into a DCI's property to retrieve it.

CHAPTER THIRTY-FIVE

Charlotte parked the car at The Shore Café, deciding that it would be better to leave it on the shoreline rather than pulling up on the main road where everybody would see the liveried vehicle. Driving a car marked with the logo of The Bay View Weekly wasn't the smartest strategy for retaining anonymity, but without a car of her own, it was a case of needs must.

She'd passed the railway crossing in Hest Bank many a time, but it was the first excuse she'd had to cross over the line and see what was on the other side. There was plenty of parking overlooking the bay, and the small café was a surprise find. Benches lined the shoreline with splendid views of Cumbria across the water; it was another hidden jewel which had passed her by.

She walked over the level crossing and took a right-hand turn, passing the small cluster of shops and businesses as she made her way up the main road. Seeing the steady flow of traffic, she was pleased she'd decided to tuck the car out of the way. It wasn't as if she was breaking into Kate's house; it was more a case of not inviting unwanted attention. Two cars were parked at either side of the road, but she couldn't see anybody sitting in them, so it seemed safe to assume Kate's house wasn't under surveillance.

The cherry tree was visible up ahead, its branches overhanging the pavement. The house was a large, semi-detached property, and the red door confirmed it was the right place. As instructed, she walked past it, all the while checking the windows of the elderly neighbour to make sure there was no sign of him. After scanning the road and path to make sure it was clear, she darted into the neighbour's driveway, rushing past the side porch towards the cover provided by the small garage at the rear.

The properties were more exposed than she would have liked. The shrub growth and foliage of Maxwell Henderson's property had provided good cover for her snooping. However, Kate's house gave no such comfort, making her vulnerable. The gardens were short, bounded by the railway at the rear, so she figured her best option was to stay close to the house and creep underneath the windows at the back. The four-foot high lap fence between the gardens was high enough to be tricky but it wouldn't be impossible to climb it. She was glad to be performing this operation alone; her ascent of the fence was undignified and awkward, but it did the job and she made it into Kate's garden.

The water butt that Kate had described was connected to the gutter next to the back door. She felt underneath it, but couldn't find the key. The water butt was mounted on two concrete blocks to raise it off the ground. She explored around the blocks. The key was there, slipped in between them. It was as if it had been moved from its original location.

She inserted the key into the lock and opened the door. What if Kate had a security alarm? Surely she'd have remembered to mention that? Relieved at the silence as she entered, she closed the door behind her and left the key on the worktop. So, this was where DCI Kate Summers lived. The space was clean and modern, with signs everywhere that it was a family kitchen: an array of cereals containing sticky honey, frosted sugar and chocolate, an Action Man perched on top of the coffee machine, and a Roald Dahl book on the kitchen table, with a letter opener inserted between the pages as a bookmark. School letters, achievement certificates and schoolwork were stuck on the wall above the radiator, surrounding a hung print of Piet Mondrian's most famous painting.

It was very much like the house she and Will had occupied in Bristol around ten years ago, when the children were young. All the signs indicated a busy family life and the accompanying mess and mayhem that came with it.

Charlotte hadn't got a clue what Kate's husband did for a living or even what he looked like. She'd couldn't recall seeing Kate out with the children either, and she'd given away very little about her home life. The evidence suggested the family had left in a hurry. The breakfast bowls had been rinsed, but not wiped and put away. Post had been opened and discarded at the breakfast table, and she could see recently delivered letters piled up at the front door. She walked through and picked them up, rifling through the bundle almost habitually, as if it were her own.

As she placed them next to the telephone, she noticed the light on the answer machine was flashing. On an impulse, she pressed the *Play* button. It wouldn't erase the messages and it might be something that she needed to pass on to Kate. She listened through.

Hi Kate, it's Superintendent Kelly here. We need to speak urgently. Please call me as soon as you get this.

The messages increased in sharpness.

DCI Summers, Superintendent Kelly here. You need to contact the office. It's gone to the Chief now.

There was a call from the school.

Hello Mr and Mrs Summers, just a quick call to let you know we received your email and we'll look forward to seeing the children again when they come back from France. You can fill out the term time absence paperwork on your return. Cheerio.

This was all as she'd expect: the police trying to raise her amid the humdrum of regular life. Then an unexpected but familiar voice came on the machine.

Hello Kate, it's Sam Halford here again. Just to let you know the site lease is already up for review; the contract formally ends next month. Can you believe it's twenty years since we first spoke? Okay, hope that helps, mind how you go.

What the hell was Sam Halford from the wind farm doing calling Kate Summers at home? And he'd called her Kate too, without any of the formality usually adopted when addressing a senior police officer. This sounded personal as well as professional. Any guilt about checking the messages subsided. This was something Kate would need to know.

She didn't want to spend any more time in the house than she had to, but she couldn't resist glancing in the rooms as she followed Kate's instructions. It was a regular family house, furnished in a modern and simple style. Carpets were plain, yet dark. She knew that trick of old; any parent in their right mind avoided light carpets. The furnishings were modern, with no dark wood to be seen anywhere and plenty of tasteful colour.

Charlotte wondered what Kate Summers was like when she was among her family in the security of her own home.

She'd like to know this woman better. Kate had helped her through her own family crisis and now she hoped she could return the favour.

She crept up the stairs as if she had no right to be there, then changed to a confident stride as she remembered she was doing this at Kate's request. It was a three-bedroomed house with a clean, modern bathroom which had been assaulted by an array of plastic toys lined up around the edges. Streaks of toothpaste around the top of the sink gave away the presence of youngsters. She smiled to herself, thinking how Kate would be wiping those away for a good few years yet; it was still a bad habit she had to chase Olli and Lucia about.

She peered inside the main bedroom, noticing that the quilt had been pulled over hurriedly. It was hard to resist the temptation to go in and straighten it out. A noise outside made her stop outside the room and listen. No, there was nothing. She moved on.

Kate had told her to go into the bedroom with the model aeroplanes hanging from the ceiling. She could spot it now across the landing. As she made her way towards it, she heard the slam of the back door downstairs. Then voices, two male voices. She was no longer alone.

CHAPTER THIRTY-SIX

December 1999

Kate checked her watch for the fourth time in the last ten minutes. Brett was running late. If they were going to get away with what they'd agreed, it was going to take meticulous timing, especially as she had to squeeze it in around her shift. Considering the new millennium didn't begin for another six hours in the UK, some of Morecambe's residents were making an early start. They'd be lucky if they made it past ten o'clock, let alone midnight.

Kate hated having to nurse soft drinks. She'd bought a pint of iced coke – there was no way she was touching a drop of anything if she was working that night – but she was already bloated from the gas and she wished she'd opted for an orange juice instead. Brett arrived, flustered. Kate stood up and hugged him, pulling him in close before he even had time to unzip his coat.

'I'm running away, not being executed,' he whispered.

'I don't want you to go, you know that.'

'We don't have any choice; we've discussed this already—'

'I know, I know, I'm on board. I just can't face the prospect of not seeing you.'

'It's only for a while, Kate, just until we get the legal stuff taken care of. Think of it like ripping off a plaster; it'll hurt at first, then it'll be fine.'

Brett ordered a pint of beer and Kate wondered if there was any point in cautioning him.

'Make that your only drink,' she warned. 'You need your wits about you tonight.'

Brett settled himself at the table and took a long sip of his beer.

'I deserve this after the afternoon I've just had.'

Kate watched him. Now he'd warmed up from the cold weather outside, he was jumpy. He'd been so certain before, but now he seemed to be having doubts.

'Have you got the documents from Tiffany?' she asked.

She'd seen the plastic supermarket carrier bag nestled at Brett's feet, and she knew what was in it.

'Yes, it's all in there. Birth certificates, passports and everything else we might need. Tiffany sealed it in a brown envelope and asked me not to open it until we're leaving town.'

Brett handed it over. Kate peered inside, to confirm that the envelope was in there.

'Let's run through it one more time. I take it nothing has changed?' Kate said. She took a sip of Brett's beer. 'This coke is way too sweet. I'm not buying a pint of my own; I don't want to drink that much.'

'Tiff seemed on edge when I saw her earlier. She managed to slip out with one of the kids to the supermarket so she could give me the envelope containing the documentation.'

'I'd expect her to be on edge, given that she's about to run away from her husband. I'm tense enough, and all I'm doing is meeting you before you go. So, nothing has changed with the plans?'

'No, it's as we discussed. Tiffany and David are going to the village event to show their faces. David has to leave before midnight – at about ten o'clock we think – to attend another event in Morecambe with some business contacts. I'll be waiting in the car park at the village hall. We've bought new child seats for my car. When I see David leaving, I'll text Tiff and she'll pretend one of the kids is ill and leave the party. She's been putting clothes for the kids in a suitcase which is hidden in the garden shed. We'll pick that up and then come and see you on our way out of town. Your break is at about eleven o'clock, you said, so we'll meet you opposite the Winter Gardens then.'

'You still think it's best for me to hang onto the paperwork?'

'Yes. We absolutely can't risk David getting hold of that at the last minute. Just suppose he worked out what's going on. Tiff would have a real problem proving anything. So I need you to hang on to that package until the last possible minute. Besides, I want to hug my big sis before I go.'

Kate nodded. 'I'll leave it in my mailbox at the front of the flats. Here's the key. Just post it through the slot when you're done, but don't lock it, because I haven't got a spare. Pick it up on your way out of Morecambe after we've said goodbye.'

Brett took the key and put it in his pocket.

She tried to think what could go wrong. 'And if I get

caught up in something and I don't get my break at eleven o'clock? What if I can't be there when you need me?'

'We discussed this. You said you thought it would all be relatively quiet until the chimes of Big Ben, then all hell is likely to break loose. In a worst-case scenario, we'll find you, wherever you are in town. It's going to be so busy tonight that nobody will even notice us.'

'Okay, I think that's all bases covered,' she told him. 'You're sure you want to do this? You realise it's going to start a complete shitstorm when you take David Irwin's children away from him, don't you?'

Brett seemed to clam up when she said that.

'What is it, Brett?'

'It's nothing. There's something about Callie and Jane I need to tell you, but it can wait until later.'

Kate was about to push him further on the issue, but he carried on speaking.

'I don't want to worry you, but Tiff's very anxious about David. She thinks he's going to make a move soon. She's not sure what he's up to, but things are happening with the contract on the farmland. Her brother's been putting her under some real pressure too. We must leave tonight. If we don't, I think we may miss our chance.'

Kate spent another half hour with Brett before she had to go home to get ready for her shift. She wanted to make certain her phone was charged too. She couldn't let her brother down, despite her doubts about the action he was taking. At least she'd have one last chance to hug him later that evening.

As she walked back to her flat, she hung onto the plastic bag as if it were the most precious thing in the world. She understood how securing the family's documentation gave

Tiffany the upper hand, but it still felt like she was handling some form of contraband.

Within the next hour she changed into her uniform, reported for duty and had a final briefing at the station. Soon she was heading towards the sea front with another female officer who was accompanying her for the first hour of her shift. Before she knew it, it was ten o'clock. The evening had all the hallmarks of being a good-natured affair, judging from the early drunkards they'd already encountered. She split off from the second officer, making her way along the sea front and checking in on the various pubs along the way. If she timed it right, she'd be close to her flat when it was time for her break and could easily get ready for her liaison with Brett.

But not long afterwards, her phone started vibrating in her pocket. She wasn't supposed to be carrying it with her on duty, but for one night – for her brother – she was taking the risk. It was Brett. She pulled into a dark shop entrance and answered.

'Kate, they've done something to Tiffany. Everything's turned to shit. I need your help.'

Charlotte recognised the first voice: Vinnie Mace. Whatever was bothering these people about DCI Summers, they weren't going to let it rest. Had they been able to monitor her phone conversation with Kate somehow? Surely that was impossible. She'd used a random pay phone in Lancaster and Kate was on some disposable mobile phone. She'd never seen anything on TV that could intercept a phone call like that. It must be a hunch. Or, as she'd just realised to her horror, perhaps they'd been tailing her, waiting for this very moment.

When Kate had warned her about being watched, she hadn't thought they might be focusing on The Bay View Weekly's offices. She'd made such an effort not to go back to the guest house, yet she'd neglected the most obvious target: her other place of work.

So, the question was, did they know she was in the house? Because if they did, she was in big trouble.

She listened. Vinnie's voice was distinctive, but she couldn't make out the second male voice. The pair sounded relaxed and familiar with each other. She was pretty sure she hadn't yet encountered the other man.

Charlotte's heart was thumping, but she had to focus. What had Kate said? It was a brown envelope hidden in the Monopoly box. She scoured the room, searching for the board games. There it was, its distinctive red and white box peering out from under the bed. She grabbed at it, opened the board and shook it. As Kate had promised, a plain brown envelope was hidden inside. The words *Receipt* had been written by hand on the envelope, presumably as a decoy in case the house was searched. It sounded like Vinnie and his companion had started that process already.

'Come out, come out wherever you are, Charlotte!' Vinnie called.

A shiver ran through her. They knew she was in there. She should have locked the door behind her. They were searching the house as they went along, with the surety of men accustomed to violence and certain of overpowering their prey. But they couldn't be sure which room she was in.

She folded the brown envelope and tucked it in the back of her jeans. Now she had to get out of there. For one moment, she considered calling the police. But by the time they arrived, even if they only took five minutes, Vinnie would have her. Or he'd have the documents at least.

She was on her own, holding the information that Kate had entrusted to her. As quietly as she could, she moved towards the bedroom window. There was a flat roofed porch at the side of the house. The bedroom window wasn't aligned with it, but if she could lower herself down, she'd be able to land on the roof, or at the very least it would help to break her fall. She reached for the window latch; it had a child safety restraint on it. It would open, but not fully.

'We know you're in here, Charlotte. We're happy to

play hide and seek if you want to, but it's going to make us much more bad-tempered by the time we find you. And we will find you; it's not an excessively big house.'

Charlotte wanted to call out to him and tell him where to get off, but she couldn't give her location away. Until they set eyes on her, she could be anywhere. They were making a sweep of downstairs and hadn't got to the stairs yet. She was terrified that the floorboards would squeak and give her away. If only she could think of a way to remove that window restraint.

She wasn't sure how old Kate's children were, but it sounded from the tone of the answerphone message from school that they were in primary school, maybe aged nine and upwards. And if her son made model aeroplanes, he would be old enough to use a simple craft knife. It had been the same with Lucia, who liked plastic modelling kits more than Olli did. They always had a simple modelling knife to remove the parts and cut any excess plastic prior to gluing. In a young boy's bedroom, with no other options, it seemed to be her best chance of cutting through the window obstruction.

The men were making a commotion downstairs. It sounded like they were ransacking the house as well as looking for her.

'Did you remember to wear gloves, Charlotte?' came Vinnie's voice from the bottom of the stairs. 'We did. Which means when this burglary gets called in, guess whose prints are going to be all over the place?'

They were coming up the stairs. She didn't have much time to find the modelling equipment. Next to the wardrobe was a small desk. She walked over to it. There was some half-done homework, something about basic algebra. That sounded like Year 6 to her, age 10 to 11; old enough to use a craft knife.

A cardboard shoe box was tucked under the desk. She'd have ignored it if it wasn't for the splash of grey-green paint on its side, a colour she recognised from the palette used to paint Spitfire model planes. As she took the lid off the box, she could hear Vinnie's running commentary as the two men made their way up the stairs.

'I imagine you're thinking of calling the police. It'll take them at least ten minutes to find their way out here, however much of a panic you're in. We only need five minutes, Charlotte, so I'd save up your call credit if I were you—'

'Screw you!' Charlotte thought. She couldn't give the game away though. Even if they'd been following her, they must have been some way behind or she'd have spotted them.

She rummaged through the shoe box and found two gnarled tubes of modelling glue, several tiny pots of modelling paint, some spare transfers and – she almost whooped with delight – a small, plastic model knife. It was sharp enough to cut the plastic window restraint, but not so sharp as to allow a young boy to do himself any serious damage. She slid off its protective sheath and moved as fast and silently as she could to the window.

Vinnie and his companion were in the main bedroom, so they had the daughter's room to get to before they reached her. She placed the knife's blade on the plastic retainer strip, and, after some sawing and some cutting, it gave way. She pushed the window wide open and looked down. It was better than she thought; the porch was mainly to the side of the window, but she could lower herself straight onto it, so she would be on the edge of the flat roof.

Vinnie's taunts were growing more confident now, as he moved into the daughter's room. They both knew that with every room he cleared, he was closer to finding her.

Charlotte climbed onto the windowsill, grasping the frame to pull herself up, then reversed her body so she could lower herself onto the flat roof. She made every move with great care, holding onto the frame, knowing that she had to move swiftly, while avoiding giving the game away. It took all her strength to support her body for the short time that she was hanging from the window ledge, and she was relieved when her feet found a solid surface.

She could hear the voices of the men from inside the house. To give herself a few minutes head start, she reached up as far as she could from her position on the flat roof, stretched out her fingers, and grasped the window with just enough force to push it back into the frame. They'd work out where she'd gone, but it might just throw them off the scent long enough for her to make her escape.

Charlotte was about to make the much shorter jump to the ground when curiosity overcame her. She wanted to see who this other man was; after all, if she was being followed, it was best to know who was doing the tailing. Perched on the edge of the flat roof she pushed herself up on tiptoes, raising her hands to pull upwards on the window ledge. She only just managed to peer above the bottom of the window frame to see them entering the room. There were two of them, Vinnie and some anonymous hired muscle. She almost slipped and fell off the roof when she saw what Vinnie was carrying; it was a gun, with a silencer attached.

She lowered herself so they wouldn't see her face peering through the glass. It was time to run; the stakes had just been raised and Charlotte had no intention of hanging around for a cosy chat.

CHAPTER THIRTY-EIGHT

Vinnie Mace would work out what she'd done in a matter of moments. Charlotte lowered herself back down then knelt on the flat roof and spun herself round, scraping her stomach on the guttering which ran around the outside of the porch area as she lowered her body to the ground. Thank goodness it wasn't a long drop.

As she landed safely she glanced back. Vinnie had spotted her through the window, but she had a head start while they ran down the stairs and out of the house. It was time to put those Saturday morning parkruns to good use.

She ran down the drive, along the pavement and towards the level crossing, fumbling in her pockets for the car keys. However this panned out, it was going to be a close thing.

As she ran across the level crossing, the alarms began to sound. A train was on its way. She scanned the immediate area as she pushed on, trying to work out if the closing of the crossing would be to her advantage or not. There was a foot-bridge above it and a large group of elderly walkers had just decided to divert their path over it. Charlotte decided to risk it, narrowly making it across the track as the dual automatic gates came down behind her. She thanked her lucky stars that she'd parked opposite The Shore Café, just a short run away. Within a matter of seconds she was revving the vehicle and ready to go.

She looked left. Beyond The Shore Café was a narrow lane, but she couldn't see how far it ran or whether it reached a dead end. If it was a through road, that was her best chance of escape. If it was not, then it would become the snare in which she got trapped.

She needed to think quickly. The train ran along the shore; as far as she could recall, there were no more rail crossings along the Hest Bank road. It was probably a dead end. Trusting her instinct, Charlotte drove up to the closed gates of the level crossing. The alarm was sounding, and the elderly walkers were lining both sides of the foot bridge, waiting for the train.

Her heart sank as Vinnie stopped at the gate opposite. She could lip-read the words that came out of his mouth; they weren't nice. His eyes narrowed as he stared straight at her. Would he shoot? Not with a footbridge packed with witnesses; he wasn't that reckless. Men like Vinnie Mace worked in the shadows. If there was one thing she had no intention of underestimating, it was the man's intelligence.

She revved the engine and released the handbrake, ready to let out the clutch the moment the barrier was high enough for the car to pass underneath. Opposite her, she could see that the hired thug had now joined Vinnie, and they were working out a plan. The second man was middle-aged and out of breath. He shouldn't be much of a threat if it came to a chase.

Vinnie, however, was clearly primed for action, like a wolf ready to pounce on its prey. The pair of them were figuring out their approach, taking a gamble on how long it would take the train to pass. If it was delayed, Vinnie had time to cross the bridge and apprehend her in the car. She pressed the electronic switch which activated the central locking. They weren't getting inside that vehicle without a fight. Their alternative was to try to stop her as she drove over the level crossing. She had no intention of slowing for them; to make it clear, she revved the engine heavily, like some boy racer about to make a noisy circuit of the town.

Vinnie opted for the bridge. She checked the doors again, ensuring that they were locked. The thug seemed to be going for the less energetic front assault, but he already looked in need of a good sit down. Vinnie was half way over the bridge. A bead of sweat dripped from Charlotte's forehead onto the car seat, then there was a sudden mass movement of elderly people as one of them spotted the approaching train and they all moved over to one side of the bridge to get a good view of it. She almost burst out laughing as an old gentleman with an expensive-looking camera took Vinnie's arm, evidently asking him to take a photograph of him and his wife.

As soon as the train had passed, the gates started to lift. She watched Vinnie as he made his way down the steps, seconds away. He'd declined to take that photograph. Charlotte continued to rev the car engine, glancing from Vinnie on her right-hand side to the hired muscle in front. As Vinnie slammed one hand on the top of the car and grasped at the door handle with the other, she released the clutch. It bit so sharply that it made the tyres screech when she moved off.

Vinnie was shunted to the side, and she closed her eyes as his companion made a half-hearted attempt at standing in her way. It happened in a flash; he dithered, and she struck him with the right wing of the car. She gasped as he was thrown to the side of the road. Her instincts were to stop and check, but as she glanced in her rear-view mirror, she saw him get up. Whatever she'd done, she hadn't hurt him badly.

Charlotte paused at the junction, trying to choose between left or right. In a liveried car, she could be spotted from way back. She took a left turn; they'd expect her to drive back to Morecambe, but she couldn't afford to get stuck on slow roads. Her best bet was to join the motorway as soon as possible, shake them off and take refuge somewhere while she came up with a plan.

That plan had to include the police now. She had no other choice, not when she'd taken it too far already. These men were intent on getting to her. She didn't have a clue why, but somebody had marked her out for special attention, that was for sure.

Constantly checking her mirrors, Charlotte ignored the speed limit and drove the car as fast as she dared in a residential area. If she got stopped by the police that wouldn't be a bad thing. It would at least give her protection. Up ahead were traffic lights and a slow junction. She cursed as the lights changed against her, watching all the time for her pursuers.

There were three cars behind her, nondescript vehicles in a variety of colours. A black SUV with tinted glass pulled up at the rear of the queue. She couldn't see clearly enough to be certain it was Vinnie driving, but it must be; people like him used that type of car like it was part of the company uniform.

The moment the lights changed, she was away, grateful for the three-car buffer between them and aware they wouldn't be able to pass on such a busy single carriageway road. She was now checking her mirrors rather than looking straight ahead, watching the dark SUV tail-gating the car at the back of the queue, seeking any opportunity to pull out. They'd be stuck like that until Carnforth.

Charlotte wasn't sure what she would do once she hit the motorway. She ran through her choices and decided driving to a police station was the best option. She'd have to outrun them then seek sanctuary with the police, hoping that whoever Kate had warned her about couldn't get to her. Did Carnforth still have a police station? She couldn't remember, although it used to have one. It was too much of a risk. She'd head for the motorway and make her way to Lancaster Police Station.

Her mobile phone rang. She reached for it with her left hand, but was distracted as the SUV made a manoeuvre which caused her to wince. Vinnie had an extremely narrow gap, but he took it, forcing the car which he overtook to brake sharply so he could pull in just in time to miss an oncoming vehicle. She placed both hands on the wheel, not daring to take the call. Her priority was driving and staying on the road.

By the time they'd passed through Carnforth, the SUV was further behind, no doubt caught by the traffic lights which had been in her favour this time around. By the time she reached the motorway junction, she could no longer spot them in the traffic at her rear. A lorry had joined them at the junction in the town, so as far as she could tell, she'd shaken them off, for now at least. A sense of elation came over her as she joined the motorway traffic, using her advantage to pull ahead and get in front of a row of trucks which would give her cover on the road. She began breathing normally again as she surveyed the busy traffic behind her. There was no sign of the distinctive SUV.

Knowing she was out of her depth now, she decided she was definitely going to drive straight to the police station. The tension from making it to the motorway slipped away and she began to relax a little, relieved that the worst was over. For a couple of miles, she drove almost in a trance. Then, out of nowhere, the black SUV emerged from behind a lorry. It was soon alongside her. Charlotte glanced across and saw the second thug staring at her menacingly from the passenger seat.

The SUV suddenly swerved towards her. Her instinct was to move left, but the lorry had now pulled in and sounded its horn to alert her that she'd almost cut him up. They were travelling too fast for safe distancing. Then a small Fiat pulled into the middle lane without signalling, right in her path. As she veered to the right to avoid it, Vinnie took evasive action, hit the central barrier and went careering across her front. She slammed on her brakes; a glance in her mirror showed the van behind was about to smash into her rear, so she floored the accelerator again, roaring ahead of the Fiat and sending the car careering in front of the lorry in the first lane. The last thing she was aware of was the SUV clipping the kerb of the hard shoulder and swerving to avoid the lorry, as her own car ran at speed up the grass banking to the side of the motorway. Then everything went quiet.

CHAPTER THIRTY-NINE

December 1999

'What's happened, Brett? Calm down, then do your best to explain it to me.'

It was taking her best police training to stop him breaking down at the end of the phone line.

'Everything's gone wrong. David didn't go to the meeting as we'd expected. When Tiff came out with the kids, David and Joanne were waiting for her. They drugged her with something and she crumpled to the floor, then they put her in the car and David drove off with the kids in the back. Joanne followed them in the second car. What do I do?'

'Are you driving now?'

'Yes, I'm following them—'

'Christ, Brett, have they seen you? Be careful.'

'No, I'm keeping back, with my lights dimmed. I haven't got a clue where they're going. This doesn't feel right; why would they do that to Tiff?'

'Just watch the road, Brett, be careful.'

'Hold on, they're pulling over. I'm going to hang back and see what's going on. They've pulled up by some woodland and there's another car there. I'm going to have to switch off my engine and turn off the phone, but I'll call you back.'

'Brett, where are you? Brett?'

Kate cursed. The wait for Brett to call again was agonising. As she listened to the chatter on the police radio, she prayed that a radio call wouldn't come in that she'd have to respond to.

She walked past the Winter Gardens, willing him to get back to her. She ran back up the road to her flat, quickly changing into civilian clothing; she could not risk being seen with Brett in her police uniform when - if - they said their final goodbyes.

Finally, her phone vibrated. She answered it before it had completed the first ring.

'What's happening?'

All she could hear was Brett, he was out of breath, running. Then a noise. Gunshot? Surely not; it must have been a firework.

'Brett, what's happening?'

'Oh, Jesus, Kate, I've got to go. Whatever they were doing here, it's all gone wrong. I have to go—'

'Brett? Brett? What the hell is going on?'

The line went dead.

CHAPTER FORTY

Charlotte came to with a start. It was as if someone had pressed a pause button, but the moment she reactivated, the fear and panic returned. Her heart was pounding. The seat-belt was locked; she touched her forehead and pulled down the sun visor to check herself in the small mirror. There was no blood and no obvious damage.

Peering through the window, she discovered she was half way up a grassy bank, sloping downwards towards the busy motorway. The traffic was still flowing, so they hadn't caused a pile up, thank God. Then the most important detail of all flashed through her head: Vinnie Mace. Where was he?

Desperate to know, she moved her head from side to side, trying to figure out where his vehicle had come to rest. Perhaps he'd swerved and been able to pass by. If so, she'd bet any money that he'd be trying to find a way to get to her before the traffic police did. The seat belt was jammed from her full weight pressing on it. She pushed herself backwards and tugged at the belt until it came free.

The traffic was slowing further up ahead, and a lorry

had pulled over into the third lane with its hazard lights on. Charlotte opened the car door and climbed out onto the grass bank. There were fresh, muddy tyre marks from where she'd veered off the road. Miraculously, the car was undamaged. She hadn't crashed into anything, the air bag hadn't activated and she couldn't see any damage to the tyres or wheels. Would somebody have called the police? There was no way of telling. She would stick to her plan, head directly for Lancaster Police Station and then tell them everything that was going on.

Up ahead where the lorry had stopped, it seemed things were about to get moving. If that was Vinnie up ahead, it was best to get the car started. But she couldn't afford to get caught up in slow-moving traffic, so she climbed back inside the car, started up the engine and tentatively made her way down the bank.

Driving slowly to check for damage, she moved back onto the hard shoulder, keeping her hazard lights flashing and staying alert for other vehicles in the first lane. She straightened the car up, then started driving along the hard shoulder. As the traffic slowed on her right-hand side, she drove straight past it, ignoring the other drivers sounding their horns at her for jumping the queue. She didn't care; there was no way she was creeping past Vinnie Mace in a snake of cars.

It was the right call too. Beyond the lorry with its hazard lights on, she saw Vinnie and his hired muscle protected by its shield, standing in the third lane and checking over the car. From the glimpse she caught of it, they seemed to have struck the central barrier, but the car was on the road and probably still driveable.

She put her foot down, travelling along the hard shoulder at over 60mph, overtaking vehicles in the first lane and ignoring all the drivers sticking either one or two fingers up at her. She deserved it but she didn't care; her top priority was to get away.

Her new mobile phone was ringing again. She ignored it. Bearing in mind the speed she was travelling at along a part of the motorway that was supposed to be for broken down vehicles, answering a mobile phone whilst driving might just be a step too far.

As the traffic on her right-hand side began to speed up beyond the blockage, she merged with the first lane of traffic, relieved to be back in the regular flow again without Vinnie's car in her rear-view mirror. Her entire body felt like it had touched an electric cable, in a fusion of adrenaline overload and sheer fear. Then she started to tremble, as if the energy had been sucked out of her in an instant. Checking the road behind, she took the first exit into Lancaster, passing the Holiday Inn and turning sharply into the business park beyond it. She spotted a catering van in one of the car parks and pulled up close by.

As she got out of the car, she looked towards the main road. The car was hidden by shrubs and foliage, so Vinnie would never spot her here.

At the van, she felt in her pocket for one of the notes she'd drawn out of the cash machine and asked for three Snickers bars and a bottle of water. Healthy eating would have to wait; she needed sugar and she needed it fast. Her legs were so weak that she thought they might give way beneath her. She'd experienced this sensation too many times before. It was the massive crash that came after an overload of fear. Somehow, her body always found what it needed to survive, but this terrible moment of weakness always followed, as if her body was spent and couldn't take any more.

She gulped down the first chocolate bar in a matter of seconds, but only made it part-way through the second.

'You can swallow, luv,' a van driver teased her, as he drank his tea in a polystyrene mug at the side of the catering van. She was tempted to bite his head off, but recalled how that had played out for her last time she'd done it in an industrial estate café. One thing was for certain, she'd need to produce some damn good articles to keep Teddy sweet after he discovered what she'd been up to in the company vehicle.

The chocolate bar sugar rush kicked in and the strength returned to her legs. It was time to get herself to the police station. If guns were involved now, things had gone too far. This was going beyond scaring people off; it was deadly serious. Besides, if the police were able to apprehend Vinnie Mace with an illegal weapon, that would give Fabian Armstrong a major headache at the very least. She resolved to call an immediate halt to the Lone Ranger act; her next stop would be the police station.

She walked back to the car, relieved that her body could carry her weight once again. After she'd finished the last part of the second chocolate bar, she took a swig of water from the bottle, then checked her phone. There were three missed calls from the same number. As she started up the car, the phone rang again. It was the same number. She pulled up the handbrake and answered.

'Yes?'

'Charlotte, it's Vinnie Mace.'

She almost vomited up the chocolate bars, as her stomach cramped with fear.

'What do you want, you bastard? Why don't you just leave me alone? I'm no part of whatever's going on—'

'Oh, but you are, Charlotte. You're in much deeper than you could ever know.'

'What do you want? I can't help you—'

'How about that paperwork for starters? That was naughty, finding it before we did. We won't be contacting your insurance company about the damage to our car, by the way, so no need to worry about your no-claims bonus.'

'Just get lost, Vinnie. I can't help you.'

'Take us to Kate Summers. Wherever she's hiding, we need to speak to her.'

'Over my dead body, you prick—'

'Well, that can be arranged, Charlotte.'

She knew that it could too. She'd seen enough already to know it was no idle threat.

'I won't help you, you bastard. I've had enough. I'm going straight to the police.'

'I don't think you'll want to do that before you've heard what I'm going to say.'

Charlotte struggled to stay calm, wanting to scream until she had no voice left.

'We've got your husband. You must have suspected it. Well, if you want to see him again, you'll do exactly what I tell you. And – plot spoiler – it doesn't involve calling in at Lancaster Police Station.'

CHAPTER FORTY-ONE

Charlotte had been in this dark place before, so she was beginning to understand the feeling well. Even worse, she was becoming accustomed to the way these people worked. Threats, intimidation, violence and illegal weapons... it was an underbelly of life in Morecambe which lay hidden deep beneath the surface.

Vinnie Mace had just ended the call. There was no cheery *Goodbye* or *See you later!* sign-off. This was all about exerting pressure, turning up the heat, making her sweat and forcing her into mistakes. The routine was the same, too: threats to loved ones or people close to her, then initial intimidation followed by direct violence. She wondered if these thugs honed their skills in the school playground. She'd seen similar tactics used by secondary school students. Only their stakes were much lower: some stolen dinner money here, a punch in the stomach there. Was this where it ended up, with guns and murders?

She opened the last of the chocolate bars. Of course they had Will; they were going to use him to get what they wanted. And of course she couldn't call the police, because they had that sewn up too. The moment she raised the alarm, whoever the police mole was would catch wind of it and pass on the alert to their evil buddies.

It always came down to this. You had to decide if you were going to fight them or roll over and play dead. Charlotte knew her rage at what they were doing was so intense that she would always have to leap into the flames. They had her husband, they were using him to make threats; that infuriated her. Whatever the risk, whatever her logical mind told her, her anger ruled the day and she refused to be cowed by bullies.

She thought back to the time as a child when she'd been mercilessly targeted by a male bully. He would pick her out when she was separated from her group of friends, then goad her and intimidate her. This went on for months and like any sane person, she would deflect, avoid the bully when she spotted him ahead and do anything to avoid confrontation. But one day, she'd seen this same boy intimidating another pupil, somebody much younger than her who she didn't know. She'd been so incensed that the moment he moved on to her, she formed a fist and punched him so hard in the neck that he dropped to the ground, temporarily unable to breathe and convinced he was dying. She knelt at his side as he struggled to recover and whispered to him, fighting to contain her anger.

'Never let me see you doing that again. And next time you see me coming, get out of my way.'

That had been the end of it. She'd completely humiliated the boy, denying him the arrogance from never being challenged. The feeling came back to Charlotte now, even though she was trembling in the car seat, petrified at the thought of what might happen next. Part of that fear was fuelled by the certainty that she wasn't going to run any more. It was the fact they'd got Will that incensed her most; she could tolerate it when the threats were directed at her.

She called Lucia on her phone.

'Hey, Mum. This is an unusual time for you to call.'

'Hello, Luc, I just wanted to say hi. How are you enjoying Lancaster? Is Olli ready to throw you out yet?'

'No offence, Mum, but I love the independence of it. I just come and go with nobody watching me, and I like it.'

'That's as it should be. At your age, nobody wants their parents around all the time—'

Charlotte stopped dead. What if she and Will didn't make it out of this? What if Olli and Lucia ended up on their own as a result of what was about to play out? She wouldn't give the prospect any head space. There was something incredulous about her situation, yet she couldn't imagine it resulting in death for her or Will.

'Are you okay? You sound... different.'

'I was just missing you being around, and I wanted to check in. I love you Luc—'

'Oh God, don't go all soppy on me. I've only been gone a couple of nights; you can't be missing me that much already.'

She would understand one day, when she had her own children.

'Is Olli around? I'd like a quick word with him if he's free.'

'He and Willow are at the cinema. Neither of them had much on today, so they sneaked off while it was quiet. I didn't fancy the film, so I'm getting some studying done.'

A swell of pride surged through Charlotte, sweeping aside the sense of impending conflict.

'Lucia, I'm going to tell you something, but you must promise to keep it to yourself.'

'What? Are you sure you're okay?'

'I'm telling you this because you understand. You were there with me at Heysham Port. You and I shared something terrible that night.'

'Oh hell, please tell me you're not caught up in something again?'

After a brief pause, Lucia put it together.

'This is why Dad isn't answering his messages, isn't it? This has to be connected to what happened at the parachute jump. What have you done, Mum? Is this to do with those kids vanishing?'

Charlotte hesitated a moment, trying to find the right words.

'I'm so sorry, Lucia, but yes, I've got us involved again—'

'For God's sake, is Dad okay?'

'He's caught up in it too. I didn't plan this; it just caught up with me. One moment, it's a dot on the horizon, the next moment you have a monster on your back. I'm sorry, Luc, but I'm going to put this right.'

'Don't you dare do this alone, Mum. Call the police, get some help. Call DCI Summers again—'

'I can't. She's caught up in this as well. She's the one I'm helping.'

'Shit. Is there nobody else you can speak to?'

'Not the police, not yet. Kate Summers has warned me not to. There's a mole somewhere at the police station. But I need you to help me.'

'Of course. I'll come with you if you want.'

The swell of pride rose in her once again. Her daughter had come on so far since they'd been thrust into the terrible situation with Edward Callow and his men.

'I have to go alone. But I need to tell somebody, in case it doesn't work out.'

'Oh God, Mum. Please don't do anything stupid. You're supposed to be at home with your Horlicks and hairnet. I'm the one who's meant to be getting into trouble.'

Charlotte laughed. It seemed a ridiculous thing to do, bearing in mind what was just about to play out. But Lucia was right, she was far too old to be caught up in events like this.

'If I don't telephone you or text you in one hour's time, I want you to call the police—'

'What will they do to you if they get you?'

'I'm going to meet them. They want something from me.'

'Are you going to give it to them?'

'Not if I can avoid it. But I must see if they've got your dad. It might be a bluff; I can't take that chance.'

Charlotte heard Lucia sniff and could tell that even though she was getting upset, she was trying to hide it over the phone call. As hard as it was, she had to ignore it for now, and avoid letting her emotional guard down. She was steeling herself for what was to come.

'I'm going to photograph these documents and send them to you by email while I've got a decent signal. They want me to meet them out at Sunderland Point while the tide is out—'

'Why there, of all places?'

'That's where I asked them to meet me. They wanted somewhere remote, and I know a man called Jed who lives nearby, so I can get help if I need it. I also have a plan to hide the documents. It seemed like the best thing off the top of my head. I'd have been completely exposed where they wanted the meeting.'

'Fair enough, as long as you know what you're doing.'

'Not exactly, but I don't have a choice. I'm going to call

you or text you just before I get to the causeway at Sunderland Point. It's easy to lose the phone signal out there, so I'll do it in plenty of time. After that, I'll call you in another hour. If I don't make that call, ring the police anyway. I'll need help if I can't speak to you by then.'

Lucia appeared to be thinking it through at the other end of the line.

'What do I tell them, Mum? What shall I say?'

'If I don't make that second phone call to you, it won't very much matter. Tell the police to go to Sunderland Point. Send those photos to DI Comfort. I hope he's trustworthy. If he's not, I'll just have to hope Kate Summers can put this right on her own, wherever she's hiding.'

'I love you, Mum.'

'Who's getting soppy now?'

They finished the call and Charlotte took a swig of water. She was ready to save her husband.

CHAPTER FORTY-TWO

Charlotte had taken a calculated risk telling Vinnie to meet her at Sunderland Point, but it would have been far worse if she'd agreed to his suggestion of the abandoned factory.

There was time to think through her options as she wove through the traffic in Lancaster and made her way back towards Heysham. She'd do everything she could to prevent Vinnie from getting his hands on those documents. And even if he did, she wasn't letting him have all of them. As she glanced at the clock on the dashboard, she realised Lucia would be waiting for her update. The traffic had obliged her by flowing freely, so she was making good time. The exchange with Vinnie would be brief, as all her others with him had been.

'Your husband is safe, but only for as long as you keep helping us, Charlotte.'

She hated the familiar way he spoke, as if they were friends. She didn't see them becoming best mates any time soon.

'What is this about? Why am I even involved?'

'Because you know Kate Summers and can help us get

to her. You thrust your hand in the wasp's nest, Charlotte. Now you're surrounded by them and they're angry and agitated. Watch you don't get stung.'

'Was it you or one of your hired hands who tried to drown me at Sunderland Point?'

There was silence at the end of the line.

'I have no idea what you're talking about, Charlotte.'

'Come on Vinnie, if you're going to threaten me, at least have the balls to admit what you did.'

As she spoke the words Charlotte could see that she'd never be given a job as a hostage negotiator. She knew her tone would agitate him, but this was her first opportunity to vent her own rage at an enemy who preferred to lurk in the shadows.

'Come on, Charlotte, that's not my style. If I had wanted to kill you, you'd have just disappeared. Nobody would know what happened to you. No body, no evidence, no scraps for the police investigators to find. Remind me to tell you more about my time in Afghanistan. I had quite a reputation among the locals.'

A sharp chill ran through her body. She could imagine some of the names the Afghans called him; she could think of a few choice words herself.

'The last time I looked, you were the last psycho trying to kill me—'

'I can assure you that I'm not a psychopath, Charlotte. In fact, I have psychological profiling tests to confirm it. Do you? And, so far, there hasn't been a reason to kill you. Why would we want you dead? We want you to take us to Kate Summers, but I assure you, that shouldn't require your death. Nor the death of your husband, come to think about it. Though it depends on what happens next.'

Their phone conversation played over and over in her mind; she had to commit to a plan.

'Tell me what you want.'

'Kate Summers. And if not Kate Summers, whatever it was she sent you to find in the house.'

'She didn't—'

'Don't even start, Charlotte. We know she has documentation. We've been watching the house, but we assumed she'd send a copper for it. Imagine my surprise and joy when I discovered it was you. I want that paperwork. And I want to know where Kate Summers is hiding.'

'I don't have a clue where she is.'

'But you can contact her?'

Charlotte didn't answer.

'How do I get Will back?'

'You give me the papers. And you tell me where Kate Summers is.'

'I don't know—'

'Jesus, Charlotte, I dealt with Afghan insurgents who were better at lying than you. That didn't stop me cutting off their fingers, mind you. It doesn't half encourage the flow of information.'

'Did you ever consider that psychological report might have been sent to the wrong address?'

She hated this. Constant threats and intimidation, just like the school bully. If the opportunity arose, Vinnie would get his punch to the neck. She wasn't sure how it would happen, but when the moment came, he'd get it. She hated people like this. They both scared her and compelled her to take retaliatory action.

To her surprise, Vinnie accepted her choice of location for an exchange of information. They fixed the time.

'All you have to do is to hand me that information and

pass on whatever contact details you have for Kate Summers. A phone number at the very least. And don't even try giving me her normal phone number; we've had that for some time now.'

Had they got hold of Kate's private number from the police mole that Kate had warned her about?

It seemed so easy. Yet she hadn't got a clue what she'd be doing if she handed over that envelope. Neither did she know what Kate's fate might be; she couldn't risk giving away all her cards. She pulled over at a corner store and hurriedly bought a pack of plain, brown A4-size envelopes and a small book of stamps. She opened the package she'd found concealed within the Monopoly board. It had been a good hiding place.

She tore open the envelope from Kate's house and pulled out the paperwork. There were four items. The first was a copy of a last will and testament, signed by Lilian Armstrong in 1986. The second was a set of deeds for some land, possibly the farmland where the wind turbines were now based. There was some sort of contract, presumably construction-related given all the technical words in it which made little sense to her. The last one was a psychological report with the name Tiffany G. Irwin handwritten at the top. It was dated 1999. On the inside of the envelope's flap was some writing: a postcode, a padlock code, what looked like a door number and a four-digit code, perhaps a PIN or something similar. It was a good thing she'd taken care when opening it up; she usually ripped open her morning post with little regard for the contents.

She had to pick one thing, just one thing to give Vinnie which hopefully wouldn't give him an essential piece of the puzzle. With no clue which was safest to hand over, she opted for the contract. It was like playing Russian Roulette.

She placed each of the four items into a separate envelope, hiding the first in the lining of the well where the spare wheel was kept, and addressing a second to the guest house for her personal attention; that way it wouldn't be opened by Isla as guest-related correspondence.

Charlotte left the other two envelopes on the passenger seat at her side, bending the corner of the one she was going to hand Vinnie so she didn't get them mixed up. She hoped she would be early; she had a special plan for that third envelope. Before moving off, she searched the junk that had been left in the side pocket of the car and found a pizza delivery leaflet, no doubt removed from the windscreen wiper of the car. She wrote the number on another scrap of paper from among the junk, then pressed that into her back pocket, alongside her phone. At least it was a new phone and the charge was holding up. It would get her through that day.

Passing through Overton, she thought about the best way to handle Vinnie. Don't wind him up. Play hard to get, and make him think it was painful to hand over the documents she'd chosen. Convince him to reveal where Will was being kept as a hostage.

Her resolve evaporated as she drove along the causeway towards Sunderland Point. Vinnie had claimed ignorance about the attempt on her life. So, who had done it? She was convinced the tall woman was her attacker, but she had assumed they were all working together. Was something else in play here, something that she hadn't pieced together yet?

She pulled up the car at the far side of the causeway. The tide was out; that was good timing, at least. There was no sign of Vinnie. She checked the time and texted Lucia.

All fine here. Give me one more hour. If I don't make

contact then, call the police. I'm at Sunderland Point. Love you, Mum xxx

She peered across the causeway and saw Vinnie's sinister black vehicle beginning to make its way over. She'd have to hurry. As she scanned the beach, she could see a couple walking a dog in the distance. The two young guys with their jet-skis had just been out for a ride. They seemed to be taking a short break from annoying the visitors and locals and were heading back to their house.

Charlotte made her way over to Jed's boat. Watching Vinnie's car all the time, she pushed the third envelope inside a metal box on the deck of the boat. He could pick her up by her feet and shake her all he wanted; he'd only get his hands on the contents of that one envelope now.

She walked away from Jed's boat towards the edge of the waterline. The couple had gone through a gate further along the stony shore. She'd rather hoped they would stay in sight. And in spite of the way one of the wetsuit-clad men looked her up and down and sneered to himself, she wished the two jet-ski guys would postpone their break and be annoying for a little longer; she could use the company.

Vinnie was on his own. She wanted him out in the open, so she stayed at the edge of the water, forcing him to walk over to her. Even from that distance she could see his cocksure smile.

I'll soon wipe that silly smile off your bloody face, she thought, as his feet crunched through the stones. This was it; it was time to face her enemy.

CHAPTER FORTY-THREE

'I hope you're not wasting my time?' Vinnie said.

'Well, hello to you too. I've got the envelope and the phone number, just as we discussed. Now, how do I know that you're not going to waste my time?'

'Because I have the upper hand right now and you might want to play a bit nicer—'

'Look, Vinnie, I want my husband back. Somebody like you might not appreciate this sentiment, but if I had to kill you to do that, I would, believe me—'

Vinnie raised his hand in the air.

'Enough of the pissing contest,' he began. 'Let me see the envelope.'

She held it up. As he stepped closer, she snatched it away from him.

'What's in it that's so important?' she asked.

'That's what I'm about to find out,' Vinnie replied. 'Hand it over, please.'

'Where's Will?'

'He's safe. We don't make a habit of killing people—'

'Like Evan Farrish?'

'Charlotte, I don't know where you're getting your information from. Evan Farrish was nothing to do with us. I assumed it was just some shitty drug dealer or something. I assure you, we had nothing to do with his death.'

She stared at him. The ability to tell bare-faced lies was probably a part of his job description, but he seemed genuinely surprised by what she'd just said.

'I don't know what to believe any more. Look, I'm going to give you this envelope. Then I want you to tell me where Will is. When you do that, I'll give you Kate's number. I can't tell you where she is. If I knew, I'd have led you there by now; you must know that much?'

Vinnie nodded. She had no choice but to trust him. He held out his hand.

Charlotte scanned the beach. The couple with the dog were still nowhere to be seen, but they couldn't be far off, as the dog had reappeared up ahead and was playing in the water.

She handed over the envelope. He opened it up and removed the contents.

'Is this it?'

She nodded.

'It was hidden in the Monopoly box in the child's bedroom. You know that's where I was, and that I climbed out of the window from there. I'm telling the truth.

Vinnie dipped his hand back into the envelope.

'There has to be more than this.'

'That's all Kate asked me to retrieve. I haven't even checked inside it myself yet, so I have no idea what you're looking at. Now, tell me where Will is.'

'You stupid bitch. Did you honestly think you were going to drag me all this way out here for nothing?'

'Everything all right here, gorgeous?' the self-confident

jet-skier asked. They were back from their break. Never had she been so pleased to see a pair of dickheads. One of them was carrying a fuel can.

'Yes, for now it is, thank you.'

Vinnie looked pissed off. The couple with the dog had reappeared through the gate. He couldn't do anything nasty with witnesses around.

'This isn't enough,' he said, quiet and controlled now. 'Give me the phone number.'

'Then you tell me where I find Will, yes?'

He nodded.

She reached into her pocket and handed over the scrap of paper. If he pushed further, she'd have to offer up the second envelope which had been concealed in Jed's boat. Vinnie examined it. A jet-ski started up at their side as one of the guys prepared to head out into the water.

Vinnie checked his phone.

'Wait here, I can't get a signal. I'm going to move towards my car, to try to catch one. Don't go anywhere.'

She watched as he crunched through the shingle back up to the concrete parking area. He took out his phone, walked around for a while, then dialled. She prayed that the pizzeria would be closed and that he'd get a ringtone. That would at least convince him she hadn't just made up a random number.

The other jet-ski rider was messing around with his vehicle, having set aside the fuel can out of the way of the water.

'Care for a ride, sexy?' the arrogant one shouted over.

'Whatever were you thinking, Charlotte? Did you really reckon you could fob me off with some pizza delivery service phone number?'

'Maybe that's where she's hiding...' Charlotte began.

She could see her bluffing time was up. She'd have to stall him with the information in the boat.

'Just shut your mouth, Charlotte. You and I are going for a ride. If you want to see that husband of yours again, it's your only choice.'

'Not on your life,' Charlotte began.

Slowly, confidently, Vinnie pulled the front of his jacket to one side, revealing a gun with a silencer attached.

'With the noise those bloody engines are making, I'll be away before they even realise I shot you. Now, walk with me back to the car. This is your only option now; I want the rest of that information. We're going to have to do it the hard way.'

Charlotte looked at Vinnie, then at the couple with the dog. They were still some way off. The first man had the jet-ski in the water and was revving up the machine. It sounded like mosquitoes on speed, the noise pervasive and irritating, the fumes pungent and choking. No wonder Jed hated these guys so much.

She took one last look into Vinnie's eyes and saw he was deadly serious. He touched the gun again to remind her that he meant business.

For a moment, she hesitated. They knew she had more information, so he had the upper hand. And they had Will, or at least Vinnie claimed they did. Even if Vinnie was telling the truth, they would never harm him because it was the only way to get to her and to stop her talking to the police. She'd have to settle for stalemate for now, but there was no way she was getting in Vinnie's car.

'One moment, I have something in my shoe,' she said, bending down. Then she picked up a stone and threw it at Vinnie's head. She heard the thud as it struck his skull, making a sound as if it had hit concrete. She got up, turned, then ran towards the jet-skis.

'Had a row with your boyfriend, my darling? Hop on—'

'Fuck off!' Charlotte screamed at him, pushing him off the jet-ski. He fell into the water, thrashing around as he tried to get up.

'Oi, love, that's out of order,' his mate called over, fuel can in hand.

Vinnie was recovering, and if he was pissed off before, his face was filled with thunder now. She revved the jet-ski and it surged forward.

'Hey, that's mine, bring it back!'

Vinnie had reached the second jet-skier now.

'Move away!' he ordered.

Charlotte revved her engine and the jet-ski began to move forward. She hadn't formed a plan when she'd taken it, thinking only that it would put some distance between her and Vinnie and she'd get off further along the shoreline and make an escape in a taxi or by hitching a lift. But he was following her. A man who had experience of a parachute jump must know one end of a jet-ski from another.

She revved up again, and the jet-ski lurched forwards. Since there was a safety clip attached to the bodywork, she might as well use it. The only thing she could clip it to was the belt guide on her jeans. Vinnie was revving the other jet-ski behind her. She pulled back the throttle, and the vehicle roared forward. Heading away from the peninsula was her best bet, to avoid being trapped.

She'd never been on a jet-ski in her life before, but the water along the tidal inlet was relatively calm and the machine seemed stable. It was a good job, because Vinnie was behind her now. She hadn't a clue how fast it went, but the digital speedo on the dashboard suggested there was a lot more acceleration left in it.

There was a sudden and violent sound in the jet-ski's bodywork. The shock made her jerk the steering wheel, and she almost fell off. She looked down as she braked and saw a bullet hole. Vinnie was shooting at her.

She pulled back the throttle, sensing he was gaining on her. The water was choppier now, making it harder to stay steady. The grey sea opened up ahead. This was not what she'd planned; the thought of being so far from land, with no life jacket, was terrifying. She threw up, overwhelmed by a gripping fear that she'd done the wrong thing; she should have complied with what he wanted. There was another crack close to her foot. Jesus, he'd just missed her body. A fibreglass shard behind her leg marked the point of impact.

She didn't dare look back. The choppy waves made it hard even to steer a straight course, as if the sea was fighting with her, working to slow her down. As the jet-ski bounced in the waves, she began to curse at herself, at Vinnie, and at the ridiculous situation she'd got herself into. The sea splashed her face and she could taste the salt in her mouth. Her eyes were sore from its sting. The sea was vast, but it was one thing viewing it from the shoreline and another thing being in the middle of it, confined to a tiny floating vehicle while being chased by a man hellbent on shooting her.

She couldn't keep this up much longer. Her hands were cold from the sea water, her clothing soaking wet and heavy. If she fell off now, she'd drown; she wasn't strong enough to take on the might of the sea. If only she could stop, give up, and go home, but that was no longer an option. They'd take her to wherever Will was – if she even survived that long – and torture the information out of her. She'd give it too, in those circumstances. If they threatened to hurt Will or herself, she couldn't take it; she would have to give up Kate. She despised herself for it, but she just wasn't brave enough.

The shots were terrifying when they hit the jet-ski. She hadn't heard the gun fire over the noise of the engine. The first she knew that a bullet had been fired was when a piece of bodywork splintered and flew up at her face.

He was after the fuel tank, aiming to disable the jet-ski, not trying to kill her. A man like Vinnie would have hit his target by now. And the second guy had been re-fuelling his unit when Vinnie stole it from him; was it low on fuel? If so, he'd need to turn back or risk getting stranded at sea. She checked her own dashboard, trying to figure out which dial told her how much fuel she had remaining. A fourth bullet struck the upholstery just behind her. He was getting too close now. She had to take a gamble; it was time to get rid of Vinnie Mace.

Vinnie had to be short of fuel, he had to be. Which meant her only chance to get away was to outrun him. At some point he'd have to cut his losses and return to land. The guys at the shoreline had probably called the police already. Vinnie would know that as well as she did. And then there was Lucia; she would alert the police if the jet-ski guys didn't. All she had to do was escape from Vinnie and avoid drowning in the process. It sounded so easy.

Vinnie was still on her tail, like a persistent terrier intent on flushing out a rabbit from its burrow. The waves were bigger, darker and more terrifying than she could have ever imagined. They made the jet-ski lurch up and down and side to side; it was like riding one of the bucking-bronco machines at a fairground, and she'd only ever lasted seconds on those. Her legs were clamped around the body of the vehicle and she was hanging on for dear life.

Way ahead, in the distance, she could see white shapes on the horizon: wind turbines. They had to be the Morecambe Bay turbines that Sam Halford had told her about. How many bullets had Vinnie fired? The roar of the sea was so loud that it drowned out everything else. She was heading for those turbines. Her fuel levels seemed fine, so he couldn't have landed a hit on the fuel tank yet. If she could make it to the turbines, they would be her sanctuary. Lucia would alert the police after her hour was up, and they'd figure it out eventually, if she hadn't drowned by then or frozen to death.

From nowhere, an enormous wave crested when she wasn't expecting it and it seemed, if only for a moment, that the jet-ski was moving backwards. She gasped at the disorienting sensation, releasing her grip on the throttle. As the jet-ski slowed, it was harder to hold the steering wheel steady, and as a second wave washed over her, the vehicle tilted to the right and shook her off. The safety harness tugged against her waist. She prayed the denim strip wouldn't tear her away from the vehicle and leave her to the mercy of the waves.

She seemed to be underwater forever, but she held her nerve, waiting to surface again. As soon as she rose above the water, her hand reached out for the jet-ski. It was still upright.

'That's enough, Charlotte,' Vinnie shouted. 'You tell me where you hid those other papers, or I'll shoot you now and leave you out here. You'll be rotten in the water by the time they find you, if they even find you at all.'

It was difficult to hear him at a distance, but he'd stopped his jet-ski and the engine was idling. She battled to hold on to her own unit as the sea forced her up and down, more powerful than she could ever have imagined.

'Screw you, Vinnie! I know you're short on fuel. You must be short on bullets too. I'll take my chances.'

'Okay then, you asked for it.'

He raised his gun and took a careful aim. She was a sitting duck. She closed her eyes and thought of her family.

CHAPTER FORTY-FOUR

The bullet didn't come. She waited in the water for over a minute, willing him to miss. But there was no sound. No bullet had struck her or the bodywork of the jet-ski. She opened her eyes, wiping the water from them. She could see from Vinnie's face, even from that distance, that he must be out of shots.

'Ha, fuck you, Vinnie! You're out of bullets.'

She reached for the side of her vehicle, wondering how she could pull herself back up in such hostile waters. Vinnie secured his weapon, revved up his jet-ski and moved towards her. She tried to get traction on the side of her unit, but the waves were too much for her. Vinnie was moving in, but she could see even he was having difficulties now.

'That's enough, Vinnie,' she shouted over, trying to coordinate her speaking so she didn't get a mouthful of water. 'You keep Will safe and we'll renegotiate this. You're out of fuel, you have to head back now.'

'I'll be waiting for you on the shoreline,' he shouted over. 'I'll sort you out, bitch. If not now, I can wait. I'm a patient man. I'll come for you when you're least expecting it.'

She'd heard it before: the school bully again, threatening to terrorise her. Well, she'd got a punch in, but she hadn't disabled him. It would have to do. The information she'd concealed was enough to keep Will and Kate safe for now.

Bracing her legs against the jet-ski once again, she at last found the strength to haul herself back on it and untangle the safety clip from her leg. Let Vinnie Mace sneer at her all he wanted. He couldn't get in close enough to do anything to her. She started up her engine once again, and checked the revs, making sure everything was good to go. While it was a struggle to fight against the movement of the waves, she could see Vinnie was having difficulty too. Even a former Marine couldn't get the better of nature.

She glanced across and gave him the finger. He'd turned her into a swearing, abusive, screaming woman, but the swear jar could get stuffed for now.

'Look after Will!' she shouted, 'or you'll get nothing more from me, you prick!'

She revved the engine again and cautiously moved forward, getting the measure of the waves as she did so. It was no James Bond exit, but she was still on the jet-ski and she'd got the last word in for now. She steered towards the wind turbines, which seemed much closer than before, and didn't look back until the first of the massive structures was rearing up ahead of her. Vinnie had cut his losses and gone. She'd been aware of him in her peripheral vision for a time, but he'd given up and turned back. Thank God she'd taken the fully fuelled unit.

The chill made her face feel like it was carved from stone, and she felt sick from the motion of the waves and the salt water that she'd swallowed. As she approached the first turbine, she spotted a boarding platform at its base. She could pull herself up on that and wait for them to work out where she was. At least they'd find her body if she froze out here, and her family wouldn't be left wondering what had happened to her.

A small storage area on the jet-ski was partially open at her side, clipped by one of Vinnie's bullets. It had two small flares inside. The young guys might have behaved like morons, but they knew their safety-at-sea procedures, that was for sure. Charlotte stuffed both flares into her front pocket. She spotted a ladder leading to a metal base around the formidable structure and reached out to grab it, struggling as the jet-ski bobbed wildly in the waves. As soon as she'd caught hold of a rung, she took a deep breath and unclipped the harness which had kept her secured.

She forced herself upright, trying to ignore the stiffness in her legs as she lunged forwards onto the base. At that exact moment, a wave washed the jet-ski away. She had no other choice now; either she found the strength to pull herself up or she would perish at sea.

She thought of Lucia, waiting anxiously for her text or call, willing her to be safe. With a loud cry, she summoned every bit of energy in her body and hauled herself up. She was safe; she'd made it. For now, she had a slight advantage, a tiny bit of bargaining power. But Will and Kate were still in danger and Vinnie had shown he would stop at nothing to get his hands on those documents.

The climb up the ladder was terrifying, but she had to reach that platform; she'd be dead if she didn't.

After what seemed like an even greater height than she'd climbed with Sam Halford, Charlotte heaved herself onto the platform, shivering uncontrollably. She'd made it;

she'd somehow survived the ordeal. Near the turbines, she could see a maintenance crew in a boat. They could take her back to the shore, away from Vinnie, preferably on the Cumbrian side of the coast. She checked the flares; they still seemed dry.

Moving her hand to her back pocket, Charlotte fumbled for her phone. Now was the time to see how waterproof it was.

She even had a signal. Jed had told her he got his best signals out in the bay, but it had sounded implausible. Charlotte fumbled around with the flares, trying to figure out how they operated. She set them off, one after the other, and breathed a sigh of relief as she realised the maintenance crew had seen her and were assembling on their platform now, ready to come to her rescue.

She checked the time. It was 56 minutes since she'd last texted Lucia. She hadn't got the energy to call yet. What would she even say?

Her fingers rigid and cold, she painstakingly typed out a message for her daughter.

I'm safe. I know where your dad is. Don't call the police. I'm going to bring him home on my own. I'm going to fix this.

The story concludes in Bound By Blood, available now as an e-book or paperback.

AUTHOR NOTES

Okay, I promise I'll give Charlotte a break at the end of book three!

She's been through the mill already in this story, and there's more to come.

When I started writing this trilogy, I always knew what the final scene would be, and I can't wait to write it.

If you thought the last encounter on the container lift was tense at the end of Truth Be Told, wait until you see what I have planned for Charlotte and Kate at the end of Bound By Blood.

As with the first trilogy, I promise to tie up all the loose threads.

You won't be left wondering what happened to Character X or who did what to Character Y; all will be revealed in the last book in the trilogy.

Sunderland Point continues to play an important part in this story. It offers such a variety of opportunities for action that I couldn't resist revisiting it.

So many of the scenes in my books are based on my own

experiences whilst working for the BBC as a radio journalist.

For instance, I have had a spin on a jet-ski, and it was that which inspired the chase scene at the end of the book.

I hasten to add that I wasn't chased when I got my chance to go for a ride, but it was in the days before digital recording equipment, and I did have to balance a rather large reel-to-reel tape recorder on the steering section to allow me to record.

I kept my fingers crossed that day that my recording equipment didn't fall into the water, because the boss would not have been pleased.

Charlotte's trip to the wind farm and her climb up to the top of the turbine was based on the last reporting job I ever did before I left the BBC to work for myself.

I tried a lot of hair-raising activities whilst reporting, including abseiling from the Humber Bridge, but it was climbing up a wind turbine which caused me to baulk, much like Charlotte does.

It was literally like climbing a ladder to heaven and I wasn't sure that I was going to make it to the top.

I forced myself to climb to the top of the ladder - as Charlotte did - and I didn't regret it; it was a tremendous experience.

However, it's just as scary climbing back down again.

My editor commented that Charlotte and Nigel seem to eat a lot of sandwiches during their work and I feel this is a good opportunity to offer an insight into the life of a journalist.

The constant snacking is for real!

When you're out on early jobs or rigging outside broadcasts, the most popular person on the team is the one who brings regular supplies of food and hot drinks.

Journalists are always meeting people for coffees and when they're on the road, they have to snatch food breaks wherever they can.

Ask any journalist about bacon butties and they'll tell you the same.

It's interesting that The Midland Hotel – which plays such an important part in the first trilogy – was derelict during the years in which the flashback scenes are set.

Morecambe was going through a hard time back then and the building which now forms such a spectacular local feature was fenced off, vandalised and falling apart.

If you ever get the chance, do go for afternoon tea at The Midland Hotel. Its sea views provide a spectacular experience.

By the way, that story about Will, Charlotte, KFC and the chips?

That was my wife and I as broke students in 1983.

It cost 10p for the chips and the KFC staff really were kind enough to throw in a free cup of water.

The funny thing is, it was great fun at the time.

Steven Terry makes another guest appearance in this story, and ever since he first popped up in the Don't Tell Meg trilogy, he's been a character who I love to write about.

With Steven, you're never quite sure if what he's saying is for real.

He has a habit of dropping bombshells on my characters at key moments in the plot, but they like him a lot and are always keen to get his insight, however scary it is.

Much of this book involves Kate Summers' life as a young police constable, and it was great to have my younger brother on hand to advise on some of the details.

He retired from the police in 2020 but it only seems like

five minutes ago that he was trying to get fit and earn his place in the force.

He gave me all sorts of insights into the day-to-day life of a constable, and it was great to be able to ask him questions like *How easy is it to go off on a personal errand while you're on shift?* and *Do police constables go out on the beat on their own?*

These things sound so simple and routine, but having been a journalist for most of my working life, I tend to know more about the senior levels in the police than I do the lower ranks.

For instance, I regularly interviewed the Chief Constable, the Deputy Chief Constable and various detectives leading high-profile cases, but I've had very little contact with the officers who do all the practical work.

As ever, it's important for me to stress that while much of this book is inspired by personal experience and conversations conducted as a reporter, the entire scenario is completely fictional and a figment of my imagination.

If you're not signed up to my author emails already, you can do so at https://paulteague.net/thrillers.

That's the best way to find out about new releases and special offers, so if you enjoy these stories, I recommend that you get registered.

In the meantime, get ready to tuck into the big finale in Bound By Blood, where you finally get to find out what's going on with the Irwin family.

Paul Teague

FREE GIFT

Are you enjoying the second Morecambe Bay Trilogy? You can now access an exclusive gift showing you many of the locations used in the book, with many amazing photographs of Sunderland Point.

Grab your FREE copy of Charlotte's Sunderland Point Scrapbook …

This downloadable scrapbook will show you all the key locations used in the second trilogy.
You'll get to see what Sunderland Point looks like as well as several other key locations, such as Happy Mount Park, Hest Bank, Lancaster University and the stone graves at Heysham.

To grab your copy head for https://paulteague.net/SB2 on your PC.

ALSO BY PAUL J. TEAGUE

Morecambe Bay Trilogy 1

Book 1 - Left For Dead

Book 2 - Circle of Lies

Book 3 - Truth Be Told

Morecambe Bay Trilogy 2

Book 4 - Trust Me Once

Book 5 - Fall From Grace

Book 6 - Bound By Blood

Morecambe Bay Trilogy 3

Book 7 - First To Die

Book 8 - Nothing To Lose

Book 9 - Last To Tell

Note: The Morecambe Bay trilogies are best read in the order shown above.

Don't Tell Meg Trilogy

Features DCI Kate Summers and Steven Terry.

Book 1 - Don't Tell Meg

Book 2 - The Murder Place

Book 3 - The Forgotten Children

Standalone Thrillers

Dead of Night

One Last Chance

No More Secrets

So Many Lies

Two Years After

Friends Who Lie

Now You See Her

ABOUT THE AUTHOR

Hi, I'm Paul Teague, the author of the Morecambe Bay series and the Don't Tell Meg trilogy, as well as several other standalone psychological thrillers such as One Last Chance, Dead of Night and No More Secrets.

I'm a former broadcaster and journalist with the BBC, but I have also worked as a primary school teacher, a disc jockey, a shopkeeper, a waiter and a sales rep.

I've read thrillers all my life, starting with Enid Blyton's Famous Five series as a child, then graduating to James Hadley Chase, Harlan Coben, Linwood Barclay and Mark Edwards.

Let's get connected!
https://paulteague.net